# ALINA MARTYN

# Towards My Now

# Contents

# I

# Trigger Warnings

*In this book there is mentions of; sexual assault, domestic violence, murder, graphic descriptions of consensual sex, and torture. It's a mafia romance with dark romance themes; forced proximity, enemies to lovers and a touch of best friend's sister tropes.*

*If any of that bothers you, you may not want to continue.*
*If you don't, no hard feelings. Your mental health matters.*

# II

# Dedication

*To all the girls who want to be a badass bit*h who
doesn't need a man, but also very much wants a big
man to hold her and tell her she's a good little sl*t.
Yeah, it's confusing for me too.*

# 1

# Before

### The Meeting

### Auggie

"You're going to be doing this, Auggie. Stop arguing." Talia snaps at me. My beautiful older sister, is standing at the foot of my bed with a large duffel bag and packing random stuff into it. Without my permission. I'd moved back in with our parents at Talia's insistence before she fell off the face of the earth and so I'm not feeling super hyped to move *yet again*. The guards she had on the house had long since left, and the letter that I received was hidden under my pillow.

"I don't want to. I'm fine here." No where was safe so I might as well not move again. They were going to find me regardless so it didn't really matter.

"I don't give a fuck if you're "fine here", Augustine." Oh shit, she's using her 'mom voice'. The tone she uses when she wants me to do something and isn't going to back down.

"I'm not going to go live somewhere else with someone I don't even know just so that I'm safer. I've been safe here for a long time now. Why do I have to leave?" I point out. Talia had just come back into my life after certain circumstances had forced us apart. Namely, both of our ex-boyfriends. She's insisting that I need to be put into a type of witness protection, with a personal guard twenty-four/ seven until she's sure the threat of her ex is gone.

"Auggie," Talia looks like she's about ready to pop a vein at my defying her, but a tall, hunk of a man with long hair tied up into a bun with his tattoos peaking out from the bottoms of his sleeves and the top of his neckline, stands up from my desk chair.

"Okay, okay." Kieron, my sister's husband, says "Here's what's going to happen. Talia, you're going to go get Trent from the car and bring him up so Auggie can meet him. I wouldn't be very happy with just accepting what we're proposing as well. Maybe if she meets him, she'll feel better. Auggie, you're going to pack a bag. We don't know how long you're going to have to be gone, but I would think you'd want to decide what you bring." Talia crosses her arms over her chest in frustration, but does what he says. When she leaves the room, I sigh deeply.

I don't necessarily want to agree with this man who I've met only one other time but he did bring my sister back to me, so I'm doing my best to give him the benefit of the doubt. I like him, don't get me wrong. But because of my history, I'm skeptical. Of everyone.

"She's just trying to keep you safe." Kieron says softly, not quite looking at me but not avoiding my eyes.

"And she's doing that by giving me a babysitter? If I'm in that much danger, why can't I just stay with her? You seem to be the type that will kill someone for looking at her wrong. I'm sure I'd be safer with her than on my own."

Kieron ran a hand down his beard in exasperation, but I cross my arms over my chest and refuse to back down.

"You're not wrong in that regard. I will kill anyone who threatens her in anyway. And I won't even break a sweat." He puts his hands in the pockets of his leather jacket and shrugs. "But, I'm… My job isn't always the safest. So, we decided to be as safe with you as we can and going into hiding is the best course of action. It won't be forever, just long enough for me and my guys to determine if Talia's ex's family isn't going to retaliate."

"Retaliate for what?"

Kieron opens his mouth like he's going to say something but snaps his jaw shut before he can say anything. "Don't worry about it."

"Should I be worried you're too dangerous for my sister, Kieron?" I cock my head to the side and squint my eyes in his direction. I'm not stupid; obviously he's in a gang or the mafia or some other shit, but I trust that Talia's taken care of. I see how much he loves her. How he's always scanning their location and perimeter, how he makes sure she's always within arms reach. To be completely honest, I'm shocked that he'd let her go to the car himself.

"She's protected. She's safe. I swear on my life and give you my word." He puts his hand on his chest and the look he's giving me is so sincere, I can't help but believe him.

I swing my long hair over my shoulder and nod once.

"So, does the person that I'm going away with, is he okay with it? Is he an ass? Does he know what's going on?" I might as well accept that this is happening. I start packing, taking the random bits and bobs out of the duffel that Talia was angrily shoving in there before. I'm a pretty skilled packer at this point.

"He knows. He's actually my best friend and right-hand man. I know you'll be safe with him. He's a good guy. I wouldn't trust your safety with anyone less."

I nod and purse my lips while I focus on my bag, not making eye contact.

"If he's your right-hand man, why is he going to be wasting his time with me? Is it really just because I'm your wife's kid sister?" The last fucking thing I need is for a man to think he's in control of my life, *again.* "I can take care of myself. Hell, just tell me where to go and then I'll stay put by myself."

"No can do. I promised your sister you'd be protected all day, everyday and this is how I keep that promise. What I don't understand is why you're fighting us this hard on it." He crosses his arms over his chest and cocks his head at me like he can see all my secrets going through my mind with just a look.

"I just don't see why you are making such a fuss. It's just me." I shrug and turn my back on him, trying to get away from his gaze.

He doesn't know, he can't know.

There's a small break in speaking until I look to him to make sure he's still there even. The big bear of my brother-in-law was looking at me earnestly with confusion and sincerity lacing his demeanor.

"You're important, Auggie. To your sister, but also to me.

I take family very seriously and I want to make sure you're okay." His dark eyes narrow as he looks into my own dark eyes. "What's going on?"

"Nothing, nothing is going on. I just don't want to be a prisoner again."

"Again?" He picks up on the word that slipped out without meaning to, and his whole energy changed again. Kieron had been like a friend and I could almost see us having a good brother/sister relationship. But after the word slipped out, he became *scary*. His hands flexed at his sides, his spine straightened and I swear he got even taller, his eyes darkened with promise of violence. He looked every bit the big, bad, leader of whatever.

"I just mean," I speak quickly to try and get us off this topic, away from the very real history I've had of being in a golden cage. "Uh, like when the other people were guarding me and the parents. We had rules and weren't allowed to do certain things. I don't like that. Can't I be in charge of myself?"

Kieron's eyes stayed narrowed, like he didn't quite believe me. But luckily, he let it drop.

"You won't be a prisoner, Auggie. I'll have an apartment rented in a small town, there will be minimal internet activity and there will be safety procautions taken. But that's for you and Trent to decide about and talk more. He, and I, aren't wanting to trap you. It's not permanent, just until we can make sure that you're going to stay safe."

We'll see about that. I do my best to not roll my eyes because I've heard these pretty words before.

Instead, I nod and keep packing.

If I have to do this, then I'll do my best to make it work for me. I won't be bowing down and just rolling with whatever is demanded of me. If I'm going to do this, I'm going to stay myself. I swear.

Fuck everyone else.

"Auggie, this is Trent." Talia's voice floats through the room and I turn my head to see the hottest man I think I've ever seen in my life. He's not the type that I thought I was attracted to *at all.*

Where I always thought I liked the tall, dark and handsome type, mysterious and quiet, but apparently, I don't know myself as well as I thought.

He's tall, taller than Kieron even, and broad. Like he was built of pure muscle, but his light skin is free of tattoos or piercings. His eyes are piercing and bright, looking around to assess the situation and looking out for threats. I feel like with one look he could unravel me.

His red hair is short on the sides, but long on top and he's clean shaven to show off his sharp, square jaw. I'm pretty sure my jaw drops as I check him out.

His eyes are locked on me as well, and I try to make myself more presentable and less... awe-struck. There's a tortured look in his eye; one that says this guy has a fucking story to tell. He clenches his jaw and his eyes dart around the room like he's trying to find an escape exit.

"Trent, this is my sister, Auggie." Talia says brightly, pulling me in and dropping her chin to my shoulder. "He's a good guy. He's saved my ass a few times now." She whispers to me, but everyone in the room can hear her words.

I nod, still unsure as to what I can say here. It's obvious that he doesn't want to be here. Not that I necessarily want him here either.

"Nice to meet you." I hold my hand out and wait for him to

take it.

But he doesn't.

Instead he just nods and goes to the side of the room like an awkward giant.

"Alright." Kieron says, clapping his hands once in front of him in attempt to disrupt the tension. "Baby, let's go get some of the stuff downstairs put together. Trent, why don't you stay here with Auggie and get to know each other a little bit?"

"That's a good idea. Auggie, do you mind if we get the technology shit sorted?" Talia asks, her mood lightened significantly now that I'm doing what she wants.

"Sure, do what you need to." I shrug, and the moment she lets go of my waist, I get back to packing. It's like my entire being is tense and tingling slightly from how close this man is to me.

And it's not like he's even that close to me. He's on the other side of the room, for fucks sake. But my body is reacting like he's standing in my space.

When the lovebirds finally leave, and it's just us, the tension in the room increases tenfold.

"So…" I start, but keep my eyes focused down on my task. Pick my clothes, fold them, roll them, put them into the duffel, repeat. "Kieron and Tali say you're their friend. How long have you known Kieron?"

"A decade at least." His gruff voice says, and his words are clipped as if saying any additional words physically hurts him.

"Long time. I take it you just met Tali?"

"No, I met her in college."

"Oh, cool." I'm starting to get frustrated because he's refusing to engage, he's refusing to give me anything. It's making me want to close off, too. So, I stop talking. I stop trying.

It's a good five to ten minutes before he opens his mouth again.

"So, how much younger are you than Talia?"

What a weird fucking question.

"Two years." Fold, roll, stuff, repeat.

"So, you're three years younger than I am."

"I guess so." I shrug.

"Great. Fucking babysitting." He says under his breath and I nearly drop the shirt I'm folding.

"Excuse me?"

"I said, "Great. I'm going to be fucking babysitting you", aren't I?" His words aren't even veiled in a fake sense of humor like any polite person would do. He's just opened fire between us and I can feel my rage building.

It's one thing for me to complain about being babysat but another for the person that is meant to be in charge of my safety, complain about babysitting me. Especially after he found out I'm barely younger than him. The absolute prick.

"I'm going to give you one chance to change your words. Want to try again?" I snap. I'm not going to let him walk all over me. Been there, done that.

"Nope. I'm pretty happy with my words." He snaps right back and I feel my blood pressure rising.

"I can't fucking believe you."

"Better believe it, because you and I are going to be stuck together for the foreseeable future. I'm not going to mince my words to protect your feelings or sensibilities. I expect you to follow what I say, when I say it, and not to fuck around. Do you understand?" I barely keep my mouth shut.

"You're giving me whiplash here, big guy. First, you were

so fucking quiet and demure. Now, you're an asshole who doesn't know when to shut up. This should be fun." I say, rolling my eyes and zipping up the bag.

"Just do what I say and stay out of my way." He shoves his hands in his pants pockets and the eyes that I was just admiring, just fantasizing about and getting lost in, are sharp and cruel. I'm not going to break though, I'm not going to let him think he's won.

His words aren't even a fraction of the harsh words I heard hurled my way before.

"I think you have it the other way around. Now, get the fuck out of my way." I pick up the bag and put the strap over my shoulder. Before I can forget, I go to my bedside table, open it up and pull out my deep blue vibrator. "Can't forget Trusty here, can I?" I smirk and feel a sense of victory when I see Trent's jaw drop and he's almost embarrassed looking. I unzip my bag and shove Ole Trusty in there, before patting the spot that it is very clearly pushing through the canvas.

"Let's go." I crook my finger and his jaw clenches again, his eyes narrow, but he doesn't say anything.

Good.

# 2

# Chapter 2

Trent

"Would you *please* just give me some fucking space?!" Auggie screeched in my face, her voice breaking.

I clenched my jaw and tried to remember anything that might bring my blood pressure down. This girl…hot-fucking-damn, this girl. She is going to be the death of me.

A very early death at the age of 28 because of a stress-induced heart attack. All because of the small little 5'5", blonde spitfire that Kellan has been having me protect 24/7. Not to mention, I'd volunteered because I'd do anything for Kieron and Talia.

Kieron's my best friend from college, and when I'd found out he was the son of the Irish Mob boss, I'd immediately sworn in. I liked the danger, the power, but most of all, I liked the found family. I was lost by myself in Boston; an orphan putting himself through college and life as best I could. When

Kieron held out a hand to save me from the wreckage that was my life, I held on. Talia was his girl, shit, his *wife* now and she'd been through hell. Within that hell, Kieron had started a war against the Italian Mafia. While we worked hard to figure out a way to keep everyone safe, I'd had to go undercover with the Italians and it had fucked with my head more than I realized.

So, when Skipper came to me with this assignment, I jumped on it. It was supposed to be chill; hang out with Talia and Kieron, keep her kid sister safe from any Italian backlash, and get my head on right. Chill, easy, a cake-walk.

Then I met her. Auggie.

Augustine Rosalie Jones.

And I knew it wouldn't be as easy as I thought.

Auggie is Talia's little sister. The sister Talia had killed a man for, the sister Talia had protected with her body and soul in exchange for the Italian Mafia's protection.

Pinching the bridge if my nose and sighing, I willed my blood pressure to lower.

"Auggie. I can't just let you walk around by yourself. We've been over this."

"I just need to go to one store and i do not want you to go there with me." She stomped her foot like a toddler. She actually *stomped* her foot like a child.

"Just buy your dirty books and let's go." I take great, immense pleasure in the deep blush that covers her cheeks. Auggie is old school, preferring paperbacks to electronic books and while I find it endearing, it also means whenever we travel we stop at at least two bookstores. The girl doesn't have any budget when it comes to books apparently because we always, and I mean *always,* leave the store with one or two, if not an armful, of new, smutty, books.

Auggie straightens her spine and pushes her hair over her shoulders.

"I don't know what you're talking about." She says with her arms crossed under her breasts, pushing them up slightly. I have to force myself not to look, not to check out her supple tits.

"Sure you don't, Princess." I smirk, toss her a wink, and move out of the way so she can walk through the front door of the bookstore.

"Fucking asshole." She mumbles as she passes by, blushing so hard I'm sure her hair is going to catch fire soon. I try my very hardest - or do I? - to keep the laugh from leaving my lips, but I lose.

The good part about being hauled to all these bookstores is the serenity that passes over Auggie.

She almost becomes a new person. She's calmer, clearer-minded, *happy*. Surrounded by old, well- loved paperbacks, losing herself in adventure after adventure, is truly what makes Auggie happier than any other time I've seen her.

Even when we head to the beach house to see her sister, there's still a darkness in her eyes, a wall she won't let drop. She's constantly looking over her shoulder, even though the whole reason we're here is for me to guard her and keep her hidden. She's always on edge.

Except when she's in a bookstore.

I make quick work of looking around, making note of exits, patrons, potential weapons, before relaxing my shoulders and sliding my hands into my pockets and heading into to ink and paper sea to find Auggie.

"Princess?" I call out in a sing-song way, and can almost *hear* the eye-roll.

"Over here!" She calls from the side, her words equally sing-songy.

We'd determined that when we were out in public, I was to play her boyfriend. It allows for me to get close to her, and stay close to her, but it also demands that we *play the part.*

It's not always a burden but damn, some days I can barely get a word in before she snaps at me. In fact, I kind of love getting to play boyfriend/ girlfriend just because of how much it annoys her.

"Oh, there you are. Another book about sex and romance? I swear baby, I think you're trying to give me a hint. Is that it? Do you need me to rock your world more often?" I tease her, wrapping my arms around her, and speaking just loud enough that I know the guys in the next aisle heard me.

Auggie elbows me, *hard,* in the stomach, my breath leaving me as the air is forced from my lungs.

"Maybe I just need to show you some things, *baby.*" She snaps back, gripping the book in her hand tightly and walking away.

"Never underestimate the girl that reads dirty books. They're freaks. In the best, most satisfying way." One of the guys from the aisle said, holding up his hand, palm open as if he was waiting for me to send him a high- five through the air.

"I'm telling you." He said earnestly. And before he could continue, I nodded and moved away.

Some people love to give advice when it's not needed. Or wanted.

"Kyle!" Auggies voice screams out my code name, the name she is supposed to call me in public when she thinks someone's following her.

Or worse.

I don't wait another millisecond before I bolt in the direction of her voice, running as fast as I can.

Auggie is standing in an aisle, a civil war and military genre aisle which I know she would never voluntarily go down, with a cocky, frat boy herding her into the shelves, trapping her against the shelf and his body, leaving just enough room that it wouldn't seem improper. An emotion I can't place rises in my chest.

"Stephanie, are you okay?" I pull her from him and pull her into my arms. My anger is surprising, but my protective instincts are not.

She's shaking as gladly accepts my shelter, and I see fucking red.

My attention turns to the asshole who is standing there looking just as pissed at me as I am at him.

"What the fuck do you think you're doing?" I snarl at the guy, watching his demeanor change from "I will fuck you up" to "I fucked up" as he takes in my height and how I easily have a good 20 pounds of muscle on him. I may not look like a typical mafia member; I have red hair and all my tattoos are small and hidden by clothing, but I make sure that if I fight someone, I can fucking win. And my size shows that.

"Hey man, I was just-"

"Just what? Just making a girl feel uncomfortable? Just getting into her personal space? Just trying to get with *my* girl? Who are you?" I snap, pushing him back. He stumbles a bit before righting himself, cooking his arm back in a fist at one last show of masculinity.

That's fine. His face will break under my fist just like any other douchebag.

"You looking to die today?" I take a step forward, getting into his space, all while keeping a hand on Auggie.

"Kyle, please. I want to go." Auggie's voice, shaky and unsure - so different than her normal tone, helps me calm enough that I can step back, never taking my eyes off the frat-boy prick.

"Are you hurt? Did he hurt you at all?" I ask, dreading and anticipating the answer.

"He just couldn't comprehend what no meant."

"You didn't tell me you had a boyfriend. A leprechaun at that." The idiot digs his grave a touch deeper.

"Did. He. Touch. You?" I say through gritted teeth. I'm sure the grip I have on her hand is starting to hurt, but I this emotion is filling my chest and the fact that I'm so worried, so possessive, is weirding me out. We need to leave before we draw a crowd and then shit will really be bad.

"No, Kyle. He didn't. Drop the caveman act, let him live and *let's go.*" Her voice lowered as she looked around us and I know she's right, we need to leave, but I want to hurt him for the meer fact that she was uncomfortable.

"Leave your books, baby, I'll give you my card and you can order whichever ones you want."

# 3

# Chapter 3

Auggie

I'll never admit it out loud. Ever.

But Trent smells fucking fantastic. Like clean rain and warm spice. It's what I imagine a thunder and lightning storm to smell like. As we leave the bookstore, he has me tucked under his arm with his bicep on my shoulder, a hand dangling in the valley of my breasts possessively, shielding me from the world and keeping me warm. It was cold in Newburyport; the sea air making the autumn breeze crisper.

"What did he do?" Trent asks, nearly asking under his breath.

"You saw the worst of it. He was an asshole." Regardless, I screamed out Trent's fake name because I'd been so freaked out, thinking it was Marcos. Back from the fucking grave, just to finish killing me *properly* this time. Something is wrong with me.

20

I expect Trent to snap, to snark at me, to lecture me about drawing that much attention to ourselves in public, like he's done in the past when I talk to people that he hasn't vetted, but he doesn't. Not this time.

He just keeps walking, holding me tightly to him.

I feel bad, although I'd never show it, that Trent got this job. Watching me, protecting me from whatever shit my sister has gotten into. The plus side is that he can protect me from Marcos's gang, too. I mean, he doesn't know he is, he *can't* know he is, but he's already protecting me from the Italian Mob, so one little gang shouldn't be a big deal... Right?

They're after me because they're certain that I betrayed them and am responsible for Marcos's death. They think that when Marcos discovered my imagined betrayal, he beat me within an inch of my life, left *me* for dead, but I had somehow turned around and killed him. Or I know who did. Truthfully, I wish I had killed him myself. More than likely, they wanted to gut me because they think I turned on Marcos. Marcos was paranoid to the enth degree before he beat me, and so it doesn't surprise me that whoever took over the gang assumes I betrayed him and is demanding my head. That just wasn't what happened, but it's futile to try and reason with a gang member who would rather shoot you between the eyes than take the chance that you really did turn.

In reality, I remember Marcos getting home that night, arguing, and so much fucking pain I passed out. When I woke up, I was in the hospital with Talia crying at my side and she told me he was dead. For all I know, he could've walked into oncoming traffic after attacking me. Death by bus. I doubt.

I have no fucking clue...but they think I do.

"Just tell me, how mad are you?" I whisper to Trent, wanting to know what level of lecture to expect when we got to the safehouse.

"I'm not mad, Steph." Trent says quietly, his use of my fake name a reminder that we are in public and to wait before talking more.

"Right." I barely conceal an eye-roll, but the colored contacts bother my eyes too much to do that.

The rest of the short walk was in silence, comfortable silence, but silence nonetheless. Being a city girl through-and- through, the lack of skyscrapers and traffic as offsetting at first, but the longer we stay in Newburyport, the longer I never want to leave. It's quaint, slow, steady. And so freaking beautiful that I can't imagine not waking up every day with the sun peeking up over the horizon, the warm colors changing slowly on the water.

When all this is over, I'm getting myself an apartment and I'm going to live here. Screw New York, screw Boston. I want to be here.

The path home is my favorite; a long sidewalk right up against the weathered shops as we look out to the ocean on the other side of the street. It's breathtaking and peaceful. Something I always seem too have in short supply. Especially after I had met Marcos. So now that I've been given a glimpse of how life could be, even if it isn't completely on my own at the moment, I realize that I can be free here.

I can be *myself* here. I haven't been able to really be me in a long time. With Marcos, it was always a Stepford-wife level of perfection he expected from me, no matter what. And I tried. I really did.

I changed and was as obedient and subservient as possible, even though it went against my nature. I'm not like that naturally. My parents called me their problem child, their independent wild child, the one that 'goes her own way'. In other words, I'm a brat that's independent and I don't need others to tell me what to do.

But Marcos... There was something about Marcos that intimidated, interested and made me infatuated with him. The complete change didn't happen overnight, but one suggestion, one nasty remark, one eyeroll at a time. When Talia told me he had died, a part of me – I now recognize it was the brainwashed part of me – was sad he'd left me. I'd been so controlled for so long I was scared about what that meant for me. He wasn't there to tell me what to wear, what to do, how to be anymore. I had been controlled and handled for so long that when that was taken, it was like the rug was pulled from under my feet.

However, a bigger part of me rejoiced that I could swear and give my opinion, that I could learn and grow, and I could be independent again. I could get a job doing something I liked and leave the house whenever I wanted to. I could be my most authentic self.

Very, very shortly after moving in with my parents, the threats started. A note taped to the apartment door. His brother, Hector, telling me to get my stuff and leave. He wanted to me tell the truth and if I did, he'd be merciful. A shiver runs through my body as I remember the fear I had day in and day out, worried about finding a note waiting for me somewhere.

Back then, Talia had dropped off the face of the earth it seemed like, and I had no one else to turn to. Some kind of shit went down with her though, because one day a bit after I'd woken up in the hospital, some guards in leather stood outside my parents front door like we were badass kings and queens that needed protection.

No matter what tactic I tried, I couldn't get any of them to tell me what was happening. It went on like that for months, until Trent showed up. This big lug of a guy who looked grumpy and exhausted with hair so light red, it looked blonder than it was because of the redness, and the darkest brown eyes I've ever seen in my life. His jaw is strong and the moment I saw him I was struck with awe. He was hot, objectively speaking. And if the first sentence out of his mouth hadn't made me want to throttle him, I'd probably have climbed him like the thick, muscled, gorgeous tree he is.

But, the first thing he said to me was; "Great, I get to be a babysitter."

His hotness factor went down significantly after that.

Now, after learning about why he's here to protect me, I realize that it could be annoying to have to watch after your best friend's little sister. I don't even know if he had a choice in the matter, or if he was ordered to protect me. But, it's not like I asked them to have him follow me. I didn't want him to, and I shouldn't be subjected to his mood swings for something I didn't ask for.

Especially when he's broody and bossy and always rolling his eyes like he can't believe what I'm saying. And he's always poking fun at me like an asshole.

Case-in-point, making fun of my books.

Trent grabs his keys out of his leather jacket, opening the door to the safehouse quickly, before checking over our shoulders and ushering me inside.

The house isn't much; a small 2 bedroom, apartment-type setup with a dingy kitchen and one questionable bathroom.

But the basement… The basement has been retrofitted to be an "Auggie-Jones-protection-command-center". I've never seen anything like it in real life; the escape windows covered in newspapers to block any sort of visibility from the outside, four huge-ass monitors all showing something; footage of the hidden security cameras outside, and other things I don't really know about but there's no doubt that they're vital to my safety.

It's like a dungeon down there, dark and the only light coming from the blaze of the monitors, so I steer clear. It's not too much better upstairs, but I prefer the little bits of daylight that faintly streams in through the blind- covered windows.

"Are you going to say anything? Or just pout like a child?" I snap when we are firmly inside and he locks the door. I am fully aware that I'm poking the bear, but I can't help it. Trent's never this fucking calm.

"What do you want me to say here, Auggie? You called me in terror, and I wanted to beat the shit of a little frat boy, who I need to now look into to make sure there's no Italian ties. That's it. Case closed, nothing more to say." He pulled his jacket off as he talked and I tried not to stare as the muscles that shifted with every movement of his arms.

"I didn't mean to make a scene." My voice is quieter than usual.

"Oh, don't get soft and shy on me now, Princess." Trent, honest to god, smirked. At me. That's never happened. He's always been exasperated with me. Like he can't fucking wait for this to be done and over with.

That smirk is dangerous. I steel myself against the attraction I feel at that look and try to listen to what he's saying.

"The code names are there for a reason. You were scared,

you called for me. That's what you are meant to do."

I'm pretty sure I wasn't meant to freak out seeing a guy that resembled my dead gangster ex-boyfriend. The 'frat guy' Trent called him, hadn't done anything, hadn't touched me or said anything vulgar. Sure, he was in my space, but it was more that he looked so much like Marcos that I freaked out.

I can't let Trent know about his gang coming after me. I don't know what he would do if he realized there was another threat… Maybe he'd throw his hands up and tell Kieron he was out, maybe he'd just walk away. I don't know, but I do know that he's already protecting me from any threat since my sister pissed off the Italian Mafia, and that means I have some level of protection.

That's right, she pissed off the *Mafia.* Sweet, perfect, 'I'm going to do what I want' Talia, had gotten involved with the Mafia, by way of her ex. And her now husband.

Her ex had died too and rather recently. Talia never told me how he died, and I never asked. She is far too happy with Kieron, and he treats her like a fucking queen. There's no reason for her to dwell on the past at all. Me on the other hand… I'm still trapped.

"Although," Trent starts, putting his hands in his front pockets. The fucking veins on his arms popping out farther against his muscle, how does that even happen? I can't take my eyes off them, and then scold myself mentally for being attracted to him in that small way.

"Can I ask you why you felt threatened? What did he do exactly?" Trent asked me almost shyly. Like he didn't want to care, but was too curious not to ask.

"He reminded me of someone." I say as I peel my own jacket off.

"That's all I get? Really? You cry out my name and are shaking like a leaf when I find you all because he reminded you of someone?"

I flip my long blonde hair over my shoulder, pushing past Trent to the kitchen and delay answering him my filling up a cup of water. He's so close to rolling his eyes, I can tell. The stern, serious lines of his face deepen in frustration. Well, fuck that. I don't owe him an explanation.

At least, not yet.

"Yep." I say, my fake confidence back.

"Not enough. I'm here to protect you and that doesn't just mean guarding you. If someone is after you, if someone is making you feel threatened in any way…" Trent crosses his arms over his chest and bends his head forward in a leading expression. He wants me to keep talking, he wants me to open up to him, but he hasn't exactly proven to me that I can yet. So, he's going to have to be content with what I give him.

"No one is after me." I lie through my teeth. "No one cares about Talia's kid sister."

"You know that's not true." He really does roll his eyes then. I feel my nostrils flare at the action. Normal people would probably try to comfort me, tell me 'No, Auggie, I care about you.' But not Trent. Not the emotionless, red-head who only seems to care when I'm in immediate danger or when he's able to piss me off.

"Look, I'm sorry I made a big deal about earlier. The guy just took me by surprise and I panicked. Won't happen again." I say with finality. I want this conversation to be done. I want the thought of Marcos and the stupid fucking gang he belonged to, that he ran, out of my mind. I've been under house arrest for so long. I just need to let off some steam, forget about all the bullshit for a few hours.

Getting laid wouldn't hurt either.

It's been *months* and living with this annoyingly handsome specimen of the male species and arguing with him all day… My vibrator is getting one hell of a workout. I'm a progressive woman, okay?  I can hate someone, but still find them hot enough to get off to.

"Auggie, that's not what I meant and you know it." Trent says.  His hands are clenching by his sides, but he makes no movement otherwise.

I'm so tired of this.

"I'm going to go lay down, okay? Don't think I've forgotten about getting the books somehow with your card, big guy." I say with a laugh, walking to my room. Before I can close the door, I hear him whisper, fearfully, "She's going to fucking bankrupt me."

# 4

# Chapter 4

Auggie

"Look, I understand we have to keep a low profile. I understand that the whole point of this is to keep us out of the eyes of the public. But what I don't understand is why you're so dead-fucking-set on making this so much harder than it needs to be." I'd asked him to pick up one thing. One thing from the grocery store, but instead he is intentionally being a dick and choosing to be ignorant.

It's been a few months of us living together now, and it's not necessarily getting better. We're more used to each other, sure, but the mood swings of Trent and my forced isolation are taking their tolls. I constantly feel like I have to walk on egg shells around him, like I don't know what's going to set him off, but then I have to remind myself that I refuse to be anyone but authentically myself. So, he gets to hear my opinion. A lot.

What's making this shit worse is that since the bookstore incident, Trent won't let me out of the house. Not even my one trip a week to go to the grocery store with him.

There are just some things I don't need him to buy for me. Tampons are one, but the sheer amount of chocolate that I consume is another. He says it's, "too dangerous and an unnessesary risk."

He said he'd get what I wanted, and so far, he has. But we're three weeks in and I'm going stir-crazy. I asked him for one thing, stuff to make cinnamon rolls, pre-baked cinnamon rolls, or even the canned stuff (at the last resort, though). I remember specifically asking him because he chuckled, then sighed, like I was a child asking for a candy bar at a store and he was the exhausted parent. I about punched him.

But I'd asked nicely and the past few weeks he'd gotten me the stuff I requested. So, I assumed it wouldn't be an issue. Imagine my surprise when he walks in all proud and puffed up like a goddamn peacock without the one thing I'd asked for.

"Auggie, they didn't have the type you specified." Trent rolls his eyes as he turns to put a bag of chips in the dingy cupboard, slamming it shut unnecessarily hard.

"Cinnamon rolls. In a can, fresh baked, hell, even the ingredients to make some. I told you I preferred that. I specifically told you the ingredients I needed. How did they not have anything at all?" I snap. I know I'm poking the bear, but honestly.

He's making it incredibly hard to trust him with even the smallest things, but he wants me to trust him with everything?

That shit is earned.

"Auggie," He says, and I can hear the warning in his tone.

"Seriously, Trent. I just asked for one thing. Is it that hard to have some kind of fucking empathy or emotion? Jesus christ." I drop the empty bag on the small table and storm off, slamming my door behind me.

It's an overreaction, I know that. But with what happened at the bookstore, with the feelings and secret fears I have surrounding Marcos and the threat from his gang, it's just becoming too much. I wanted to take my mind off of it for two fucking seconds, make my favorite comfort food, and I was going to stay put. I just needed a reprieve from my emotions and the lack of control I have. Not complain. But he decided me asking for something was too much, and so instead of telling me straight up that no, he wasn't going to get it, he let me think I'd be able to only to pull the rug out from underneath me.

It's just rude.

I take some deep breaths, trying to calm my irrational anger, but it's like my brain just keeps spiraling.

I'm in the deep end of my anxiety, and it's going to take me a little bit to climb out of it. My chest is starting to feel tight, the blank, empty walls around me seem to be closing in on me the longer I spend in this box. We've been here for a few months and we are still living like we are squatters. Kieron made sure that we had furniture, comfortable beds, TV's, etc., but it's bare bones. There's no warmth. I have a sleeping bag on the mattress and a memory foam pillow, my own TV in here that rests on a small bookshelf that houses my collection of books I've acquired throughout our time in hiding.

For obvious reasons, we can't just go out and shop for all that stuff; sheets and comforters, décor, or even print out pictures. Not matter how much I wish we could. It would make me feel less like I'm being held prisoner.

I hear the door shut and all three of the locks *click* as Trent leaves, again, and locks me inside. At least I'm alone.

There's nothing really to do, except read. So, I pick up the paperback on my side table, admiring the half-naked man covered in tattoos on the cover, and get lost in a world where the man will do anything for his girl, including burn down the world to keep her happy.

* * *

A soft knock wakes me up. I must have fallen asleep reading, and cringe slightly because now I don't know where I was at in the story.

"Auggie?" Trent's soft voice carries through the thin door as he knocks again.

"Yeah?" I answer, my voice groggy with sleep still, but I push myself up as much as I can. A violent yawn rips through me.

"Can I come in?"

Why the hell not, it's not like I really have much of a choice. "Sure," I unzip the sleeping bag just a little more and try to make my hair somewhat more presentable. My hair is getting to be so long that I'm considering chopping it off. I don't know if I'd be able to do it myself but I know for a fact that Trent wouldn't let me go out and get my hair done.

He slowly opens the door and his annoyingly handsome face peeks around the side.

"Hey,"

"What's up?" I try to cover up another yawn. I thought the

nap would've helped my tiredness, but instead it just seems to have made it worse.

"I wanted to apologize." The moment the words are out of his mouth, I feel my own mouth drop in surprise.

"Excuse me?" I ask incredulously, because I need him to repeat it. I'm sure I misheard him. Trent doesn't apologize for the dickish things he does. He just pretends like it's normal and gets on with it, forcing me to do the same. After a few weeks, I realized pretty quickly that I needed to let some of the little things go so that when I fought back, he knew I meant business. I needed to be strategic and not hold on to my anger quite so tightly. For my own sake.

"Don't be a brat." Trent rolls his eyes at me, but one of his hands comes up to cup the back of his neck nervously. The t-shirt he's wearing is just tight enough that it cups his biceps nicely and shows off his tapered waist. When he lifts his arm, a sliver of his stomach is shown; the pale, clear skin showing right above his jeans. No tattoos there either.

Interesting.

"I'm not. I need to make sure I'm not hallucinating. I don't think I've ever heard those words leave your lips. Especially not to me." I scoff, without meaning to. His eyes turn darker, his jaw sets, and his nervous energy seems to disappear.

"Look, I don't want to fight with you. I wanted to apologize for not getting your cinnamon roll shit at the store. I'll be honest with you, I forgot and was too much of a dick to admit it. While you were sleeping, I ran out and tried to grab some, but they didn't have any at the store bakery. I didn't know… I didn't know that it was that big of a deal. But, the more I thought about it, the more I realized that it wasn't really about the actual cinnamon rolls, was it? It's more about your freedom to do even the little things that you want. And I haven't been very… understanding of that. So, I apologize and I'm going to try to do better."

The dark, trapped feeling that had pulled me under was dissipating with his words and his admission.

"What did you get?"

A small smile lights up his face and he gestures with his head for me to follow him.

** * **

"I didn't know you liked to bake." Trent has taken up residence in one of the chairs in the kitchen, watching me putter around making my sweet comfort treat.

"I don't. Not really. I can't cook to save my life unless it's like three steps and doesn't require the stove. But cinnamon rolls, I can make them and they always turn out perfectly. I don't know why or how, but they're my favorite for a reason." I chuckle, kneading the dough softly. It's a fine art, baking, and one that I'm not overly confident in.

"Why cinnamon rolls?" Trent asks, and I momentarily halt my movements as I think about how to answer.

"Honestly?"

"I mean, I would hope so." Trent shrugs and leans his head on his hand.

"My dad used to make cinnamon rolls when was stressed. Or on weekends at the very least if the week wasn't too outrageous for him. I would sit in the kitchen with him as he hummed along to the classic rock songs on the radio and when he let me help him, it was always such a fun time. We'd talk and laugh. It was like any troubles I had would melt away. When we had to be guarded by the other guys, my dad was baking them daily. I think he was stressed about Talia, but didn't know what to do. So there for a while, I just stood with him, kneading the dough, forming the rolls, dusting the cinnamon and sugar. We worked silently, but we gave each other strength to have hope that she'd be okay." Instead of looking at Trent in anyway, I keep my eyes focused on the task at hand. I turn the dough over once more and put it in the bowl beside me, covering it with a towel and setting it to the side to proof.

"There, now we just have to let it rise for a bit."

"Thank you." He says softly. "Thank you for telling me that."

"Can we do a trade? I told you something, so you tell me something?" I ask, wiping my hands on a rag. Trent's eyes narrow and I can see the brick wall building behind his eyes.

"What do you want to know?" He asks, crossing his arms over his chest as if he needs another layer of space between us.

"Why don't you have any tattoos?" I tilt my head to the side and run the rag through my hands before folding it and setting it on the counter.

"What?" He's shocked. Shocked that I would ask that question when there are clearly so many more questions that I want, need to know the answers to.

"Well, Kieron alluded to the fact that he's this big bad boss man, and it doesn't take a genius to realize you guys are either in the mafia or you're in a *very* influential gang. I'm leaning more towards mafia because you guys have this air of 'being born into it' around you. That's neither here nor there, though. I mean, typically guys who are in the crime circles, they're covered in tattoos, piercings, body modification. But so far, I haven't seen one tattoo on you. Do you have like a little ladybug on your ankle or something?" I cross my arms loosely, leaning my hip on the counter and smirking like a fool.

"You think I have a ladybug on my ankle? Really?" He successfully sidesteps my deduction about his company and organization, but that's okay. I'm not really looking for those details just yet.

"You seem like the type." The smirk on my face blooms into a full-blown smile as I try to keep the laughter from my voice.

"You know what, you're right. A little ladybug on one ankle and a small glitter butterfly on the other." He teases, throws me a half-smile and a wink.

"I fucking knew it." I kick off the kitchen cabinets and go to stand right in front of him with my hands on my hips. "Let me see."

Trent chuckles. He actually *chuckles* at something I said. He's not laughing at me this time, he's laughing at a joke I made. The deep laugh is mesmerizing, and I want to make him laugh again and again.

"You caught me, Princess. I don't have any tattoos. At least not yet." He puts his hands up in mock surrender.

"Why not? I figure that would be like a rite of passage or something in your... job."

"Kieron has never made me do anything that I don't want to. I have been in terrible situations, but he's never made me be in them. The same with tattoos. Kieron's covered, Cillian, his cousin, is covered. Hell, even Bryan has a sleeve. But I have never found anything I wanted to be inked into my skin permanently. At least not yet." He said the last part again, like he had a specific idea in mind, but had yet to make it a reality.

I nod, "What do you want?"

"What?"

"You talk like you have a tattoo already picked out but you're getting cold feet about it." I shrug and Trent's eyes are blown wide and his mouth is twists a little in the beginning of a smirk.

"Well, you are overly observant aren't you?" He shakes his head and runs his fingers through his hair. A nervous tick I've discovered. "I do have an idea, but it only just came to me a little while before we met. I've… I've been through some shit and I'm working through it. So, until I feel like I've worked through most of it, I'm holding off." My interest and curiosity is significant peaked.

"What is it?" I ask nosily. I wonder if it will be a typical tribal piece I see a lot of guys have, or flowers with skulls. I saw that a lot in Marcos's men. They all had skulls, guns, knives all over them.

"I think… I think I'll keep that to myself for right now." He says shyly, like he's worried he might offend me for wanting to keep something private. "I'm sorry,"

"Don't be sorry! I'm sorry I pried. But, I think you'd look bad ass with one though. You look like you could crack a skull with your bare hands as you are right now, but with a tattoo, you'd be a beast."

His eyes change, an emotion that I can't quite place is swimming in the dark brown of his iris's. Satisfaction and pride are the closest things I can think of.

"I'll have to keep that in mind." He says, his voice lower than it was before and a tension between us grows.

"Yeah, I think you should." I drop my gaze down to my shoes, but I can't help the smile on my face.

"Do you have any?"

It's a very nice change of pace for us. This back and forth, the interest in each other. Not just trying to understand why I blew up at him or why he shut down on me.

"I do. But I'm not going to tell you where." I got a butterfly; this beautiful, watercolor piece on my ribcage as soon as I was able to leave the hospital after I thought I was free from Marcos.

Turns out I was wrong. I wasn't free. I probably won't ever be again. But I love the hell out of that tattoo and what it symbolizes for me.

"Will you tell me what it is?" Trent comes over to stand in front of me, and the gaze he's raking my body with, as if he could see my bare skin through my clothes, is heated. His eyes trail down my body, taking in every piece of uncovered skin, but his gaze lingers on my stomach, my hips, my thighs. He's truly checking me out and it feels like he's interested. If I saw a guy looking at me like this in the club, I'd be taking him home.

I giggle softly, and look up into his dark eyes; they're so full of intrigue, of interest, of… lust.

"No, I don't think I will." I say with more seduction than I knew I was capable of. And the air between us crackles with tension.

"I'll find out one day." He whispers. Too afraid to break the tension between us. But his words are like tossing gasoline on the fire building within me.

"Maybe you will."

# 5

# Chapter 5

Auggie

I think I'm going to go out of my mind with boredom.

Honest to god, I think I've watched every Disney movie, sitcom, drama, I have access to. I've read all the books I have. I even took Trent up on his offer to go get me some new books because of the creepy guy situation. I looked up a few titles the store had and wrote down explicitly what I wanted. That way we didn't have a repeat of the cinnamon roll situation.

When Trent had gotten home, he gingerly handed me the bag, with a slight blush on his face and shook his head softly.

"What? Did you get them?" I take the bag and open up seeing all four titles tucked neatly inside.

"I did. But you didn't tell me they were going to be half-naked men on the cover. Most embarrassing thing I've ever done." He peeled his jacket off and draped it over the chair. "You could've warned me. I mean, I guess I should've realized, one is literally called 'Stepbrother's Darling.'"

"You got that one? Yay! It's about a girl who falls in love with her three stepbrothers even though they're kind of bullies. The reviews were good and I can't wait to read it for myself." I pull out the books unashamed in my reading choices. I love romance stories; I love falling in love with these characters and the sexy times that ensue.

He had blushed, making the light red of his hair look even more red, and he basically sprinted from the room down to the dungeon.

Needless to say, I devoured the books and now I'm back to square one.

Trent has been making it a point to hang out in the common areas a little more, and it's nice. I feel like we are definitely starting to move into more of a friend territory instead of two people that hate each other and are forced to live together.

The only thing is… he's also taken to doing his workouts in the living room, too. Dear god, save me. He's doing one right now, sweat dripping from his skin, rolling down the caverns between his abs as he does abdominal twists. *Fuck me.* I thought I was attracted to him when he was wearing clothes. Seeing his bare chest, I know for a fact I'd let this man wreck me.

He could do whatever he wanted to me and I would say, 'thank you.'

I'm totally not checking him out. I'm not.

But then he lays down on his back after his set and breathes heavier, all while looking at me and I know I was. And worse, I know that I was caught.

"You okay?" He asks, one of his eyebrows arch up.

"Uh huh." My mouth is dryer than the fucking desert.

"What's up?" He sits up and leans on his elbows and I swear, I'm drenched. He's all pale, smooth skin and hard muscles that ripple when he moves. The way he's propped up, it makes his arms and shoulders look even bigger and his stomach even leaner.

*Don't look, don't look, don't look,* I chant to myself to try to keep myself from checking out his shorts.

"I'm bored." My voice squeaks, completely ignoring the cool, collected vibe I was trying to portray. One of his eyebrows lifts up and an infuriatingly attractive smirk crosses his face.

"You're bored?" He asks, still a little breathless. I nod, perching on the side of the chair, letting one of my feet dangle.

"Well, I'm sorry Princess, but my job to keep you safe, not necessarily save you from boredom."

"Oh, come on!" I groan and throw my hands in the air.

"Did you already read those books?" He lays back down and brings a knee to his chest, his eyes glued to the ceiling, and I sneak a peek down to his grey athletic shorts.

*Hot damn.* I can see the outline as he moves, and it's impressive. It's also reminding me exactly how horny I am, and how I can do nothing about it. Not that I wouldn't accept that invitation if he offered, but I sincerely doubt he ever will.

"All of them."

"Damn, Auggie. Those were four, full-length novels that I picked up not even a week ago. What did you do, refuse to sleep?" He puts his leg back down to rest and pulls up the other.

"There's nothing else for me to do here, Trent. I can't go outside, I can't work, I can't go on the internet except for the streaming services you guys have somehow hooked up in a way where it's not traced to us. I can't do anything but watch

TV, read, and bake." I grumble. I don't mean to complain, I really don't. But I'm going stir-crazy. At least at the penthouse, I had access to a full gym, a pool, internet, my phone. I was able to do anything, as long as I didn't leave the premises.

Not that I'm comparing my hell with Marcos and the protection I'm reluctantly receiving from Trent and Kieron.

"What would you like to do?" Trent stands up and walks over the table, grabbing his water bottle and downing half of it in one gulp. His Adam's apple bobs with each swallow and I'm transfixed.

Maybe I need to cool it with the smut books until I'm able to…do something about this intensity. This longing I feel.

Who am I kidding? I'm going to continue to devour those books until I can't any longer.

"Right now, or in general?"

"Well, it's only one in the afternoon." Trent points out, looking at his watch.

"So, I'm guessing we can't go out? Just for a walk? Please?" I do my absolute best to give him puppy eyes, pushing my bottom lip out and threading my fingers together under my chin.

Trent looks at me for a moment, and just when I think he's going to tell me no, he groans and I know I've won the moment.

"Can you give me half hour to shower? And we're going for a walk, no stops, no interactions with others, just making a loop around town. The *edge* of town." He points at me with a finger lifted from his water bottle.

"Yes, of course." I nod, too happy to finally be leaving to argue.

"I'll be right back." He shakes his head and I do a little happy dance before I leave the room to go put on real clothes myself.

* * *

"Oh my god," I moan when the fresh air fills my lungs and the warm sun hits my skin. It's a stark contrast between the cooler air, but I love it.

I tip my face up to the sky, soaking in as much sunlight as possible.

"I know we haven't been able to be outside a lot, I'm sorry." Trent says softly. I open my eyes and look to him, expecting him to be looking around, but instead, his eyes are locked on me.

"It's okay. I understand." I say, equally as softly. "But, you should know by now that I'm like a plant. I need sunlight, food, and water to really thrive."

He laughs, loudly and more like a cackle, but it's warm and his eyes are full of light. I like that I was the one that made him feel like that.

"A plant? No, Auggie, you're definitely not that laid back and low maintenance. There's a reason I call you 'Princess', you know."

I scoff. "Rude." But smile at him and decide which way we're going. I pull him to the left and we start our stroll. God, it's beautiful here. The sea crashing against the shore, pushing ice blocks up on the sand. The air is clean and the sky is clear. It's perfect. Everything I want.

I can't wait until I'm able to live here freely. Go out and find my preference of grocery store, a gym, my favorite bookstore, actually go to the club and meet people. God, it's been so long since I've organically met anyone. It's always been set ups or 'allowed" people from Marcos. But, even then, it's been years.

We're silent as we walk. Trent's arms are covered in his leather jacket and I have one of my arms looped with his. It's drilled into my head that the moment we step outside, we are Stephanie and Kyle, not Auggie and Trent.

Honestly, it's not that much of a hardship these days.

"So, tell me about yourself." We can't keep going through the motions, can't keep living like this, like we're becoming friends, but not actually getting to know one another. Sure, I like figuring things out slowly with Trent. I know how he takes his coffee in the morning, I know how he likes to kick up one leg on the couch or coffee table while watching TV, I know how he snores softly when he's really tired. But I also know there's a haunted look in his eyes, a fractured piece of him somehow that's changed who he is.

Like speaks to like.

"What do you want to know?" He asks guardedly, side-eyeing me as he tries his best to look at me but also keep an eye on our surroundings.

"Anything. Everything. How'd you get wrapped up in this mafia stuff?" I'm throwing it out there, hoping I'm right. By process of elimination, there's no way I'm wrong.

Trent pales even further. "What?"

"If I've deduced it correctly, Kieron brought you into the fold, right?" I do my best to keep a smirk off my face, but I know I've pegged the situation correctly.

Trent is angry when I look back to him. The teasing and light in his eyes is completely gone, leaving only that cold, emotionless detachment and anger left in its place.

"What? What is it?" I ask, holding onto his arm a little tighter, hoping to show him I'm concerned. I don't want him to pull away, to hide behind his emotionless mask and what I'm beginning to think is faux distain for me.

"You don't have a fucking clue what you're talking about. I'd shut my mouth and say 'thank you' if I was you. Kieron could have very easily thrown his hands up, but he's a good guy, one of the best, and instead of just doing what I say and using common fucking sense to *not* bring up what you are, you're pushing for more." He snarls. I feel my hand drop from his arm in shock and take a step out of the space we were sharing. I don't recognize the man in front of me. His eyes are narrowed and the pupils are blown open so wide, it's making his light eyes look black. Trent's shoulders are hunched over, his hands in his pockets, but even through the leather, I can see his muscles shift. It makes him look even more threatening than his sheer broadness already makes him look.

My mouth drops to say something, anything, to give him a rebuttal, but honestly, I don't have anything to say. Anything I can say.

"I think I'm ready to go back to the apartment now." I manage to push out, my words soft and breathless, but even I can hear the agony.

"Finally, you have a good idea." He snaps, and turns on his heels, stomping away from me.

I don't know what just happened. But I'm surely not deterred from finding out.

* * *

The short walk home is completely silent. Trent makes sure to stay in front of me, but not too far. He's taking the space from me he needs, but as always, he's still making sure I'm safe.

The asshole just can't seem to leave me alone, even when he's pissed off.

I didn't think that question was too out of the norm. It wasn't like I asked if he was in the mafia in a crowded movie theater where everyone can hear you whisper. We were on a sidewalk, with no cameras around, no other people, fuck me, I thought we were fairly secluded, but I guess the only place Trent feels safe at all is the apartment.

Message received.

The apartment comes into view and Trent, who was already speed-walking, forcing me to keep up with him, speeds up more before pulling his keys out and starting the process of unlocking our safehouse.

"Are we going to talk about this?" I mutter.

"There's nothing to talk about."

"There obviously is."

"Shut up." He snaps, and the key turns one final time before the bolt unlocks.

"I'm getting really fucking tired of your attitude. You can't be hot and then cold to me whenever you feel like it." I push in front of him, turning to stop his entrance to the apartment and forcing him to look at me.

"Let me inside."

"Are we going to talk about this?" I put a hand on each wall of the small hallway, showing him I'm not kidding.

"Let me in." He growls, and I can see from his posture that he wants to just push past me, but something is stopping him.

I drop my arms and stand to the side, letting my hormonal, confusing, giant of a man, through. But I don't give him much space, following close behind him so that we can have this long overdue conversation.

"Okay, are you going to speak now or would you prefer that I say what I think is going on and you can grunt or snap or whatever to tell me if I'm right or wrong. Because this," I gesture between us, "this needs to change. We are good for a few days; joking, laughing, becoming friends, and then I ask one question, one question to try and get to know you better and you change from Dr. Jekyll to Mr. Hyde. I can't live like this. It's not fair, Trent. So decide now, do you want to actually be friends, to talk and laugh and enjoy this time, or do you want to keep fighting every step of the fucking way because you think you have to act a certain way to be this big, bad protector. Make your choice and stick with it." I poke my finger, *hard*, into his chest and turn on my heel, leaving him to figure it out. No one can decide for him, no matter how much I might want to smack some sense into him.

"That means letting me in. Letting me get to know you. I want to know you. But it's really hard when you don't want to know me." I say softly before I close my bedroom door and give him the space that he's so desperately wanting.

* * *

I step out of the shower, wrapping the towel around my naked body, and wipe a hand over the condensation on the mirror to reveal a distorted vision of myself. Like a funhouse mirror reflection of myself where I barely recognize the person looking back at me, but I know it's me. My eyes look sunken in, my skin is paler, my hair is borderline out of control in it's length.

Taking a deep breath, I shake my head. I'm so done with this. This emotional power struggle and back and forth. This physical toll that all these events are having on me. I'm so done.

I try my best not to break, not to show any outward signs of breaking, of weakness. Because Marcos would always retaliate when I would. He'd hit me or tighten his reign on me a little more. Cut off my world even more. I'm not going to sit around and let Trent do the same thing. Even though I know he'd never raise a hand to me, never strike me physically, it doesn't mean that his verbal lashings don't hurt.

Maybe I'm just kidding myself with trying to be his friend, trying to be anyone to him other than his charge. I'm not going to keep putting myself out there if he's never going to let me in. I have to have some kind of self-preservation.

But, why does Trent's distain for me hurt far worse than Marcos's fists on my body?

A soft knock draws my attention to the thin door that separates me from Trent.

"Yes?"

"Are you decent?" His voice is different, shockingly so. When he's pissed at me, his voice is dark and dangerous, full of violence and an edge that tells me that he'd like to let go of his control. When he's teasing me, it's light and full of laughter. Even when he's rolling his eyes at my words, there's always an undertone of friendly banter. But now…

Now he sounds like he's in pain. The way his voice breaks as he asks the question makes my heart hurt for him.

"Yes." As the word leaves my lips, the door is already opening and Trent's huge frame is filling the small space. His eyes linger on my exposed chest and shoulders, and I can feel the heat rush in between my legs at his gaze. He looks hungry. He looks stricken. I wrap my arms over my chest, subtly pushing my breasts up and together under the guise of making sure my towel stays put. Trent's eyes get stuck on my cleavage, and I can almost feel him ripping the towel apart and having his way with me; fucking me roughly on the bathroom counter, his powerful thrusts sending my breasts jiggling with each movement of his cock in me. I quickly turn to the mirror again, and try to ignore the bright blush on my cheeks. "So, what couldn't wait until I'm fully dressed?"

Just because I care about how he's feeling doesn't mean I'm going to forget just how quickly he turned on me.

"I'm sorry." He says, looking down as if he can't bear to look me in the eye.

"For?"

"There's a multitude of reasons, but first and foremost, for how I snapped at you like a self-righteous dick on the walk. I was surprised, is all." He has the decency to look sheepishly at me, like he knows I won't just accept it right off the bat. Trent knows me enough by now to know that I'm going to demand answers. Then, maybe, I'll forgive him.

"Why were you surprised?" I put my hands down on the small counter and stare at him through the mirror, my fiery gaze intent on burning him, but instead, it seems to calm him. His body relaxes and he takes a deep breath before answering.

"Because, Auggie. You figured everything out simply by watching. You're a very intelligent woman, and I'm sure you've already figured out about 95% of why we are here, who I am, and what this is all about. But, with that knowledge, or I guess, with me explicitly telling you this stuff, comes a lot of danger."

"I'm always in danger." I say softly, and the secret meaning of my words isn't lost on me.

"Not because of me." Trent says strongly. "I can't have you in danger because of me." His head drops down and softly, I hear him whisper to himself, "No one else."

There's definitely a story there. One I'm desperate to know.

"Trent, I'm already in this. My sister is married to the head of a Mafia gang. I'm probably always going to be in the sights of someone now. Anything you tell me isn't going to change anything except *our* relationship. *Our* friendship."

"What if it changes how you see me?" His eyes are burning with emotion as he looks at me in the mirror.

"It would only show me the real you, big guy." I shrug.

"And if you... don't like the real me? If you don't feel safe with the real me?" He looks nervous. He actually looks nervous as if he cares what I think of him. It takes everything within me not to show how shocked I am at that. He's never shown any indication that he cares about my opinion, especially not my opinion of him as a person.

"Who's to say I like this version?"

A smile crosses his face; the tension in the air broken finally.

"That's fair." He chuckles and comes to stand a bit closer. My skin prickles with the movement that brings him into my space. Closer than I thought he would be. I could feel his heat on my bare skin and I resist a shiver.

"In all honesty, I think I'll like the real Trent more."

"More?" He says breathlessly.

"I mean, yeah, big guy. I like you. When you're not being a massive asshole." I shrug slightly, but my body is still rooted in place by his stare and how close he is.

"I didn't think that was possible." He whispers, and the expression on his face kills me. It was surprised, self-destructive, and full of longing all at once. He didn't know what to do or what to feel, but then again, neither do I.

"What, trying to not be an asshole?" I chuckle, but the laughter gets caught in my throat.

"You liking me. In any way."

My smile drops, and guilt churns my stomach. Does he actually think that I wouldn't care for him? Had I not been as obvious as I thought I was being by nearly begging him to be my friend?

I swallow the lump in my throat and push my long hair over my shoulders; trying to prove I'm confident, even though this emotional back-and-forth is making me feel more vulnerable, and more insecure by the moment.

"Well, you didn't make it easy. But yeah, Trent, I'd like the opportunity to get to know you better because I like who you are. I don't want you to share anything you're not comfortable sharing, but I need the truth from you. You're asking me to put my life in your hands, to blindly follow you, but you're not giving me enough to go on."

I watch in the mirror as his whole body seems to slouch with tension as he realizes I'm right. His head hangs forward, like his neck can't hold his head any longer, and it rests on my shoulder.

We stay there, locked in this semi-embrace until Trent stands straighter, his eyes determined and a decision looks like it's been made in his mind. I hope he'll let me in on what that decision was.

"Get dressed, and meet me in the living room." He says

roughly, turning quickly to leave the bathroom.

"Why can't we just talk now?" I turn quickly to ask him before he can leave. I look at his back, the broadness of his shoulders that look like they hold the weight of his whole world on them.

His hand stops on the doorknob, but he doesn't turn around. His other hand rests at his side, and is clenching into a fist tightly.

"Because, Auggie, I need to be able to tell you this story without distractions."

"And me in a towel is a distraction?" I scoff, disbelievingly.

"More than you know." He says and leaves the room before I can even comprehend his words. But when the door latches shut, the words are stuck in my brain, playing on a loop. Changing everything.

# 6

# Chapter 6

Trent

I move across the room swiftly trying to get away from the floral smell of Auggie's shampoo. It feels like it's stuck in my nostrils, tempting me, and making me go even crazier than I already am.

Liquor, I need liquor to have this conversation.

Before I go and pour myself what will be my very heavy-handed, but the only drink of the night, I go to the dungeon and make sure that the apartment is as secure as possible. So, I check the cameras, make sure the house isn't bugged – well, I re-check like I do every single time we leave the house, I check my email to make sure Bryan is still checking into the prick that cornered Auggie in the bookstore.

When there isn't anything for me to procrastinate anymore, I climb the stairs up to the living room, and see Auggie sitting on the couch with a book in her hand, waiting for me.

I keep my eyes on the prize though, and pull open the cabinet above the fridge that houses the one bottle of whiskey we keep. Or I keep. Auggie's never had a drink stronger than a wine cooler here at the apartment. I hate wine coolers with a passion, so one day on a grocery run, I decided I needed a bottle of whiskey, just in case.

In case of what, I didn't know. I do now.

I pull out a small plastic cup and fill it far more than two fingers.

I'll need it to get through this conversation. Fuck.

How am I supposed to tell this girl, a girl that I'm realizing I have some confusing feelings for, all about the torture I've endured all for the sake of her sister? I did it willingly, and not because I cared for Talia in any romantic sense, but because I care about Kieron. He's my best friend. The guy I know would have my back for anything and when the time came for me to have his back, for the love of his life, I didn't hesitate. Because I know he'd do the same for me. Besides, I was there when they got together, and I saw how wrecked he was when they were apart.

But in doing so, my whole brain is now fucked up.

I gulp down the amber liquid, hoping that it gives me some courage to answer her questions and not revert into the dark headspace that became my home for a few months.

"You don't have to tell me anything." Auggie's soft, melodious, *calming* tone gave me strength. I knew I don't have to. But I want to. It will make so much ore sense to her, why I'm like this, once she knows.

"I know."

"If you're that uncomfortable…"

"You wouldn't want to know more information? Come on,

Princess, we both know that's not true." I take another drink, more controlled and a more acceptable amount this time. "But I appreciate the sentiment."

Auggie looks at me sheepishly, but also kind of happy, maybe that I know her better than she thought.

"What do you want to know?" I ask again.

"You'll tell me the truth?" She presses. Her dark eyes are so big and deep that I have to hold my cup a bit tighter so I don't fall. I need to keep a clear head, or as clear as I can with alcohol, the necessary alcohol, involved.

"I'll always tell you the truth."

"Is Kieron the head of a gang?" She fires that off quickly. It's obvious that she had that question locked and loaded.

"No."

The surprise is clear on her face, disappointment that she was wrong is fleetingly there, but then her eyebrows furrow together in confusion. "No fucking way he isn't."

"He's not." I chuckle, and take another sip. "He's the Second-In-Command of the Irish Mafia in Boston. It's much more than just a gang. And technically he's not the leader. He's the Second."

And her mouth drops open slightly before snapping shut. Auggie's quiet for a minute, and I take a moment to just watch her try and sort through it all in her head.

"Makes sense." This woman never ceases to amaze me.

"It makes sense?" I repeat.

"Yeah," she nods, "I mean, he has the power to somehow keep multiple people safe, order others around, he's tattooed from neck down, and he's always packing. Jesus. Talia knows, right? Obviously, she has to know."

"She does." Another nod, another sip of the amber liquid.

"Wow." Auggie looks off, before she whispers softly enough that I know it's not meant for me to hear, but I do anyway. "She never said anything."

Choosing to let her run this conversation so I don't have to expend any more emotional shit than I have to, I wait patiently for Auggie to ask her next question.

"What's your title, then? You work for Kieron which means you're in the Mob too."

"I don't think I have a title exactly. The way that Kellan, Kieron's dad and our Skipper, runs it, I report to Kieron, who reports to Kellan. It's like a pyramid, but my job is sectioned under Kieron's rank. The closest title I can think of would be enforcer. I'm the one who takes what Kieron says and makes it happen. Through persuasion or force." Another sip. I lean back on the worn cushion, and let my head rest against the back of the couch.

"So, you torture people."

"If I need to."

She raises both eyebrows, and she crosses her arms over her chest on the opposite side of the couch. I'm waiting for her to tell me I'm a monster, I'm disgusting, I'm a *bad person*. All things I'm well aware of, but I start to build defenses anyway. That this is my job and I do what needs to be done. Usually, the people I'm hurting deserve it. Usually they're terrible, horrible people who are taking up space in this world and I relish in being the one to rid the world of them. That I feel powerful when the scum of the earth tremble before me, and I make them bleed. That I do what I'm told, that I'm good at it and I'm good at keeping people safe. My heart starts to beat faster as I mentally preparing for a fight.

How dare she say anything about my character? She doesn't

know what I've been through, she doesn't know what an honor it is to be the Second's right-hand man, to have the complete trust of someone so powerful. She doesn't know what I've done to work for the power and position I have. How I've earned it. This Princess hasn't had to work a day in her life; going from her parents' house to Marcos house where I *know* she was taken care of monetarily, to here where Kieron and Talia are footing the bill for everything. I'm prepared with comebacks to insults that have yet to be spoken, but I will not feel guilty over my chosen lifestyle. Over my family.

"That must really suck." That's all she says.

*That must really suck.*

Like I didn't just tell her I torture and maim people on the regular.

Her eyes are full of compassion and warmth as she looks at me and takes a deep breath before continuing.

"Do you… Is it everyone, or just the really bad guys?" She asks softly.

"Just the really bad guys." I whisper, still shocked and surprised at her reaction. "Just the people that truly deserve it. And I won't lie and tell you I don't enjoy making those kinds of people hurt."

Her eyes cloud over like she's stuck in a memory, before she shakes her head slightly and moves one of her arms to her neck, using the back of the couch as a rest.

"So, what happened?"

"What do you mean?"

"You look like you have a million stories behind your eyes. And now that I know what you do, I'm wondering if something happened to make you so hot and cold, so closed off. Not that you need one particular incident, I'm sure you've seen your fair share of terrific events."

"I'm not… closed off." I deflect, taking the last drink of whiskey from the plastic cup before filling it back up halfway. I don't want to get wasted, but I do need to take the edge off.

"Yeah, okay." She scoffs. "When we first met, Talia and Kieron were singing your praises; how good of a guy you were, how great friends you are, how well we would get on, how sweet and full of life you were, how you're the only one they would trust to protect me. Then you walk in, and you shut down, get angry, insult me. That doesn't seem like someone who would be friends with my sister, no offense."

"I insulted you?" I'm taken aback slightly. I don't really remember much of that first meeting, too engrossed in my guilt to be much use to anyone, but Talia and Kieron had said time was of the essence, and I wanted to get right into my next assignment. Faster than I should've. I'd just come off a few days off, and was nursing a hangover headache and nausea. My head had felt like it was going to explode, my mouth was dry like I'd swallowed a cotton ball, and I felt like I was sweating whiskey, not to mention I hadn't eaten because whatever I put in my mouth came right back up. That handle of whikey I'd demolished, mostly the night before, was sloshing in my stomach to torment me.

I just remember Kieron and Talia picking me up early, driving me across the city, then left me in the car. Kieron wasn't happy with my choices, but he didn't say anything. So, I'd fallen asleep after a bit, and Talia had come back looking angry and frustrated before pulling me inside. So to recap; I was hungover, clouded and overwhelmed with guilt and trauma, and woken up not-so-nicely abruptly.

I'm pretty sure I blocked that entire day out because I wasn't on duty. Not yet at least.

"Yeah," Auggie scoffed unkindly, "Like you don't remember."

"I don't know if you remember, but that day I was pretty fucking out of it." I snap, all the while knowing I shouldn't.

"Well, you made it very clear that you did not like your new babysitting job. And were bound-determined to show me how you didn't choose this, and weren't happy at all." She said. Her words held an air of hurt and an edge. Even after all this time. My stomach dropped, and it's like a light-bulb went off over my head. It all made sense. Everything that's happened. Sure, I made sure to keep her at arm's length because of the annoying attraction I feel for her, and that it could have made my job protecting her harder if we were closer. But I never wanted to be cruel to her, even though we bicker and tease, I never wanted to be *mean* to her.

I feel sick to my stomach that I... that I'd...

"I'm sorry." I say sincerely. The words taste terrible as they past my tongue, but not because I have to apologize, but because of how she must feel being around me. Just like how they did...

"It is what it is."

There's nothing else that I can say. Nothing I can do to prove that I'm sorry for that initial meeting, except change how our relationship trajectory is going.

I nod, taking a small sip from my refilled cup.

"So, what was your last job?" She asks. I can tell that she's trying to push past the awkwardness, past the tension growing between us, but the mention of the place I'd left... It was like a shock to my system.

I took a big drink.

"I was undercover with the Italians. For Kieron. For your

sister."

"The same Italian group that you're protecting me from?"

"Yes," I nod.

There's a beat of silence before Auggie gets up and leaves the room suddenly. I don't stop her, ask her where she's going, I just watch.

She pads into the kitchen. I hear a cabinet open and close before she walks back in and plops down next to me, holding out a plastic cup that matches mine.

"You're going to need to pour me a strong one because I feel like this is a story and a half."

7

# Chapter 7

Auggie

It was more than obvious that this was seriously weighing on Trent. Like every movement was hard for him when he was reliving what had happened. He lifts up the bottle, and pours me a healthy amount of whiskey into the stupid little clear plastic solo cups we have instead of real glasses. Setting the bottle back on the table, Trent wordlessly lifts his cup to meet mine and we cheers.

"It is… It's a lot. Are you sure you want to know? It makes my role in the Clan seem not that bad."

Trent shifts from looking at me, to sitting facing forward on the couch with his elbows resting on his thighs, his drink loosely held in his hands.

"You don't have to tell me anything you don't want to. But, it might do you some good to talk with someone about it. It's obviously weighing heavily on you." I tuck my feet up under me and get into a comfortable position to listen. This whole situation might have come up because I forced the matter, but it's clear that Trent needs a friend. He needs someone to vent to, talk to, let help him with this huge burden, to cry with, and I don't think he's been letting anyone help him.

"I don't usually need to talk about what happens on missions to get over it. With time, the… hard parts fade and I'm able to throw myself into work, or booze, or women," His eyes widen when he looks at me like he's embarrassed he said that, and I shrug, gesturing for him to continue, "and I'm fine. But it's not happening this time."

"What's happening this time?"

"I can't stop hearing them crying, screaming as they're hurt. It's in my head all hours of every day and night. I feel like I'm going crazy." He whispers, and holds his forehead with one hand.

"Who?" I gently ask.

"The girls. The girls they'd taken to sell. Garzino made us…" Trent clears his throat and runs a hand down is face. My own jaw clenches with the vulnerability in his voice, understanding that the story he's going to share will hurt him.

I don't know what I thought he was going to say, but it wasn't that. I thought that it was going to be a gun fight that went wrong or something like that. Maybe he lost a close friend in some deal gone wrong. But hearing that he's haunted by crying, screaming, all the time, it's heart-wrenching.

Instead of prompting him, I take a deep breath and wait for him to continue. This is… so much more than I thought, so this has to be on his terms; what and when he tells me. I just want to be his friend, help him through this.

"Garzino had lost his business standing, and was scrambling

to make up the lost profits. They'd already been doing some shady shit with brothels and strip clubs, but when Kellan and Kieron pulled the contracts they had with Garzino, he got desperate. I volunteered to go undercover, to be the inside man so we could monitor the situation that was coming, to make sure that the people we care for were safe. But to do that, to be accepted and given the information we needed, Garzino had a few tests for me. To prove my worth." Trent takes another gulp of whiskey, and so do I.

Trent curls in on himself more; my giant protector, full of fight and standing, but hurting so badly that his body is unconsciously trying to protect itself. I wonder if he has anyone to protect him like he does for everyone else.

Trent takes a deep breath and looks at me. I do my best to keep my expression neutral, warm, open, *understanding*. I can't imagine being in the situation he was, but I want to be here for him as he tries to tell it.

"I had to… They brought in a girl. A young thing, shaking and scared, obviously she'd been taken and they made me watch as she was raped by Garzino. In order to get in with them at the higher level needed for Kieron, I had to really prove my allegiance to them and so I had to… I had to…" He starts to sob, the broken sounds that come from him are gut-wrenching. I don't think, I just move, and take this man into my arms. Wrapping both of my arms around his neck, I nestle his head against my chest, and lay my head over his.

"It's okay," I whisper.

"It's not. It's never going to be okay. I'm never going to be able to come back from it. I don't think I ever will. And even if I can somehow move on, I don't deserve to. I deserve to feel this horrible, this soul-eating guilt and regret for the rest of my life. I deserve to suffer like they did." He cries into my chest. The words are lost in between the sobs of this broken man.

"What happened, honey?" I coo, the nickname slipping out as I try to help give him strength to continue.

"They made me hold her down. I had to hold this poor girl down as she was broken. As she was violated in a way that is evil and cruel. I stood there, unable to do anything because if I showed any sign of weakness, they'd pounce and I'd not only be killed on the spot, but I'd ruin any chances the Clan had at infiltrating. So, I stood there. Just listening to the girl scream for me to help, for him to stop, begging for mercy. But no one stepped in to help her. I couldn't." He looks at me earnestly, pleadingly. Trent's hands take both of mine and he squeezes tightly like he wants me to understand. Like he's begging me to understand and not judge him.

"I couldn't show any weakness or they'd know something was up. I couldn't give her any sort of comfort or apology; I couldn't do anything and I… I just wanted to pull my gun and kill every motherfucker in there. After it was done, we were dismissed and I immediately threw up in my room. I was so sick at what I'd watched and done. But I thought it was over, that I'd proven myself. I was wrong, Auggie. So fucking wrong."

I hold onto him tightly, pushing my fingers through his hair and shush him softly for comfort. I can't imagine what he went through. I know I probably should be angry or disgusted that he would let that happen, but he did what he had to do. He was trying to survive himself. Trying so save my sister.

"It kept happening. Garzino wanted to break in the new girls and he always had me hold them down. Proving over and over that if I did anything out of line, he'd have this over me. That I *helped* break, hurt, and rape those girls. I… I can't…" Trent tries to pull back, pull away from me, but I hold on tighter. So far, I'd been sitting beside him, but as he gets more forceful at trying to get away, I climb up on his lap and fully hold on.

"You don't have to pull away from me. I'm here for you." I whisper. It's like my words are a balm, or the breath of air he needs, because he wraps both of his arms around my waist and pulls me tighter to his chest.

"How? Why?" He never completes the questions, but I know. I know what he's asking. How am I not running from him, not disgusted by his actions, by his choices? Why am I giving him comfort and acceptance now that I know?

"Because you're a good man." I say simply, softly.

"I'm not."

"At your core, Trent, you are. It's easy for anyone to see. You did these things for my sister. For your best friend. Your job is hurting bad guys so they don't hurt others. Those two events don't make you bad." I try to reassure him, to keep him from spiraling more. It's clear to see though, that he's too far in his grief and guilt for that.

While Trent was softly crying before, my words cause him to openly weep. I don't know what to do, so I hold him tighter and whisper softly in his ear; words of encouragement, of acceptance, of kindness.

I don't know how long we sit there, holding each other until his sobs start to quiet and we are just cuddling on the couch.

"I'm sorry," he whispers. His deep voice hoarse from crying.

"Don't be."

"This isn't your job. To deal with me and my emotions."

"Trent," I scoff, "it may not be my job, but *it is* my job as your friend to be there for you. Have you told anyone what happened?"

He shakes his head 'no' against my chest.

"Trent," I drag out his name like a whine. "You need to talk to someone about this. You're struggling, and you don't have to do it alone."

"I'm telling you." He says softly, his words muffled by our embrace. "Even though I shouldn't."

I can hear the disgust and disbelief in his voice, like he's already regretting letting anyone close to him.  Let alone *me*, someone he couldn't stand until about two weeks ago. Someone he barely tolerates.  Someone he is meant to be looking after. Someone who is just a job to him.

"Look at me," I guide his head up to look at me, and cup his face with my hands. His grey eyes look even lighter with the tears lining them.  The look on his face… it's one of a man trying to pull himself together, but he doesn't know how.

"We're in this whole thing together. If talking to me about the trauma and hardships that brought you to me, help you, I am more than willing, more than happy to sit and listen. I won't judge you, I won't lecture you. I promise you, I'm here for you. You're not alone in this. Not anymore."

He gasps softly and pulls me closer, notching his face in my neck and breathing in deeply like if he doesn't hold me tightly I'll leave.

I feel protected. I feel cherished. I feel appreciated.

I wrap my arms tighter around his shoulders and neck, keeping him to me to try and push those feelings to him.

I want *him* to feel protected. I want *him* to feel cherished. I want *him* to feel appreciated. Because no matter the shit we've said to one another, the teasing, and the yelling, it's clear now that we're just two broken souls trying to put themselves back together with missing pieces.

Maybe the two of us really do need each other in some way. We can help each other become whole again.

In the back of my mind, I know that I should tell him about Marcos. I should tell him about the abuse and the captivity. I should tell him about all that I went through and what threat I am up against. But he's so fragile right now, so open and honest. The thought of me wrecking the trust that's just starting to build between us by being overly honest, by opening up and telling him something I shouldn't... It's enough to make me sick to my stomach.

What if I tell him what happened with Marcos, and he tells Talia? What happens if I tell him about the letter and he tells Kieron, and they pull their protection? What happens if I explain what I went through, only for him to belittle me or the Trent from the first few weeks returns? I can't lose him now.

So I don't take the chance.

I keep my mouth shut and hold him close to me, hoping that he finds comfort in my embrace and that he understands that I'm always going to be here for him. Even if he decides in the future not to be.

8

# Chapter 8

Trent

After we talked, really truly talked, something shifted with Auggie and I.

I wasn't so closed off and annoyed at everything, and she wasn't going out of her way to antagonize me. We'd called an unspoken, unofficial truce, and it was nice. Peaceful. Domestic.

We'd cook and clean up the house together, we started watching movies together at night instead of how I would usually just hide out in my room after dinner, we started to talk about our lives more. I learned a lot about her in a very short period of time. And I realized that Auggie was a cool chick, a compassionate, sassy, independent, loyal woman who would do anything she could to help. She thrived under our truce, under our fragile friendship.

Auggie still complained, still moaned and bitched about how

strict I was with her safety, with how I wouldn't let her do anything. And I know I'm being a controlling asshole, but I'm not taking any fucking chances with her safety.

Not now.

So I'm trying harder to make an effort to keep her happy and entertained. We've baked more cinnamon rolls than my waistline is comfortable with, she's read at least seven more sexy books; which she's told me about in great, torturing detail that left my cheeks red and my pants tight, we've watched movie after movie. I've even asked if she wanted to start doing workouts with me, which she told me to fuck off.

Movie nights are becoming my favorite, though. We curl in on the couch, she covers herself in one of the blankets I bought on my last grocery run. And she always wants a Disney movie. Always. I don't mind watching Beauty and The Beast, The Little Mermaid or even Cinderella all that much when it makes her so happy. Every so often, she'll nod off, finally feeling comfortable with me and in my presence that she can sleep. I love those times. She stretches out, and always tucks her toes under my thigh for warmth. Sometimes, she just puts her foot on my lap, and then I'm able to touch her in some way.

It was the sweetest fucking torture I could ever have come up with for myself. This girl that I am growing to care for more and more, but my own fucked up head was making it difficult.

I know, I *know,* that I'm totally screwed. We still fight, still bicker, but I'm fairly certain that's just who we are.

I could feel she was getting restless staying in. I couldn't blame her, not really. It had been so long since we went on that half of a walk that I'd ruined.

After the whole freakout in the bookstore, I'd immediately gone into to the 'dungeon', as Auggie so lovingly calls it, and hacked into the stores security system, gotten a good look at that fuckface, and started running it through every data base I had access to. And a few I didn't.

Something about it all doesn't make sense to me.

In the clip, he walked up to her, said something, and smiled like a fucking savant, throwing move after move at Auggie, but she stood there frozen, terrified. Her eyes were wide with fear, it's plain to see even on tape. How Casanova didn't see it, I have no fucking clue. Her sass and argumentative flare was gone, and she had just stood there, clutching the book to her chest with her mouth open slightly. The dumbass had taken that as an opening, and put his hand over her shoulder, leaning in to speak more intimately to her.

And that's when she'd screamed.

For me.

We have been in hiding for a while now, and anytime we had gone out, Auggie was hit on by quite a few guys. Nothing as overtly as this guy, though. Lingering looks, extra smiles, making sure to ask how she's doing, but mostly it was angry, jealous looks in my direction.

Thinking about those times now, I eat that shit up. Smiling proudly and possessively that she's *mine*, even if it was just for show.

Honestly, everyone is drawn to Auggie. Her energy is contagious, her smile makes you feel like you've earned something, and she's *funny*. So freaking funny. If she didn't hate me quite so much in the beginning, I could see us being friends right away. Hell, if I had met her before all the bullshit that had gone down with the Garzino's, I probably would've hit on her myself.

So there's no wonder why that guy had approached her. But her reaction…

For her safety, I'd made the decision for us to stay inside until all the information on a one Sean Roberts had come back.

That conversation was as fun as eating gravel. Imagine, it was another fucking fight. Auggie's not a person that takes to authority well, so we had to compromise. I promised a night out, under three hours to a place of her choosing, if she did what I said and didn't complain about it.

She did stay inside, and completely stayed off the internet. She also complained so much that I contemplated throwing her out, and letting the Italians have her.

Except Talia and Kieron would have my balls if I did something like that. Not just that, but I'm actually *really* starting to enjoy her company.

Tonight's the night I pay up. I'd received all the boring, plain details on Sean last night. University of Maine senior, in the Sigma Gamma Upsilon, a few tickets for drunk and disorderly, total fuckboy and likes to brag about it online. He's a dick, but he's harmless.

"Go get ready, big guy, we're hitting the club." Auggie yelled after I'd reluctantly told her earlier, throwing her arms in the air before she basically victory-danced to her room. I haven't heard from her since.

And it's been four hours.

I'm almost afraid of what she's been doing in there all this time. But, a deal's a deal.

"Jesus christ, Auggie." I mutter under my breath, looking down at my watch that read ten o'clock. At night. I try to not be a dick and ruin her night before we even leave, but I'm not a night owl if I don't have to be.

I made sure to dress nicer than normal, but I wasn't going to be caught unprepared in a fight. My trusty leather jacket was decked out with any and all of my small weapons; pocket knives, brass knuckles, a switchblade, a one-barreled mini pistol. All concealed within the lining, of course. I had taken care to do my hair and shave. The dark navy Henley I was wearing was my nice one. It hugged my broad chest, and the color complimented my red hair. When the guys and I have gone out before, I've pulled plenty of girls with this exact outfit.

Tonight, however, I'm on the job. And I have a feeling that Auggie's going to make my life incredibly hard. That is, if we ever leave before midnight.

"Are you anywhere close to being ready?" I bang my fist on the flimsy door, but how much more time does she really need? "I'm not going to be shutting this bar down!"

"Hold your horses, old man!"

"I'm three years older than you!"

"Still older!" Her cheeky little laugh floats through the air and I clench my teeth in frustration.

"Can you just hurry it up?" I grumble, feeling like the Beast from the Disney movie at Belle's door with my arms crossed over my chest, and my jaw set to the side. I sigh in frustration because she's made us watch so many freaking Disney Princess movies that now I'm drawing comparisons.

I'm an enforcer for the Irish mob for fuck's sake. I've killed, maimed and tortured people, I've gone undercover and taken down plenty of other pieces-of-shit without batting an eye.

And I'm comparing myself to a Disney hero.

What the fuck.

But, then the door opens and I mentally take back everything I said, every frustration I felt, and all the cussing out I did.

Every second was worth the wait. And I really don't know how to feel about that thought.

"I'm ready, let's go." Auggie smiled, her eyes sparkling through her colored contacts. She'd curled her hair, then combed through it so the curls were softer, more fitting around her face. The blonde had new streaks of color; hot pink, purple, teal, all laying together like a watercolor work of art. Not to mention, she'd cut it. Instead of it flowing down her back, it was cropped right at her clavicle, drawing all the attention to her face and chest.

And the dress. That fucking dress was going to make me get into a fight tonight, I swear to god. And I'll gladly fight every motherfucker in there if they so much as look at her a beat too long.

The black, velvety material clings to her body like a second skin and shimmers in the light. Every move she makes draws my eye to her body; her full hips as she walks past me, her tight waist, her ass.

"Fuck me," I whisper softly with a groan. In pain, in arousal, in longing, in a feral, possessive want.

The dress had one of those necklines that looked like she was going to have a boob pop out, but was somehow really secure, and I thanked whoever was watching out for me and my face that it was. I would definitely punch a fucker if he saw her tits before I did.

*Before I did?*

I cleared my throat and shook my head slightly, painfully forcing myself to look at her face.

"You look great." Even my voice was fucking turned on and deeper. I have to get my shit together.

"Thank you, big guy. So do you." She smiled, her ruby red lips accenting her fake blue eyes, that were framed in the dark makeup that made them look even bigger.

She put in a long dangly-looking earring and my eyes immediately dropped to the slope of her neck, the clear skin begging for a mark.

*My mark.*

She turned around, and slung the smallest purse ever over her shoulder.

"Ready?"

"I guess." I ran my fingers through my red hair, knowing that tonight wasn't going to end well for me, one way or another.

# 9

# Chapter 9

Auggie

From the look on Trent's face, I'd done it.

My goal was to make everyone that saw me, stop and stare. To drive guys wild.

I *needed* to get laid.

I needed to get the idea of Trent fucking me specifically, out of my head.

His dumb face that's so soft and rugged at the same time. The short hair that I can't stop wondering if it would be just long enough for me to run my fingers through and grip tightly. His strong, corded with muscle arms holding me down, keeping me close to him as he thrusts inside me.

I shake my head, trying to halt the increasingly sexy and panty-ruining picture that is forming in my mind.

*He tolerates me. He's doing his job, and nothing more. We're just friends. Just friends. Get a grip.*

Trent opens the car door, a generic Honda; the perfect on-the-run car, and helps me inside.

"Thank you," I whisper. Now that we aren't in the house, my bravado is all gone, and I'm a bit nervous about being in a small space with him for the next half hour with this tension simmering between us.

"Anytime, Princess." He chuckles, rounding the car and hopping into the driver seat.

"That one's sticking, huh?"

"Don't like it? I think it's kind of fitting, don't you?" Trent smirks at me. Again. And if I was wearing any underwear, there's no doubt that they'd be destroyed with just that one look.

"It's certainly better than other ones I've been given."

"And pray tell, what would those be?" He asks. It's an innocent question, I know it is, but I get lost in the memories that start to surface.

Marcos calling me a slut and slob in front of his friends, and them all laughing at me. The whispered insults between him and his close members about just how pointless of a human I was. That surprising form of torture and bullying had lasted the whole evening. But, was just the start of my torment.

'Worthless', 'whore', 'ugly'. All names and words that were both whispered, and said, in my presence from then on. I had stood tall and with my shoulders back, letting my overly highlighted blonde hair flow over my shoulders, letting the words fall off me so that they couldn't tell how badly they stung.

Words are words, but the cruel smirk on Marcos's face every time the insults were hurled my way... *that* I will never forget. He let his crew talk to me like that, all the while sitting on his proverbial throne and watching me break. 'Augustina, my darling', turned to 'stupid fucking whore', and after a while, after I knew he wasn't going to change, I started to try to find a way out.

And that's when my life blew up. The hitting started. A slap here, a shove there. It escalated over the time of a week. He didn't even seem remorseful about hitting me, about leaving bruises on my body. The insults, or 'pet names' as he'd call them, were bad but didn't break me how he wanted.

The hits definitely did. The fear of never knowing what would cause a punch or a kick ate at me.

I'd called Marcos to break things off, politely, and when I did… I'd never seen him like that. I never thought he'd turn on me like someone who had wronged his gang. I never thought going to live with my sister for a while would be a big deal. I hadn't wanted to take anything that wasn't mine, I hadn't tried to stay in the apartment or demand anything… I just wanted out.

"Auggie?" Trent's soft voice pulled me from the horrible memories, his rough hand soft on my bare knee. "You with me?" My mind was jumbled, being pulled from the memories, but all I could focus on was his hand on my knee. One point of contact between us that wasn't for appearances sake. I mentally kicked myself because it didn't mean anything, it *had to mean nothing*. He was just being kind.

"Yeah, sorry. Just scatter brained, all those chemicals from adding the colors." I chuckle, but it's a very weak, and see-through, attempt.

"If you don't like being called Princess, I won't." His eyes leave the road for a moment, and even in the dark I can see how honest he's being. If I said the word, he'd never utter the word in my presence again.

My heart beats faster. The yearning I feel growing so strong that I'm sure he can see just how much I'm wanting him these days.

Another reason why I need to forget him for a few hours.

"I know."

It's not until we pull into the nightclub that I realize he never took his hand off of my knee.

———————

The thumping bass only added to my excitement as Trent paid the cover charge and we were granted entrance into the dark hallway at the front of the club. We weren't in New York or any big city so we didn't have to wait in a line, we just paid our fee and walked right in.

Trent kept a hand on my lower back the whole time we walked in, never letting me out of his grasp. I would be lying if I said I didn't completely love it.

The room was booming with music, fractured lighting, and the grinding of bodies in the middle of the room, swaying in time with the music. It smelled like sweat, cheap beer, and the mixture of too many different perfumes and colognes, but shit, I'm so excited to jump in there and join in.

"Drink?" Trent leaned in close, yelling over the music for me to hear him but my body reacted as if he had sensually whispered it in my ear. Goosebumps erupt over my neck, and I fight - hard - to make sure I don't lean back and bear my neck to him, like I'm begging for him to bite it, forcing me to submit.

I nod to Trent eagerly, and before I can tell him what I

actually want, he's already making his way to the bar in the back of the room. I know he's going to bring me a light beer, something that'll not even get me buzzed, but is *technically* an alcoholic drink.

Stupid, rational prick.

Let him bring me the beer, I'll get my tequila shots one way or another.

I push through the crowd to try and find an empty high-top table, finding one closer to the back, shrouded in darkness. *Perfect.*

I stake my claim on the table, setting my elbows on the edge and I take a look around to people watch. To try and find my stud for the night.

Of course, I feel eyes on me and I do my absolute best not to swivel my head around to search for who they belong to. My anxiety steps up a bit, knowing that anyone from Marcos's gang could be here; watching and waiting. But the colored hair and the contacts… I have to trust that they are enough to shield me.

The music is infectious, and my hips start to sway with the beat. With each note I can feel the stress and frustrations melt away.

"Here you go." Trent slides the beer over to me and I try to not let my eyes roll at his predictable behavior.

"I don't believe I ordered this, Kyle." I take the beer and drink from it anyway.

"But it's the drink you're getting. I don't need you getting into any more trouble than I know you will already." He says, taking a long pull from his own beer. We stand in silence; I move sensually to the beat until I finish my beer.

"I'm going to go dance." I tell Trent hesitantly. I need to go get on with my getting laid plan, a quickie in the bathroom should suffice and at this point, I'll even take a hot make-out session in the dark. Anything, *anything*, to distract myself from climbing the man in front of me and embarrassing myself.

I fix the soft underwires holding my breasts in the dress and don't fail to notice Trent watching me as my chest jiggles with the motion.

*And now I'm on fire.*

I watch as Trent's throat bobs, and his eyes stay locked on me, but he never moves, never speaks, so I go.

I walk into the crowd of people all moving together as one in their dancing; grinding and rubbing along each other, arms wrapped around, fingers gripping and dipping under clothes. All in time with the music.

I can't wait to join them. To get lost in the movements.

I step into the fray, pushing myself into the mass of sweaty bodies, until I find a spot and just let myself feel. There's something so freeing about the anonymity of being in the masses.

I close my eyes; sway my hips and roll my body slowly, confidently. I let my hands trail along my dress, over my hips, and my fingers drag the fabric up just slightly. Enough to tease, and for me to feel sexy. My fingers drape over my stomach, and I drag them up around my neck, moving my hair to one side, exposing my neck in the process.

The bass thumps under my feet, and the music plays loud enough that it's all I can hear.

Until he wraps his hand around my waist. A thick, strong hand slides along the velvet of my dress until it reaches its destination.

I know immediately who it is, like the pieces of my soul calls to his. His strong, thick thighs press against the back of mine, his chest against my back. One of his long hands spans my waist while the other goes to the low crease of my hip, holding me in place against him as he leads me in a dance.

Trent rubs his fingers over the material at the hemline of my dress, the pads of his fingertips barely touching my thigh. All my senses zone in on that spot. The spot that he could potentially touch.

I need a real drink. I need him to touch me. I need to get a fucking *grip.*

The way he's moving with me; rolling his body and moving mine with his was a thing of fantasies. Straight out of one of my books.

Neither of us talk, not that we can easily, but I'm scared that if I speak, it will break the bubble and he'll stop moving against me. I slide one hand up, to grip the back of his neck and pull him close to me to make sure he doesn't.

"I couldn't see you." He says roughly in my ear.

I turned my neck and arch my back so I can speak in his ear.

"I didn't think you'd want to dance, big guy."

"I usually don't."

"Yeah, clearly you're awful at it." I smirk and pull away, grinding slowly against him in time with the beat to prove the opposite. I enjoy our banter; I crave it actually, as of late. I snark at him, he shit-talks me, I give it back and, sure, sometimes we take it too far but usually, lately, it's been in good fun. But as I roll myself against him, every muscle in his body seemed to tense and he pulls away from me suddenly.

"What? What's wrong?" I turned around, our bodies being pushed back together with the others around us still moving.

"I'm going to go get another drink." He said, using both

thumbs to gesture to the bar, then running his fingers through his hair.

"Want anything? No? Okay." He stuttered and walks away.

*What the fuck was that?*

———-

*Trent*

*What the fuck was that?* It's like all the goddamn blood in my body went directly to my dick and none was left to make sure my brain was working properly.

I need a drink.

"Can I get a coke, please?" I call out to the bartender, then drop my head against my hands, pushing the heels of my hands into my eyes with a groan. No matter how much I might want a real, stiff drink, I won't jeopardize Auggie's safety.

"What did you say?" The guy working behind the bar yells at me over the music.

"Just a coke." I order again and throw a $5 bill down.

The bartender takes the bill and turns to start making my non-alcoholic beverage.

I turn around to watch her, not trusting any of the other assholes here not to try something, but I see her smiling. Fucking smiling. Just dancing out there by herself, looking like she is the music that everyone is dancing around to.

She's gorgeous, and our chemistry has always been off the charts. Thinly veiled by sass and shitty comments from both of us, but I know that she cares. I hope she knows that I care, too. I don't want to take advantage of the fact that I'm really the only man she's able to be around these days. I don't want her to have to settle. And I know I don't deserve her after the shit I've done. How could she ever trust me in that way?

But just watching her makes me feel lighter. Just watching her smile, getting to be around her in anyway she'll let me, and knowing she's happy makes me want to fight the world to keep her that way.

It's true, I've always had a more protective nature. Always willing to step up for someone, but my mind is detached about it. My emotions don't usually come into play. With Auggie, my whole being is focused on one thing - keeping her happy and safe. And with how I feel, what I shared, it's all getting messy.

As I wonder what the fuck that means, I get to watch a tall, lanky guy with a plaid shirt and black jeans slide behind her and take the place I'd unwillingly voluntarily vacated.

Auggie keeps dancing. The sexy, slow roll of her body, her skin sparkling in the dim light from sweat, the way she dances *for her*, but accepts the new guy to help guide her movements.

I'm getting turned on, just from watching her move. The guy touching her makes me want to rip his fingers off, one by one, without any weapon, just pure force. I know I can't though, so I turn to face the bar, adjusting my hard-on in my jeans before turning my eyes back to her.

In that split moment in time, Auggie went from joyful and carefree, to serious and terrified. Her eyebrows were furrowed together, and her mouth dropped in shock as her eyes were glued to where I stood. She was stiff, and my mind immediately went back to the library where she was frozen in place; the terror in her eyes is as clear as crystal. It could only have been a split second before she went back to giving the guy and the crowd a tight smile, but it was long enough for me to know something was wrong. The guy leans down and whispers something in her ear, and she nods. While the fakest smile I've ever seen is firmly locked on her face.

*What the fuck was happening?*

There's a moment where I freeze and wonder if I'm just overthinking things. Maybe she wants to go with him willingly. Maybe she is going with him for a quick fuck in the bathroom. part of me tells me to let it happen because it's none of my business, I have no claim on her, and I know it. I hate it, but I know it. Another part, a smaller part that's just now making itself known more and more these days, roars in anger and jealousy. My mind involuntarily conjures images of someone else thrusting into her, someone else biting her neck, someone else holding her tightly against them as they hold her in the air and screw into her, someone else kissing her, tasting her, loving her.

If I find her mid-fuck, I might kill the guy with how I'm feeling. It wouldn't even be hard.

But then I see the terror in her eyes and I know she's in trouble.

The guy takes her hand and starts to lead her through the crowd in the opposite direction from me. I'm already on high alert, my hand inconspicuously going to my jacket pockets for my knife, and my eyes never leave them. I slowly stalk forward, following her through the mass of people.

"Move!" I snap at the people in my path or the odd girl who steps in my way to try and get me to dance with her. I must look like a beast, all flaring nostrils, clenched fists, and stomping around without any care for others except for Auggie. I need to get to her.

Auggie's rainbow hair is still within view, so I barrel towards her. She never looks back, but the way she is dragging her feet slightly and how her shoulders hunch forward tells me she isn't going with the plaid fucker just because she wanted some. They were rushing, going towards the back of the club where it was more secluded.

I stop by the bathroom door, and press my ear to the disgusting surface, listening for moans, grunts, anything that would tell me what's going on in there.

A *thunk,* and what sounds like a door slam reach my ears. Just as I go to open the door, I hear her scream. Pulling on the handle, I see that fucker locked the door. I jingle the doorknob, hard enough to break the flimsy lock, but it doesn't open.

"Wait, stop," I hear Auggie beg and my foot goes through the crappy door like it's made of paper, and I push through the room just in time to see the plaid fuck try to shove Auggie through the window.

"Wait, please. I don't know anything about Marcos's death, please. Let me go."

*Who the fuck is Marcos?*

Auggie pulls at his hand wrapped too tightly around her forearm, and he responds by shoving her roughly into the wall under the window. Auggie's head knocks against the cinderblock wall because of him, and I mentally promise a matching injury. One worse and deadly. He's clocked me now, the door shattering sent an obvious message that I'm here to fucking rumble, and his eyes widen like he knows that I'm going to kill him. *Good.*

"Auggie," My feet haven't stopped moving since I kicked the door in and Plaid Shirt knows it. He knows his time on earth is running out.

"Trent!" She cries.

Even from here, I can see the grip he has on her will leave a mark, and that pisses. me. off.

I pull my switchblade from its secret compartment in my jacket and lunge at the guy, forcing him to drop Auggie's arm in the process.

My arm slices through the air, nicking his chest through his t-shirt. It's a shallow cut, but it'll bleed. It'll be messy. Just like I like it.

"Unless you want a matching cut along your neck, back the fuck up." I snap, making sure to position myself between Auggie, who had run to a corner behind me. "Who do you work for?  I didn't think Garzino had anyone but grease-buckets and guys in suits." I try to get his attention on me, but he's staring over my shoulder. Right at her.

"He won't forget about this, *Augustina*.  He will find you, and next time, your guard dog won't be there." The guy holds a hand close to his chest, but the blood is seeping over his fingers.  He pulls off the plaid shirt and wraps it around his hand, pressing it to his chest before flying out the window and taking off.

My mind is playing his words on repeat.

Turning to face Auggie, I want to snap and demand answers. I deserve as much, being scared out of my head that she was hurt, hell, she'd almost gotten kidnapped. But the moment I laid eyes on her, all of those issues flew away.

She was huddled in a corner, obviously trying to put as much distance between herself and the window as possible. Her arms are wrapped around her thin frame and I can see she's shaking.  Her dark makeup is running down her face, her hair is all tangled and limp. But my eyes are drawn to the massive handprint encircling her arm like a sick bracelet. The beautiful, confident, infuriating girl is shaking and crying in fear.

"Auggie?" I say, walking to her slowly and with purpose. She looks like she needs to know each move I make. "Princess?" I try, leaning my head to the side and putting my knife away.

"Trent," She whispered, her voice barely audible, but there. "Is he gone?"

"Yeah, baby, he's gone. We need to get out of here too." I reach down for her slowly, taking her hand gently, and help her up.

Whatever had happened, why she went with him, why she was so terrified…

Something didn't add up. And it was increasingly clear that Auggie was hiding something. Something bigger than I knew or suspected, and I was going to figure out what it was.

10

# Chapter 10

Auggie

They had warned me, hadn't they?

The week after I'd left the hospital, I received an unsigned letter, slipped under my door threatening me to turn myself over to them, to the Los Muertos, they'd be more inclined to show mercy.

Whatever that meant.

But the people guarding us - my parents and I - hadn't realized that I received it which meant that Los Muertos was able to get to me. Regardless of someone guarding me or not. It was a clear sign that I wasn't safe anywhere.

I didn't get a whole lot of time to figure out what exactly they wanted or why they wanted me, before I was whisked away by one of Kieron's men to keep me safe from the Italians after my sister made them mad. Then, came Trent.

Would you believe me if I said that the topic never came

up, aside from our talk a bit ago? It's a little heavier than just, 'Could you get me some cinnamon rolls and a book from the store', like all the conversations we have had up until now. I felt like it was weird and… uncomfortable to out of the blue just say, 'Oh hey, you know my ex? Yeah, his gang is trying to kill me. But I don't know why.'

Trent, Kieron, Talia and I had left my place so quickly that I didn't really think that anyone who had been watching me would follow.

I was wrong.

It'd all started so innocently tonight. It had been such a great night, until the kidnapping attempt. Trent had left after we both were getting maybe a little too into the moment on the dancefloor. I could see he wanted me – maybe still wants me? – but then he ran.

He didn't want me to follow, that much was clear. Thankfully, the dark lighting had hidden my burning cheeks and absolutely mortified look of being rejected that was completely clear on my face. So, while Trent ran from me, I stayed put and let myself get lost in the music.

For a moment I had forgotten my goal of the night. So, when a guy slid in behind me and started dancing, I didn't question it. He was cute enough, good dancer, and I liked how he felt behind me. I liked the attention.

Even if the guy I really wanted to be dancing with wasn't anywhere to be seen.

It had been barely a minute into our dance when he leaned down and whispered in my ear that he was here to collect on Marcos's murder. And "unless I wanted my guard-dog's death on my conscience, I had to go with him and not make a scene".

So, I'd gone with him.

Without a second thought.

Because it meant Trent would be okay.

But I should've known my protector was watching me closely, was monitoring my every move. Just as my head was being forced out of the dingy bathroom window, my hands and forearms getting all scratched and bruised, my red-headed knight kicked the door in, and saved me.

And now I have to come clean.

Fuck, I *really* don't want to have this conversation.

I don't want word of it to reach Talia. She's got enough on her plate.

"You calm?" Trent asks. We are sitting in the car on the drive home, and this time, the silence is so loud it's hurting my ears. It's such an awkward silence because now Trent knows I've been keeping something from him. Even after he told me his secret. His voice is rough and clipped, all of the warmth that has been in his tone for the last few weeks is gone, back to the detached, emotionless Trent from before, and I know I deserve it.

"More than before."

"Then it's a better time to talk"

I take a deep breath and let it out slowly.

"You know my ex? The one who died?" I start my stupid, freaking story that I don't even have all the answers to. I'm running for my life, but I have no idea what I'm running for, or exactly why I'm being chased. The darkness of the night was interrupted in a consistent flash of light on the streets. To calm myself I started timing the space between streetlamps in my head.

"He was in a gang. Los Muertos."

"I am aware of that." Trent said, his tone screaming 'get to the point'.

"Well, when I say he was in a gang, I mean that he *ran* the gang. Was their leader. And when he died, they assumed I had something to do with it. And now they're after me."

Trent turns onto our street, never speaking or even looking like he heard what I said. He turned the wheel with one hand, the muscles in his forearm tensing with the motion. If he wasn't so mad, and I wasn't so scared, I'd appreciate the sight more.

I can see his jaw clench in the fractured lighting from the passing street lamps. He's pissed, and rightfully so. I'm not so deluded or naive to think that I'm not in the wrong here. I'd essentially put Trent in the line of fire against a threat he hadn't known was there. I know I fucked up, but I thought that he'd hidden us so well that we would be safe from Los Muertos anyway.

I could feel the anger rolling off of him in waves. His finger gripped the steering wheel tight enough that I could see the skin stretch over his knuckles. His muscular, denim-clad thighs shifted as he moved in his seat.

I shrink back down in my chair, the tension between us isn't playful, or even barely tolerating the other like it's been. The best thing I can think to do is stay quiet and let him sort through it.

Trent parked the car, barely letting it stop before yanking the keys out and climbing out of the car.

Well, shit. This was bad. I'm in so much trouble. I feel tears prick my eyes.

There is no doubt in my mind that he's mad at me now. All that trust and friendship we'd built is gone.

"Get out, Stephanie." Trent snaps, his voice muffled through the car window. He raps on the window impatiently.

I wipe under my eyes to catch the stray tears, and take a deep breath.

He knocks on the window once more, more forcefully this time. I guess I should be grateful that he didn't just up and leave, and is at least giving me some protection seeing as Los Muertos has found me.

Climbing out of the car, I look at Trent through my eyelashes.

"Get your ass inside." He turns and stomps to the front door, but I see him check around, making sure we weren't followed.

I walk in and wait, taking off my heels. He closes the door behind us, locks the three deadbolts and pulls out his phone. I can see him flipping through the security camera feeds, and he pulls his gun from his waistband, then leaves, going deeper into the apartment.

I drop my heels by the front door, and go into the living room. Pulling the fuzzy blanket that Trent had gotten for me around my shoulders, I snuggle into the couch figuring that he'll find me when he's ready to talk.

Turns out it wasn't too long of a wait, and he did not want to *talk*.

"What the fuck were you thinking, not telling me that you had a gang after you? Jesus fucking christ, Auggie. How am I supposed to protect you if I don't have all the variables?" He yells as he walks into the room not a moment later, putting his gun back in his waistband after checking the apartment. He brings his hands to his face, rubbing his forehead with his fingers.

"Do you understand how much more I would've done to protect you? I would've changed our location, or our fake names, or even had you changed your hair more frequently. I would've done so much more if I had known we had two powerful, deadly groups gunning for you. Fuck. *Fuck!*" His hand flies into the wall behind him and his fist goes through the drywall. His knuckles are bleeding already.

I close my eyes in fright, not used to Trent acting this way. My body jolts with the sound of drywall crunching.

"You need to tell me everything. Now." Trent growls, his bleeding finger points at me accusingly.

I can see how angry he is, but in his eyes, I can also see how hurt and scared he is. For me. Trent thrives when he is protecting others and keeping them safe, and I pulled the rug out from under his feet. He is scared, scared *for me,* and hurt. Hurt that I didn't share this with him when he's shared so much with me.

As new as this behavior and roughness is for me to see from Trent, I can't deny that the show of strength and the possessive way of him speaking to me isn't hot as fuck.

"I will. I will, I promise." I walk over to where he stood, his chest heaving with exertion.

And all I can think of is making him breathe like that…but for a completely different reason. Preferably a naked, sweaty, satisfying one.

The air between us is charged, but the tension is changing. Where it was angry and volatile, now it is shifting deeper, darker. I pick up his hand that's bleeding and shift it so I can see the damage.

His light eyes meet mine. His jaw relaxes and his Adam's apple bobs. There's so much it looks like he wants to say, but instead stays quiet. His eyes are clouded with something, an emotion that I can't quite place.

He's probably feeling the same way I am; shocked at the sudden, intense heat between us when we'd always been so tense with each other.

My eyes drop to his lips and I *need* to kiss them, I *need* to see how he tastes. This man who's been doing everything within his power to keep me safe, to keep me happy and feeling free while doing it. This man, who busted into a bathroom to save me life, who just split his knuckles in frustration that he couldn't protect me from a threat he didn't know existed.

Trent's eyes drop to my lips and I lick my lips quickly before biting down on my lower lip, just slightly.

"Let me take care of your hand." I said, my voice soft and low. I'm terrified to break this bubble we're in. Just like on the dancefloor.

Trent doesn't speak. He just nods.

I walk us to the sink in the kitchen, letting go of his hands only to grab a paper towel and wet it. I grab the first-aid kit under the sink, while Trent sits at one of the stools by the counter.

Gently, I pick his hand up and dab the towel over the wounds, letting the water wipe away the dust and blood over his knuckles. I don't want to talk about Los Muertos. I don't want to tease Trent and act like we're just buddies or less than. I don't want to continue pretending I'm not going mad with wanting him, with caring for him.

I pick up the antibiotic cream and lightly dab some over the cuts.

"Thank you," His voice, husky and low, draws my gaze back to his. When I'm done covering the marks, I go to put the cap back on the ointment, but Trent's hands grab mine. I stop; every muscle in my body going tense, my breath caught in my throat, as his hands encircle mine before the tension between us snaps, and he yanks my body to his.

# 11

# Chapter 11

Trent

I can't take another moment of her touching me without doing something, anything, about it.

I don't know when exactly my feelings changed, but I do know that if I don't kiss her right this *fucking* second, I might actually die.

Feeling her body pressed against mine in that sexy little dress, and her eyes open and wide, showing me that she wants this too, it drives me crazy.

Our foreheads touch, and our breaths mingle, the air around us pulling us closer.

"Tell me you don't want this." I whisper. "Tell me to stop." I move my hand around her waist, forcing her back to arch and her tits to press tighter against my chest.

I wait for her to say something, anything, to show me she doesn't want to cross that line with me. We haven't stopped moving, pushing closer into each other, slowly - excruciatingly slowly - sliding and rubbing against each other. One of my hands go to her rainbow hair, threading my fingers through the strands, and pulling to move her lips closer to mine. She nods and closes her eyes.

The moment she gives me permission is the moment I take her for myself.

This infuriating woman who pushes me to be better, who's not afraid to stand up to and for me, who's strong and independent all while making others feel cared for.

Mine. *Mine.*

"Auggie, if you aren't sure, tell me to stop. There's no going back. Not for me." I say and I can hear just how strained and desperate I sound. Just how thin my control is, but I'd never do, or push her into something she didn't want. "I can't fight this any longer. It's killing me."

As far as confessions of love go; I don't know how great it is, but it's the truth.

Her sky-blue eyes covered with the odd brown contacts, look directly at me. Her eyes are hooded, heavy with the dark makeup and lust, and it's clear that she's just as lost in this lust-filled haze as I am. But she bites her bottom lip again.

"Don't stop." She whispers, and the rubber band of control within me snaps. My lips take hers in a kiss that ruins all others for me. Auggie climbs over me and quickly straddles my thighs, and she presses against me harder. Her cunt presses hard against my cock, and she rolls her hips, pulling a groan from my throat.

I run my hands up the pale, strong thighs that are bracketing my own. Her dress is scrunched up tightly around her hips, exposing the little bit of red lace between her thighs. The deep red patch in the middle makes my mouth water. It's proof, just like the hardness between my legs that thrusts against her almost unconsciously, that she wants me. That she wants this.

Standing up, I make sure to put both of my hands under her ass to keep her held against me, and do everything I can to not break the kiss. I nearly groan when Auggie tightens her hold on my neck, lifting herself slightly in my arms to hold on tighter.

"Where are we going?" She says breathlessly.

"My room. The first time I get to have you, I'm not going to fuck you against the wall. We've got all night and I'm going to utilize every moment of it."

I push through the small space, carrying her easily until I reach my door and kick it in. My room, like the apartment, isn't anything elaborate. The double bed I have almost fills the whole room. So, when the door slams against the wall, I only have to take a step or two before my shins hit the mattress, and I drop her.

She hits the mattress, and immediately starts scooting backward, crawling back towards the pillows, but I don't let her. I smirk as the possessive, dominant, thirsty part of myself awakens.

"Where do you think you're going?" The words come out as a growl and I see her eyes darken. Auggie looks confused, and in the dim light I can see a blush form over her chest.

"I want you," I wrap my hands around her calves, "right", I grip them tightly, "here." And I pull her whole body to the edge of the bed. Her dress moved up with the movement and gives me the most perfect view of her lace-covered cunt I could've asked for.

The way her light skin is just slightly darker than my own

makes me smirk. I like how we differ; she's small and petite where I'm tall and built, she has light hair where my red hair is more noticeable, she's able to be more tanned from the small amount of time she's spent in the sun and I'm forever deathly pale or sunburnt from the smallest of sun rays.

My favorite though, is how my large, strong hands contrast with her dainty, soft ones.

Even though she looks soft and small, her personality is anything but.

And I love that hidden prize so much.

"Trent, you don't," Auggie starts to squirm back again, but fuck that.

"I *want* to. I *need* to. Let me." I growl, pushing her thighs apart and breathing her in. I can smell her arousal, and she smells so fucking good I'm going to need to get her off at least twice before I even think of fucking her. I'm going to come so fast, it's not even funny.

"But," She starts to object again, to squirm away, and I look at her to see if this is an actual objection or just something that she's saying. Some weird 'you don't have to do that' variation about to leave her lips.

But what I see is nerves. Fear. Fear of what though?

"Please, Princess, let me taste you." I plead. Of course, if this is a hard limit for her, then I'll stop, but I don't want to miss out on this because she's scared I might have some hang-up on it. That I might be doing it out of obligation.

My beautiful girl blushes, her hands coming to try and cover herself up.

Fuck. That.

"No one has liked it." She whispers, and my heart stops. My entire being lights up with disbelief at that and anger that someone has made her feel that way.

"Then they're fucking idiotic." I move one hand closer to her pussy, and the other holds her spread in front of me. "This pussy, *my pussy*, is so pretty, so pink and wet. You smell so good. There's no fucking way you don't taste just as sweet."

I twist my finger around the wet lace and pull hard, hard enough to rip the seam and bring the material to my face. Auggies eyes are blown wide, the pupils dark with lust and want, and I know she wants me to, just as much as I want to. I suck on the dark patch of her thong, and her essence made my eyes roll back.

Auggie gasps and squirms, trying to press her thighs together for some relief, but my hands won't let her.

"Let me show you just how much I like it," I say softly, running my nose up her thigh as my mouth waters for more of her taste.

Instead of an answer, I get a surrender. Her thighs fall open, and she scoots down so I can comfortably kneel at her feet.

Where I belong. Where I want to be.

I waste no time in diving in; my tongue licking at her entrance, lapping up all the wetness that she's made just for me. My nose nudges at her clit, and I bring one of my hands up to pull the hood back.

"Trent!" Auggie cries passionately.

*Music to my fucking ears.*

I taste and tease and nip and suck at her heat until she's thoroughly desperate, then I sit back. Her fingers grip my head and hold me against her, as her hips start to rock back and forth against my face, spreading her wetness all over. I can tell she's close, her movements are getting choppy as she uses me to find her pleasure.

I slip a finger into her cunt, groaning at her tightness. Her walls clench down on my finger, and when I crook my finger against her front wall, she quivers.

"Oh, god." She cries out and squirms backward. "Wait, wait." She whispers, but what I'm waiting for, I don't know. But the way that she's moving and the way her body is gripping me tells me she's close.

My eyes find hers, and *fuck me*, the sight of her was amazing. Her lips are parted slightly, her eyes were hooded, her chest heaving hard, her hair is flared around her head as she's resting against the pillow, lost in want, in need, in pleasure.

I crook my finger again, rubbing her front wall as deep as I could go.

And she releases all over my face. Her wetness dripping down my face and my hand as I continue to finger her through her orgasm.

I fucking made her squirt. *I fucking made her squirt.* I swear to god, she is the sexiest thing I've ever seen in my entire life. I reach down and grip the base of my cock tightly, trying to stave off my own orgasm that I'm barely holding back.

With one last lick, I sit up, wiping my face and licking the extra wetness off my palm.

"I'm so sorry, fuck, I'm so sorry." Auggie sits up, pulling away and sitting up. Why the hell is she sorry? I loved it.

"What are you sorry for?" I cock my head in confusion. She surely isn't sorry about the sexiest head I've ever given.

"I haven't... I didn't... Oh my god." She put her head in her hands, hiding her face from me.

"Baby," I take her hands and pull them from her face, before I wrap my arm around her waist to drag her against me. "That was the single hottest thing I've ever seen in my life. You squirting all over my face will forever be the fantasy I use to get off. So fucking sexy."

Auggie peaks her head up, her eyes still embarrassed, but hopeful.

"Really?" She whispers.

"Oh yeah," I scoff while sliding my hand under her thigh and wrapping it around my hip "it's a big kink of mine."

I can feel her heat with every shift of my hips, her wetness coating my cock with each shudder. Auggie's breathless, gasping with each swipe of my cockhead through her folds.

"Do you want me, Princess?" I ask her, meaning for the words to come out cocky and sure, dirty-talking is what I do. But instead, they come out as a whisper. Auggie looks me in the eyes and I feel the vulnerability I've exposed in my words.

My sweet girl smiles at me softly, her eyes wide with understanding and care, as she cups my face with one hand.

"I want you, Trent. Fuck, do I want you." She whispers, "Take me."

My heart lurches at her words. She sounds so strong and so sure that I have no choice but to believe her words. We both know it's more than just sex, it would always be more between us.

And she pulls at my hair until I look at her, and her lips slam onto mine.

The understanding that she's tasting herself on my lips sends me into overdrive. I deepen the kiss, and rest my body over hers, pushing her harder into the mattress. It would be so easy, *so fucking easy*, to just slide inside her bare and feel her completely. I **want** that. But in the rational part of my mind, I know it's a conversation for another time. Condom. Fuck, I need a condom. I don't even know if I have one. I didn't expect to need one.

"Birth control?" I ask around her kisses, the moment getting away from me quickly as Auggie wraps her other leg around my hips, and pulls me to her. My cock brushes her slit harder, deeper, and I almost say fuck it.

"Implant. In my arm." She whispered, a hand snaking between us and grabbing my throbbing dick.

*Jesus fucking christ. If this is how good her hand feels...*

My head falls forward as I try not to come all over her small hand holding me. She tugs on me, just as I thrust into her hand. The moan that leaves my mouth is animal, guttural.

"It's a good thing you do because I'm going to fill you up to the fucking brim."

I slide into her easily with how wet she is. I push forward, parting her and spearing her on my cock. I watch in awe as I enter her body, becoming one with her.

My wide hands hold her thighs open so I can see everything. *Every. Fucking. Thing.*

"Trent, oh my god, oh my god, fuck." Auggie babbles, her eyes rolling to the back of her head.

"That's it. Fuck, that's it." I'm going to try to make this last because her pussy is pretty much the best thing I've *ever fucking felt* wrapped around me.

She's hot, wet, and so tight it's like a vice. I force my eyes to stay open so I don't miss a moment of this. So I don't miss a moment of *her*.

I pull out completely, only to thrust back in hard. We both groan together, and her fingers grip tightly onto my neck. With strength I didn't know she had, Auggie pulls my face to hers in a punishing, deep, dirty kiss.

I fucking love it.

My hips snap against hers in heavy, quick thrusts, her tits bouncing with each movement. My balls slap her ass each time I fuck into her, breaking her open, molding her to me. To me *only* from now on.

"I'm so close," She gasps. "I need... I need..." Her hips shift and thrust under me faster, less controlled.

Oh, that just won't do.

My hand wraps around her throat, and her eyes fly open, landing on mine in alarm. She's cautious, but not afraid of my hand on her throat as I tighten my grip around her slender throat.

"You're going to come, and you're going to come when I tell you to. Understand?" I growl.

Auggies eyes widen, and I wish, for not the first time tonight, that she wasn't wearing those fucking contacts so I could see her baby blues staring back at me.

I know she's close, her walls are tightening and pulsing around me rapidly. Driving me wild, and pushing me closer to coming. Her cunt is sucking me in and holding me hostage, not that I ever want to leave. The familiar feeling of my own orgasm approaching builds at the base of my spine, and I feel my balls tighten.

"Ask me." I order, my words clipped as I try to stave off my peak. There's no way in hell I'm coming before her. Not a chance in hell.

"Please," She gasps, her cautious expression changes into a needy, breathy, *feral* one.

"More," I demand, needing her words like I need the air to breathe.

Her eyes flash with that fighting fire I've come to like so much. She wasn't going to beg.

But I'd enjoy making her try.

"Ask me to come, baby. Ask me nicely." I slow my movements, pulling out so slowly it makes me shiver.

"Come on, Princess." I mutter, pushing back in, just an inch before holding. She whines; the needy, breathy that threatens to push me over.

I hold the base of my cock and squeeze, trying to hold back my orgasm as long as possible. Then, my cheeky, sassy girl starts to top from the bottom, and fuck me.

Her hips undulate underneath me, and she shifts her body up and down to ride me expertly. It feels so good that I shiver and drop my head to her shoulder for a brief moment. My girl wants to fight, so we'll fight. And she *will* ask me to come.

My hands shoot out to hold her hips and I force her to stay still.

"Don't even think about it." I say through clenched teeth.

"I'm so close, and you're not moving," She pouts, actually fucking pouts. Her plump lower lip, swollen from my teeth, sticks out, and I can't keep my eyes off it as she slowly bites down on it.

"Ask me to come, baby girl, and I'll let you come."

And I slam into her, as hard and as deep as I can go, my eyes seeing stars, and she cries my name.

With my hands pinning her hips down, she's not able to do a damn thing but take it. Just like I want.

Her eyes are filled with that defiant fire I love, but she's far too lost into her lust to try anything else. She glares at me slightly and I know I've won. I've won the chance to take care of her and give her as much pleasure as I possibly can.

"Fine, please! Please let me come, please!" She cries, her fingernails digging painfully into my shoulders, and any control I was kidding myself into thinking I still had, snapped.

I lose total control. And I know I'm not gentle as I pound into her. Into my girl. Into my Auggie.

"Come for me, princess." I whisper, barely holding my own release back.

My order is the only thing holding her back because once I give permission, it's like a fountain.

Auggies back arches as she pulls me closer, and she tightens around me in pulses. My vision darkens again, and I stop fighting it. My movements become less and less controlled, my hips snap against hers quicker, and I hike her legs up higher around me, making the angle deeper to prolong her pleasure.

Hearing Augustine Jones cry out my name in pure ecstasy is the thing of fantasies.

She mewls and whines and groans and I fucking lose it. My release crashes over me harder and heavier than ever before.

Breathing heavy, sweat dripping down my back, Auggie pulls my face to hers.

"I'm so glad it's you."

# 12

# Chapter 12

Auggie

I'm completely boneless.

Completely ruined for sex with anyone other than Trent. He somehow took everything that I like in the bedroom, and just elevated it to another fucking level. A level I wasn't aware of.

I always knew I kind of liked being a brat in bed, but I had no idea how much. I loved *making* him make me do what he wanted. He made me feel safe and secure while feeling absolutely sexy and admired the whole time.

"I'm glad it was you, too." He whispers, his face still hidden in the crook of my neck. "I didn't think this would happen with us."

"I didn't either." I cradle his head to mine and run my fingers through his hair. "If I'm being honest, I wanted it to, but slowly over time. It wasn't an initial thing, but I think since we became such good friends… the need to be closer to and with you became so much stronger."

Trent nodded in understanding. He lifts his head and rests his chin on my chest, making sure to keep me close. I love that he hasn't pulled out yet, like he can't stand to be parted from me now that he has me.

"They say the best relationships are the ones built on friendship and camaraderie. So, I'd say we have a pretty good shot." He says, and my heart threatens to beat out of my chest in happiness.

"You want a relationship?" I didn't dare hope that a guy like Trent wanted anything to do with me for other than a night. Maybe two if I was lucky. So, to hear him even allude to a real relationship…

"Auggie," Trent's light eyes find mine, and I'm mesmerized by all the feelings I see in them. "The way I see this, we've already been in a pseudo-relationship for months. I wake up and my first thought is you. I think about you throughout the day. I worry about your well-being, and I want to be the one to make you happy. When that guy was dancing with you tonight, I realized that my feelings for you have changed. I want you to be mine, and only mine." His expression turns dark as he talks about the other man who touched me tonight. His hands grip my hands, thread our fingers together and put our clasped hands by my head.

"I *want* you to be mine and only mine. I know this started off as a job for me and an inconvenience for you, but I think we owe it to each other to see where this goes." He punctuates his words with a soft kiss that still manages to make my toes curl.

"I know you feel this. I know you feel how strong, how

magnetic, this is between us. Don't you?" He rocks his hips, his softening cock still within me.

I nod, because I do. I always knew we had strong chemistry; it's why we got on each other's nerves so much, why we would tease and pick on each other, why we knew exactly how to poke the others buttons so expertly.

They say it's a thin line between love and hate. How true it is.

"So, we jump from acquaintances, to enemies, to friends, to lovers, to together." I smirk.

"Sounds about right." He smiles, kissing me softly again, and pulling out. I feel the loss of him and then feel the gush of our releases leave me. Trent rolls to the side, and gently rolls me to lay against him, my back to his chest.

"Are we skipping a few steps? We are already living together now. What if you get tired of me?" I ask jokingly, but really, I'm only halfway joking. I don't like being self-conscious. Don't like projecting it. But I can't help feeling like he might, I don't know, change his mind in the morning. When the dust settles and the sun shines. When he's no longer feeling the adrenaline of me almost being kidnapped.

"What if you get tired of me?" He returns the question like it's a dumb question to ask.

"Be serious."

"You be serious, Auggie. We haven't killed each other yet. We know how each other lives, all the annoying little things that come from living with each other. Now, we can cuddle and kiss whenever we want." He flashes me his panty-dropping smirk, and his hand slides around my waist, drawing me in closer.

I breathe his words in, absorbing them and letting them

fully sink in. The silence stretches on until I start to wonder if he fell asleep. I'm close to falling asleep myself, safe and content in his big strong arms. But then, he says the one thing that brings my anxiety back up.

"As much as I don't want this moment to end, we need to call Kieron and Talia and get us into another safe house, away from here." Trent said.

"No." The word burst from my lips before he even stopped talking.

Trent raised a dark auburn eyebrow at me, moving so I could roll to my back and look at him.

"No?"

"They can't know. So please, let's just, I don't know, figure it out?" I had no clue what we were supposed to do, but I couldn't add any more stress or problems for to my sister. I don't know exactly what happened that night that Marcos died, but I do know that my sister sacrificed something big for me. I wouldn't let that happen again.

"Auggie, you're asking me to disobey a direct command from my leader. Something that I could be severely punished for."

"Kieron wouldn't, would he?" I hadn't thought of that. I can't put Trent in danger as well. But I don't know what else to do... Talia can't save me every time. And if Kieron steps in, not because of an Italian advance but because of Los Muertos, they'll be saving her kid sister. Again.

"I'm not working under Kieron's direct orders. I'm working under Kellan's. The Skipper. The head of the Irish Mob. I have to call this in to him, *at the very least*." He emphasized.

"Can we keep it just between the three of us? Can I talk to this Kellan?" I'm starting to feel desperate. The need to handle this myself, and not drag others into my mess any more than they are already, growing strongly.

"Auggie, we have to leave here. My job is to keep you safe, but it's hard for me to do that without knowing all the variables. Now that I know I have Los Muertos to look out for as well, everything needs to be ramped up even more. New place, new identities, new everything. But it means fuck-all if we don't stop them. I need to have someone else on the outside taking them down." I can see that he's trying so fucking hard to be patient, to explain it clearly so I understand when really, all he wants is to just take off, and do what he thinks is best. My heart warms at the understanding of his gesture. His patience and belief in me and our new relationship to treat me as an equal.

"Fine. But Talia doesn't need to be in on this. Can you see where I'm coming from? Please try to understand."

His eyes soften in the light streaming in from the hallway, we hadn't turned it off in our haste to get to a bedroom as quickly as possible.

"I do understand, Princess. But I'm telling you that the best course of action, for all of us; is telling Kellan, getting you into a new safehouse, maybe pulling in Cillian and Bryan to help, and taking Los Muertos down." His hand cradles my face and deep in my chest, I recognize that he's right. As much as I don't like it, I know he's right.

I nod. "Can the rest wait until morning?" Trent laughs, his sudden outburst warming my heart and making me smile.

"Yes, baby. The rest can wait until the morning." He nuzzles into my neck, breathing in deeply. "But I have to go call Kellan now. We need to move quickly."

My eyelids are drooping, the events of the day catching up

to me. I turn over with a sleepy smile on my face. My eye catches a shadow that crosses over the window, I see a shift of darkness under the edge of the curtain. Just the wind making a tree branch move. It has to be. I shake it off, and pull the sheet up over my shoulders.

"You'll be back, right?" I asked, turning over to look at the back-lit silhouette of the man in front of me as he bent over to slide his boxers over his toned ass.

"As soon as I can." He leaned over and kissed me softly, cupping my chin and smiling.

————-

I felt like I'd barely closed my eyes when a firm hand closed over my mouth tightly, painfully.

A man I'd never seen before staring down at me with a sick kind of glee on his face. I try to scream, try to get Trent's attention in the next room, but the hand clamps down harder. My jaw feels like it's going to be crushed under the leather glove clad hand. I try to calm my fear, to breathe slowly through my nose, but I have to do something, anything, to make noise and get Trent in here. My captor must have seen the idea because he chuckled darkly, the air turning putrid from his breath, and I kick my legs repeatedly, trying to make any noise. A sharp sting, like a bee sting, hits my neck and my thoughts immediately turn sluggish. He doped me with something. Fuck.

My whole body starts to feel cold, too cold.

I have...to... I have to.... What do I have to...Trent. Trent! I scream his name, but realize even with the captors hand off my mouth, no sound is coming out. I can't move anything, my eyes can barely move.

The guy stands up straight, rolling his shoulders, and moving to the side. My vision is darkening and twisting with whatever they gave me, but I force myself to stay awake as long as possible. Another man comes into view, stepping around the asshole who drugged me. He's shorter than Trent, but stocky. I can't tell what he looks like, but the moment he leans forward to pick me up, I recognize him.

*Hector.*

# 13

# Chapter 13

Trent

"Stay safe." Kellan hung up the phone quickly after I'd informed him of everything Auggie had told me.

While he didn't fully understand how Los Muertos had found Auggie, he accepted my request to bring Cillian and Bryan in on her protection detail. I can understand why he was confused and angry that the protection I'd given her hadn't protected her against Los Muertos as well as the Italians.

It should've. It absolutely should have.

I run my hand over my face; the scruff feeling different than my usual clean-shaven face under my hand. A thump had sounded while I'd been on the phone, and I'm sure it was just Auggie going to the bathroom, but I'm anxious to get back to my sleeping beauty.

My chest is tight and heavy, the *need* to get to Auggie overwhelming. I'd been in the Mafia for long enough, been on enough missions, for me to know to trust my gut.

Running back into the room, the first thing I notice is a draft. The curtains flutter in the breeze of the window that I know was locked.

"Auggie?" I call out in fear. My heart stops with no reply, and I run as fast as humanly possible to the bathroom to check, only to find that she's not there.

"Fuck. Fuck!" My fist flies through the dry wall.

They took her.

They took my girl.

They took Auggie.

————-

"I need you here *now*." I snap at Cillian through the phone. I can hear how domineering I sound, how aggressive, but those fuckers took her from me. Who knows what they're planning, what they're doing to Auggie as we sit here, helpless.

After securing the apartment and checking for any kind of evidence left behind, I'd immediately called Cillian while getting dressed into full tactical gear. Lacing up my boots, I try to shove the terror that threatens to cripple me into a box, and put it in the back of my mind so that I can focus on the task at hand.

"I'm half an hour away." Cillian is Kieron's cousin, one of his best soldiers. We've worked on many missions together, and now Cillian's one of my best friends. I like to think that the four of us guys are pretty close. I can call on any of them, no questions asked, and they'll be there for me, just like they know I'd be there for them.

"Fucking step on it, Kill."

"Okayyyy." He drags the word out like an annoyed teenager.

I understand I'm panicked and short, being a total fucking dick, but every moment it takes me to get her back means another moment she's not safe in my arms.

"I'm panicking, man." I sigh, running my hand through my hair.

"Dude, I understand we need to get her back, but you are really invested in Talia's family. Is there, uh, is there a reason for that?" Cillian says, his tone surprised.

Silence.

I wasn't going to tell him just yet how close Auggie and I had gotten, but at this moment, I don't care.

"Trenton... you didn't."

"I fucking did, and you know what? I swear she's the fucking one. She's it for me. My best friend, and I know it's too soon to tell her I love her but, it's only a matter of time." My feelings for Auggie grew steadily, and creeped up on me, but they were no less powerful. Now that I've given myself permission to feel things for her, I feel *everything* for her.

"And you know what? I can't stand the fact that she didn't tell me about Los Muertos. I can't stand that she kept it from me because now she's *gone*. It's like she didn't even give me the chance to protect her really. We finally, *finally*, got to be together fully, and now she's gone, Kill. Gone. All because I left for a 3-minute phone call that I didn't think could wait."

Cillian was quiet; letting me yell at him and expose my feelings for my best friend's sister-in-law, my charge, and think through my fear and guilt that she's being hurt at this very moment.

"Trent, we will get her back, man." Cillian was sincere, his normally aloof and kind tone was hard and determined. My friend had just accepted what I told him and started problem-solving. "You need to call Bryan and get him up to speed. I'll be there in 5 minutes and we will go knocking at their door." It's five minutes now. He must have sped up.

Sighing, I utter the fear that I don't even want to acknowledge to him.

"What if they kill her?" I whisper, my voice sounding like that of a broken man.

"Then we fuck them up. Six feet underground."

—————-

"Los Muertos…" Bryan says, his voice was still deep and husky because I'd woken him up to get him up to speed, and start gathering intel.

"I want to know everything. But specifically look into their recently deceased leader and figure out who took over." I say into my phone as Cillian walks through the door, his large stature taking up more space than my own. The apartment Auggie and I share never felt necessarily cramped or small; her bubbly light-hearted personality making the space vibrant, but with her gone, it feels a more like a coffin.

"Auggie told me that he was her ex, and after he died, his gang blamed her. Someone tried to take her from the club earlier tonight."

"Jesus, Trent. A club? Were you even trying to lay low at all?" Cillian said, plopping down on the couch before shrugging out of his own leather jacket.

"Shut your fucking mouth, Cillian. I don't need your bullshit right now. I know I fucked up, and I'm well aware she's out there; scared, alone and paying the price for my stupidity." I snap.

Both guys were silent. Sure, I outrank them within the Clan so part of their silence was probably because I'd unintentionally given an order but, I really knew it was because they were shocked. I wasn't one to get so worked up about a charge. Sure, I was pumped full of adrenaline, and worry if there were any issues with protection that I was overseeing, but never so personally invested.

"Marcos Constanza. Age 30 years old at time of death. Blunt force trauma. Murder. He was the head of the gang known as Los Muertos. The papers all reported he was murdered, but there were no leads as to who actually did it. We know it was Talia, though." Bryan says, just prattling off information like that last tidbit wasn't a shock to anyone. My eyes widen, and I stare in disbelief at Kill as he just shrugs his shoulders. "Had one younger brother, Hector, who has taken his brother's place at the top." Bryan's voice came through the phones speaker, and my mind struggles to accept the new information.

"Talia killed the head of the Los Muertos gang? Did she know?" I ask the room. Obviously, Kieron had known. He'd known and kept that information to himself, probably for her own safety so I can't fault him. But, damn. That girl was full of surprises, just like her sister.

"I doubt it. You saw her when Luca found her." Cillian said, leaning over on his knees.

Do I remember? It was a traumatic night for Talia and for Kieron. I remember the three of us rushed to Kieron's beach house after we had discovered that the Italians had sent us off into a trap to get her alone so Luca could kill her. We had gotten to her as fast as we could, but she had already killed Luca. We hadn't made it in time to save her from having to fight for her life and kill him herself.

Talia had been a mess. Thrown into a PTSD episode from the past while cowering in fear of the corpse and filled with guilt.

She'd killed Marcos for Auggie. Why?

There's only one reason.

To protect her.

Marcos was doing something to Auggie and Talia had snapped. My mind started conjuring images of Auggie being forced down by some guy, being punched and kicked. Of that independent, spitfire being stripped of her fire, forced to be helpless. The Auggie in my mind calls out for me, and I officially lose my fucking mind.

"Tell me you have a goddamn address, Bryan." I growl. Cillian stands up, tosses his jacket back on, and goes to all the spots he knows I hide my guns and weapons, and starts to pull them.

"I do have one that I found… Wait. Oh fuck, you're not going to like this."

"Spit it out, Bry." I don't have time for this.

"Headquarters are in New Jersey, but Constanza's address is in New York."

"Both of those are hours away." Cillian said, his hands lowering from the top of the fridge where I kept a pistol, the very one he has in his grip. My fists clench in frustration and fear. If we picked the wrong place to go to, Auggie could be hurt in the delayed time.

She could be hurt by another choice I make.

I have to stop those thoughts, the spiral I'm going through, because it isn't going to accomplish anything.

It won't bring her back.

We need more information. As much as every bone in my

body begs me to go off and find her, I know I need to be smart.  Hector isn't going to just give her back to me.  He wants vengeance for his brother, and he going to take it from Auggie even though she has no idea what happened to him, at least not really.

But Talia might.

I snapped to Cillian, "Get Kieron on the phone."

He pulls out his phone and starts tapping away.

"Keep looking for more information, Bryan. Try tracking her, hack into any of the cameras around here. There has to be something you can do. Do it. We are going to get on the road." I fucking wish, not for the first time, that I'd known about this so I could've installed more cameras around the perimeter, and not just the front door.

"We'll find her, Trent." Bryan said, and hung up. I shove my phone into my pocket just as Cillian shoves his phone to me.

"He's pissed." He said to me, eyebrows raised.

Like I gave a fuck.  Auggie was going to be pissed at me too, but if me breaking a promise to her was the difference between saving her life or not… she is just going to have to live with it.

"How the *fuck* did you lose her?" Kieron's voice was hushed, but deadly. "You had one job, Trent. One job. Keep her safe. And I had to find out from fucking Cillian that she's missing."

Rationally, I know I deserve this. I didn't keep her safe.

Irrationally, I was looking for a fight to help me tame my out-of-control emotions.

"I didn't call to talk to you, Kieron. I need to talk to Talia." I say through my grit teeth.

"There's no fucking way I'm letting you talk to Talia right now, she's *beside herself* because her sister is gone. You know how close they've gotten since everything went down and they reconnected."

My chest, already tight, starts burning with raging emotion. My fingers clench the phone so hard I'm sure I hear it cracking. My eyes narrow as I do my best to keep my breathing under control.

"Do you think I did this on purpose? You know me better than that."

"I don't know. But I'm disappointed as hell and so mad I don't know how to handle this. I figured that since you and Talia got on so well, you'd get on with Auggie. You guys came over a bit ago, and I could've sworn that under all the teasing and eye rolls and attitude, you'd do right by her. By me. You didn't have to like her, just fucking keep her safe!" He yells and all my self- control snaps. How fucking dare he talk to me like I don't care about Auggie, like I just threw her at danger. He hasn't even asked who took her.

"How dare you. How *fucking dare you!*" My voice cracks through the air, through the phone so loudly I'm sure people could hear me outside. "I have feelings for Auggie! And I finally, *finally*, told her, got to be with her, and have her care for me back, and three minutes later she's taken from me. Don't you say I didn't do my goddamn job when I did it as best I could with the information I was given. You don't know what it's like to have your girl stolen from your bed!" My voice cracks, and I try not to let the despair I'm feeling knock me over.

"She was safe, tucked under the covers of my bed, and I left to call Skipper to get a new safehouse because some piece of shit had tried to take her from the club we were in,"

"The club?!" He snaps.

"So not fucking important right now! I left for three minutes, Kieron. Three. And they took her from me. So now, it's your goddamn turn to help me save *my* girl! I need. To talk. To Talia." I let out a deep breath. "Please."

It was silent on the other end of the phone.

"Please." I said again, softer. There was a scuffle on the other end of the phone before Talia's voice, so similar, but so different from Auggie's, came through the speaker.

"Trent?" Her voice was watery and stuffy, a clear sign she's been crying, and while my heart goes out to girl who I love like a sister, I'm too focused on getting the information to save Auggie.

"Hey Talia. I know this sucks. I know you're all mad at me. Trust me, I'm mad at me too. But we can talk about that all later. Right now, I need you to tell me everything you know about Marcos Constanza. Where did he live? Do you know about his job? What about his brother, Hector?"

"They did this?" I can't see her but the way that her voice turned hard, all the tears and sobs became anger instead of despair, told me she did, in fact, kill Marcos.

What a fucking badass Talia is.

"They did. And I swear on my life, I'll get her back. They'll regret even thinking of taking her from us. They won't be able to do much of anything by the time I'm done with them." A deep sense of promise and fury fill my vows. No one touches my girl without losing at least a finger. They were all fucking dead. In most painful, most excruciating way I could think of.

"I thought killing that asshole who decided to beat on my sister would stop this. I guess I should've realized they would try to retaliate." Her words are a shock to my system as the image of Auggie sitting bruised and bloody fill my mind.

I feel like I'm going to be sick.

"They're going to be so goddamn sorry. I promise you that." My words are a balm for her nerves, and also a dark promise. "But I need more information. I need some information from you. Do you know where Auggie would meet up with Marcos? We have two addresses that Bryan was able to find, but I'm not willing to chance that I'm wrong and…" I couldn't finish that sentence. I couldn't think of anything but getting her home safely and unharmed.

Talia sobs, but she doesn't let it take over because she clears her throat.

"I never met Marcos myself. Until that night, that is. He, and Luca, isolated us from each other in their own way. I got a phone call from Auggie telling me she wanted out, she needed to get away from him. That is was getting unmanageable. So, I snuck out of Luca's and went to the apartment they shared in New York." She tells me. The phone for sure cracks in my hand a bit as I get more information about my girl with another man.

"I didn't know they were that serious." I say softly as I try to rein in my caveman emotions.

"I don't know if they were, or that he just decided they were. I walked in on my baby sister lying in a pool of her own blood as he stood over her killing her, punch after punch."

Everything in my vision narrows sharply and I can vaguely hear crashing.

*"Trent!"*

# 14

# Chapter 14

Trent

He'd hurt her.

He'd made her bleed.

He'd damn near killed her. He tried to.

My anger and rage was uncontrollable as I tore through the small safe house I shared with Auggie. There wasn't much that would break, we didn't have much here. So, I settled for throwing the stools, smashing the TV, and reveling in the satisfying crunch it made. At the pain in my knuckles from punching the screen hard enough to make it crack. Soon, papers joined them soon as I threw file after file that I had put on the counter.

"Trent, man, calm down." I vaguely hear Cillian's voice as the blood rushes in my ears.

I pick up one of the remaining stools and throw it across the room, throwing it right at the already broken TV, and even the crash as it fell off the stand didn't satisfy my need to make a dead man pay.

I hear Cillian talking to someone in the background, it's only then that I realize he picked up the cracked phone I'd dropped in my rage.

I look around for something else to throw, something else to destroy, when two thick arms banded around my chest, pinning my arms to my sides.

"Trent, that's enough! We have a good location; we need to go." Cillian snaps in my ear, and I hear Talia scream-crying through the speaker.

"Trent, it's okay. She was okay, I'd made sure of it." She repeats over and over. Kieron's voice joins hers as he takes over.

"Trenton." I snap to attention at the sound of my Second-in-Commands 'official voice.' "The more time you spend here the more time she's in their hands. Stop, baby." He mumbles the last words, his tone lighter, clearly speaking to Talia. "He's fine. He'll be okay. Yes, obviously they got together. Ugh, fine." He speaks to his girl, and I arch my eyebrow in question, tapping on Cillian's arms so he knows I'm calm enough for him to let me go.

"Yes, I know. I owe you $10." He's still talking to Talia, and I can hear her giggle. "You just lost me money, Trent. Talia knows Auggie better, and bet you two would get together in less than six months."

I laugh incredulously, shaking my head. Cillian gathers the weapons he'd found, and quickly packs them in a black duffel bag. He tips his head to the side, signaling that he will drive, and I throw my keys at him. There's no way I can drive right now with how I'm feeling. How I'm vibrating with the need to get to her. We can't afford to get pulled over, or have any police attention. I just need to get to her.

"Talia said it all went down at the New York address, so I think we should head there." Cillian says.

"We are headed to the New York address now." I tell Kieron our plan. "Tell Talia I'll get Auggie back, I swear it." I've never meant something more, I will get Auggie back to safety if it is the last thing I do.

"I'll pack up and meet you there with Bryan. Let's go bash some fucking skulls, eh?" Kieron chuckles through the phone.

"Kieron, no. I got this."

"Let me tell you something, Trenton." Killian snaps harshly, and shit, he is pissed. "I know you have this, and you'll most definitely get your girl home safely. But just because you can take it on yourself, doesn't mean you have to. You helped me when my girl was in danger, and I'm going to return the favor. Not only that, but you're the closest thing I have to a brother. So shut up, and send me the motherfucking address." Even though his words sounded harsh, every word was said with care and emphasized with emotion.

We'd always been close, and I knew I'd do anything for that asshole but to have him turn around and be there for me, to put himself in danger *for me and my girl*, it hit a little different.

"I'll see you in a few hours."

15

# Chapter 15

Auggie

I groggily try to pull myself from sleep. My eyelids flutter open, but my arms and legs still feel like they're filled with lead.

What happened?

I look around; expecting to see Trent, expecting to see his handsome, smug face at giving me the best sex of my life, but instead, I jolt in horror. My arms are bound behind my back and my ankles are tied together in front of me. Fuck, my side is killing me. My weight is resting against my shoulder and face with my ass up like they'd just thrown me on the floor and walked away. They probably had.

A quick glance around tells me that I'm back in the apartment I was forced to share with Marcos. *Fuck.*

The floor to ceiling windows showcasing the gorgeous New York City skyline, and the millions of people below it. The apartment is gorgeous, over-the-top, and stunning with a view of the world as a God would see. Marcos would stand so many nights just staring out and down, looking down on his subjects like he was untouchable and benevolent in his violence. In his anger. In his cruelty.

When I'd been…coerced into moving in, Marcos had convinced me under the guise of protection. That people he knew, "bad people who didn't really know him" he'd say over and over, were coming after him because he'd stuck up for his family. Little did I fucking know that meant that someone had pissed off the Russian Mob and killed the wrong person, so the entirety of the Russian Bratva was gunning for him.

At the time, I was happy to move in. Happy to take this next step with him. Was it early? Sure was. But did I think we would be together for a long time? Very much so.

That was how it started.

It happened so slowly I didn't really even recognize it happening until after the fallout. After agreeing to move in with him, he convinced me to give up my job completely. Marcos promised me he'd take care of me, that I didn't need to make money because he had more than enough for us both. He convinced me that it was too dangerous for me to work. I was the well-known consort of the leader of Los Muertos. That meant I had a target on my back.

So, under the constant fear that I was in such danger, I quit.

It's not like I lived for my job in retail anyway, so it seemed like a good thing for me to be able to get to be a stay-at- home girlfriend.

The longer the manhunt for Marcos went on, the more stressed he became. Security got tighter, more intense. Communication was cut off completely. Marcos was getting more and more paranoid. I shouldn't have been surprised when the blame and fear was turned on me.

He came home from work one day, and I had rushed to greet him at the door. Instead of a kiss hello or a grunt in passing like I was met with more often than not, I was met with a backhanded slap across my cheek. When I asked what I'd done to deserve it, he had smacked me again.

What I hadn't planned on him screaming at me was how I was a traitorous cunt who was feeding information to someone named Talia.

He had hit me because he found the only text thread in my phone - to my sister - and assumed I was conversing with his enemy.

There had been no way I could've explained it any clearer, that I was talking to *my sister*, but it didn't matter. At that point, Marcos was too far gone. In the moment, I felt guilty. Guilty because I'd disobeyed him and talked to someone he hadn't given me permission to. But now, now I realize and recognize just how fucked up that is. How much he had fucked with my head.

That was the last night I ever saw Marcos. It was also the night he almost killed me.

My anxiety cranks up a notch as I look around me, and I realize I'm in the exact same spot I was in when he beat me half to death.

Only this time, I *know* I have people in my corner.

Trent will undoubtedly be pissed as hell when he sees I'm not in his bed anymore. Can't say I'd blame him; I'm pissed I'm not there, too. I should be. I want to be. Fuck, I wish I was.

I just need to give Trent and the others time to find me. Talia knows about this apartment, but I don't know if Trent will call her. I told him not to involve her, so I don't know if they'll figure it out in time.

Gruff, muffled whispers carry through the wall, and can hear at least two men speaking Spanish. One of them is really angry and the other, I can tell from the tone, is just placating the angry one.

A shiver of fear runs down my spine as I realize the angry one's voice has the same deepness and vocal tilt that Marcos's had... That can only mean...

A loud *boom* sounds, and I jump in my restraints. I will myself to stay in the same uncomfortable position and close my eyes again. My heart is hammering in my chest, I'm so fucking anxious about what is coming for me.

The door to the kitchen opens roughly, the door hitting the back wall, and I can hear a storm of footsteps echoing against the tile floor, coming right for me. I feel like I'm playing a game of hide-and-seek, but I'm physically unable to hide. I keep my eyes squeezed shut, and try to keep my breathing steady. I need as much information as I can get, and they'd only speak freely if they thought I was still knocked out.

After living with Marcos for a while, I was well-versed in his Spanish/ English intermingled way of speaking. I knew a few words in Spanish, enough to know that based on what they're saying, I'm in some serious fucking trouble here.

I mentally scold myself because if I'd just opened up and talked with Trent, really talked with him, he'd know about this place. He'd know about Marcos and Hector and all the suffering I went through. He'd know how hard I had fought to be free of it all. He'd know I didn't intentionally hide it all from him, I'd just thought they'd leave me alone.

How fucking naive I was.

How fucking stupid of me. I thought the truth that I hadn't killed Marcos would keep me safe. That they'd see reason.

And now, not only was I back in hell, but they'd finish the job that Marcos started, making sure I died in hell, too.

"Eyes open, bitch. I know you're awake." Hector's rancid breath fans over my face, telling me just how close he really is. I open my eyes slowly, my head still throbbing from the brutal treatment I must have received when they knocked me out.

I couldn't let my terror show. Guys like Hector pounce on any emotion I show, so I did what I'd done so many times before, I retreated into my mind. On the outside, I look present and like I'm paying attention, but inside I'm hiding my soul, my feelings, my heart, behind thick brick walls of sass and fire.

"You must be Hector." My throat is crazy dry and hurt, like I've swallowed sand.

"Smart girl. I wish I could say it was good to meet you, but I'd be lying." He stood up from his crouched position, and gestured with his hand for his lackey to sit me up. It was painful, sitting with my ankles bound tightly, while still trying to keep some dignity. He had kidnapped me naked after all.

Bring naked was the least of my problems. At least I thought so, until I got an eyeful of the guard on the other side of the room. A brutal, gruesome guy, balding and missing teeth with a porn-stashe, leering at me and adjusting his position so he can have an unobstructed view of my body. I look around, and realize that I'm in real, serious, painful danger. In more ways than one.

I look to Hector, making sure my face is blank as can be, regardless of the absolute terror I feel on the inside.

"So, you're the girl that got the jump on my brother." Hector sat in what looked to be a comfy, oversized armchair that was strangely reminiscent of a throne. He must have brought it in because that was, for sure, not here while I lived here. It was tacky and out of place, but I suspect that it wasn't there for its comfort factor, more for the face that Hector needed a throne. "The girl that took down the "Great Serpent"." He uses air quotes for the name that I don't recognize.

"I don't know what you think, but-" I say softly before a hand comes crashing down on my cheek in a mind-numbing slap. I hear ringing in my ears, and my heartbeat in my cheek as it heats.

"You will speak only when spoken to." Hector says angrily, the man he had been arguing with steps away from me, backing Hector up. Even if I was somehow able to get past Hector, I'd have to deal with him, too.

My eyes water with the pain, and I'm sure my cheek was already starting to bruise. But I wouldn't let them see me cry. I *refuse.* I shift my hair over my shoulders, and straighten my spine as much as I can.

"My brother was a fool. Relationships, even ones that were obviously not going anywhere, make you weak. Make you *seem* weak. But, nevertheless, he must have care for you at some time because he sequestered you here in the tower. Hidden in fear because he thought someone would get to him through you." Hector crosses his leg over his knee and rests his chin in his hand. My jaw clenches and I try to simply listen, let him monologue to give Trent more time.

"Little did you know, he didn't care one lick about you at the end. I got a call from him, demanding a bullet through your skull because he couldn't take the possibility of the Russians finding you and, therefore, finding him. He thought you knew too much. Then he found out you opened your whore mouth. You signed your own death warrant." My eyes never left Hector's as we stare each other down in a battle of wills.

His will to break me and mine to stay alive.

I take a deep breath, and let it out slowly through my nose, willing my heart rate to slow. I bring my ankles up, bending my knees as much as I can to offer myself some coverage.

"You see, my brother - the Great Serpent, Satan rest his soul, was so paranoid that he installed cameras to record every single aspect of his life. Cameras in the living room, in his car, in the bedroom, in the bathroom. Every square inch of his life was caught on camera and monitored, so that if there was any tampering, any threat, he'd know. Imagine my surprise when the day of his death, the moment you walk into the apartment, the footage is erased. From every. Single. Camera." He snaps to punctuate each word.

I want to scream that I have no idea what happened, that I have no idea that everything was being recorded, and honestly, I'm sick to my stomach knowing that I was watched at all aspects of my life back then. The thought that some guy was crowding around a monitor; watching me undress, watching me shower, watching me get hurt, and fucked against my will. And no one did a goddamn thing because they were too chickenshit to go against Marcos to care.

But I didn't do what they're saying I did. I'm not going to try and fight them on it because I need to focus on getting free. So instead, I just sat there quietly. Doing my best to subtly look around for anything that I could use to cut myself free, to get out of this situation, I peak from side to side. There are more guards here than I would think are needed for just one girl, but maybe Hector is just that paranoid.

I can't see anything that I can easily get to. I guess it's a smart move on their part, having me set against the cold glass window because with my ankles and wrists tied, I would have to inch worm, which would for sure draw everyone's attention to me. And something tells me if I flip on my stomach, the perv across the room won't stay over there.

"That footage, Miss Jones, told me everything I needed to know." Hector stands slowly from the chair, buttoning one button of his suit jacket, and he looks straight ahead above my head out at the New York skyline. "You are indeed working with the Russians."

"No, I'm not." I say through my clenched teeth, bracing myself for the hit that I know is coming. It's a beat after I speak of nothing, and I think maybe he won't hit me again.

But then, a backhand smack to my face that is harder than the first slap I received lands across my cheek, and my body flies to the side. If I wasn't held up by the window, I would've been thrown across the floor.

A coopery taste fills my mouth as I taste blood. I groan in pain. My head falls forward, and I see red staining my skin as big globs fall from my mouth.

"Shut the fuck up. You girls, you never learn. Just like that bitch in the back. She swears up and down that she had nothing to do with this either."

I breathe as much as I can through the pain, but my blood runs cold at his words. If this motherfucker has my sister tied and beaten up back there, I'll kill him myself. I may not have been able to protect myself against Marcos, but I sure as hell will protect Talia from these fuckers as much as I can.

I didn't say anything, didn't ask questions, just quietly plan

Hector's murder in my mind as he talks and paces in front of me. And the porn-stashe guy's murder, too.

"Maybe I should pass you around." Hector said, tapping his chin with his finger as if he was actually thinking about it. "It might change your fucking attitude. And it'll be a nice treat for my boys."

"I call dibs." Creeper in the corner calls out. I don't look up, I don't make eye contact, but I'm freaking terrified. I could withstand a lot of things, but I don't know how I could withstand what they're threatening. It was bad enough with Marcos, but I knew him. It's confusing and has me all kinds of fucked up, but at least when Marcos took me against my wishes, I knew what to expect. Even if I didn't want it. But these guys… Something tells me it will break me in a way that I won't be able to come back from.

Fuck, I hope Trent has figured out I'm gone. But, again, how would he know where to find me?

No one would know where to find me.

That thought is what makes me realize, it's up to me. I need to save myself this time.

I know better than to say anything. I didn't want to run the chance of him hitting me again and losing consciousness. Who knows what he'd do, or let his men do to me, if I passed out. At least, if I'm awake, I can try to fight.

"Just let her go. She doesn't know anything. She'd never even met Marcos before he died." I say softly, hoping that my demure demeanor negates the fact that I'm speaking at all.

"Now, now, Augustine." Hector *tsks*. "Don't flat out lie to me."

He takes a step forward, staring at me as one might look pityingly at a dying animal. A mix of hate and disgust crosses his face as his hand shoots out and grips my throat, cutting off my air and dragging me closer to him.

"You knew she was in contact with him." He said roughly, tossing me backward. With my hands and feet tied together, I can't do anything to brace my fall against the window. My head hits the thick glass with a sickening crunch, and immediately, there's an intense throbbing throughout my skull. Pain laced through everything with that fall; every breath, every blink, every movement.

"And you'll both pay for his death with your own." Hector growls. He reaches back behind him, and holds out his hand. I can't just sit here and let him kill us.

Think, Auggie, think.

"Why are you so sure *I'm* the one that was working with the Russians? Do you not have access to everything? Everything I did, and used was under Marcos's nose so he would have had access to my bank records, phone records, fuck, he was so paranoid towards the end, it wouldn't surprise me if he had a fucking tracker implanted somewhere in my body." I yell to Hector as I see a gun being placed in his hand.

"He did have an extraordinary amount of security and data on you. I'll give you that. But even if you aren't working with the Russians, you're working with the Italians. His murder stinks of their coverup work."

I have absolutely not a fucking clue as to what he's talking about. My head hurts too much, there are too many variables that I don't have to be able to make this crazy-ass motherfucker see the truth. Regardless, I need to get Talia out of here.

"Let my sister go." I say strongly. "And I'll tell you whatever you want to know."

Hector raises an eyebrow and *tsks* again.

"Sister? Oh, senorita. You just ensured that you both will die gruesome, revengeful, painful deaths for the both of you, Russian scum."

# 16

# Chapter 16

Trent

"How fucking far away are we?" I'm barely holding it together. My fingers are making indents on the leather seats in Cillian's car because the longer we're driving, the longer it seems. It feels like we've spent decades of our lives on the goddamn road just trying to actually get to Auggie.

"Two minutes, Trent. Keep a level head, we don't know what state she'll be in, but she will need you to be calm." Cillian snaps at me from the driver seat while I check over the guns, *again,* checking the clips and reloading the magazines.

Thank fuck the apartment that Talia sent us was on the edge of the city so we didn't have to drive into the heart of Manhattan wasting precious time in traffic. The penthouse was in a massive building; tall and encased in mirrored glass and chrome, at least fifty stories tall.

Cillian peels onto the right street, his hand circling the wheel in a flourish to have us drift into a spot as he burned the tires to a halt.

"We're here." Cillian threw the car in park and I rip the car door open, pulling so fucking hard that I almost rip it off its hinges, storming towards the front door.

"Trent, wait." Cillian hisses, looking around for anyone standing guard. "We don't know what we're walking into. We should at the very least, wait for Bryan and Kieron."

Anger, that I know is misplaced but still needs an outlet, bubbles to the surface. Not that I had ever not been truly angry since finding out Auggie was missing. I shove Cillian hard, and the mammoth of a man barely moves.

"I'm not going to leave my girl in there with people that want her dead. That's just not going to fucking happen. So, stay out here if you want, but I will not let her be alone." I snap, and point my finger in his face before pulling out my gun from behind my back.

I can see the indecision, and I can understand it. It goes against our training. It goes against reason. But my heart won't listen to my head. I don't think I would listen to reason, even if I could.

"Look, stay here and wait for them. I'm going up." I survey the area, trying to find the best place to enter the building. Just because I'm going in blind, doesn't mean I'm going to be stupid about it. There's a service entry to the side of the building, hidden in the darkness and shadows. I know we made a fuck-ton of noise coming in, but I need to try and remember to keep quiet. The element of surprise might be the only thing that helps me get the drop on whoever, or however many, there are up there.

"Goddamn it." Cillian swears, and I hear his lumbering

footsteps follow after me. "Can't listen to save your life." He mutters.

I ignore him, but he's not wrong.

We make our way to the service door, and I take a deep breath. There isn't really time for me to sit down and make a plan. I just need to be as careful as I can, as quickly as I can, and take as many motherfuckers down as I can.

"Just shut up, tell the guys what's going on, and follow my lead." I hiss over my shoulder. I don't need Cillian to follow me into certain doom here, but I'm sure fucking glad I have him at my back. "Be careful."

Cillian nods, bringing his own handgun up to the ready.

I test if the door is open and am surprised to find that it swings open easily. That means they either knew we were coming or they're just that stupid.

Slipping inside the door, and letting my gun lead the way, I take in the room, scanning it quickly for any threat. I flip to the other side of the room, inspecting it as well. Finding it empty, I walk deeper into the room, and signal to Cillian to follow.

"Kieron said they're ten minutes away." Cillian whispers, following in my footsteps as we walk through the first vacant room. It looks to be an abandoned room store-room, cardboard boxes covered in dust and grime from years of unuse stacked against the walls with broken chairs, desks and other miscellaneous, forgotten office supplies.

I push through the room, always checking the corners of my eyes for movements or traps. I can't - Auggie can't - afford for me to be caught. I don't know what they're doing with my girl, but from the way that asshole was talking to her at the bar, I don't think they're going easy on her. I know that the moment I find her, I'm going to kill anyone who dared touch her.

We have a long fucking way to go, but all I can think is, 'Hold on, Princess, I'm coming.'

———-

"Okay, I get that we're trying not to alert them, but holy motherfucker." Cillian whines and breathes deeply, holding onto the metal railing.

I can't exactly blame him. Fifty flights of stairs, going as fast as we can, taking minimal breaks, is pretty killer. My quads are going to be jacked after this, but it's well worth it to not alert anyone and get to her as fast as we can. I'm very quickly remind myself that this is why I work out. This is why I *have to* run so fucking much. Luckily, Cillian works out as hard as I do, we both take a second to catch our breath before opening the door to the apartment. On the fiftieth floor.

"Shut up, we're here." I tell him, completely ignoring that I'm just as winded as he is. I hate cardio. I hate it so fucking much.

But I vow to any deity that's listening, that if Auggie's okay, I'll add more cardio into my routine as penance.

I put my ear to the dark wooden door, obviously reinforced somehow. The dark brown of the door standing between Auggie and I is daunting and ominous. It stands out against the white walls in the dingy stairwell.

I can't have Cillian in there rushing after me blindly, hoping that the two of us are enough, I need to gather more information. I need to figure out that if it's Auggie, Hector, and four or five of his minions, I can take care of them quickly before they call for backup.

Fuck, I wish I had a blueprint. A picture of the layout. Anything to let me know what I was walking into. But I don't, so I have to play this smart.

I turn the doorknob slowly, thanking my lucky stars that it was unlocked. *Where they expecting us? Are we walking into a trap?*

I hear voices echoing through the apartment. The entryway is thankfully small and boxed in, making surveying it for threats easy, but at the same time, if someone decides to come in here, we're completely fucked. There's absolutely nowhere to hide and nothing to use as protection. The dim lighting makes the dark taupe walls even darker.

"Sister? Oh, senorita. You just ensured that you both will die gruesome, revengeful, painful deaths for the both of you, Russian scum." I hear the thickly accented voice taunt. I can't just assume that he's talking to Auggie, but I don't know who else he might be speaking to that way.

"How many are there?" Cillian whispers.

I peak around the side with my back flat against the wall to try and see as much as I can. I clock two by the far side wall, one with a gross mustache that for sure has become that fucker's whole identity. I cringe as I see him smooth it down, and smirk like he's hot shit when really, it's pretty revolting. There's another two on the opposing wall, staring straight ahead and looking like they'd rather be anywhere but here. Not that I can blame them, I'd also rather be far away from here.

Specifically, back in my bed with Auggie wrapped in my arms without a fucking thought of these assholes.

My gaze goes to the front wall, an entire wall of windows, where the voice I heard came from. A guy in a suit with dark brown hair and tanned skin, stands with his hands in his pockets looking down at something I can't see. Another guy, more casually dressed in baggy jeans and a t-shirt, stands beside him with his back to me as well.

I turn back to Cillian, silently holding up 6 fingers, and motion with him to take the left side of the room, I'll take the right and we can split the two in the middle.

"I told you fuckers already; I don't know what you're talking about. My sister and I, we aren't Russian. I haven't worked with the Russians, and I know she hasn't. Let us go or you're going to be sorry." My Auggie speaks so strongly and true, and I released a breath that I wasn't aware I was holding. *She's alive. She's right fucking there.*

My eyes must say that I'm about to thunder through the room because Cillian grabs my arm to hold me back.

"Be smart." He hisses, and I grit my teeth so hard that I'm sure my molars will be dust soon. Ripping my arm out of his grip, I nod.

Of course, my Princess has to push Hector's buttons. And I barely contain my reaction when I see him rear back and hit her. There's a maddening thud as his hand hits her skin, and I vow, then and there, that I will cut off his motherfucking hands and give them to her. A squeak comes from the floor with the thud and a panful groan as Hector stands back up.

"Who, or what, do I have to be scared of, little girl?" He laughs like he's been told a hilarious fucking joke, and I can't wait to laugh like that over his dead body.

"We've had your sister here for months and not one person has been able to get through our defenses. And they've let you be taken as well. Can't say that I'm too worried." Hector said. I can just barely see him inspect his knuckles, but I see red smeared on them. I feel myself vibrating with the need to do something. Anything. I feel the completely unhinged part of myself beg and claw to take over. I need to get her out of this situation and kill the people responsible for her pain.

"Her sister?" Cillian whispers in my face. "Is Talia here? We just spoke to her. Do they have another sister?"

I shake my head no. Whoever they have, wasn't one of the Jones girls.

"Does Auggie know that Talia is okay?"

Fuck. I shake my head again.

"What do you want? You want to punish me for Marcos's paranoia? Fine. Let my sister go, she had nothing to do with this." Auggie says and dread fills my body. We have to do something, and we have to do it now.

"Oh, fuck. Here we go." Cillian murmurs behind me as I raise my gun and aim. I fire off two shots in quick succession with the two guards against the side, neat bullet holes between their eyes, both of them dead before they hit the floor.

Then all hell breaks loose.

The creeper with the thick mustache turns to were we're hiding and starts shooting, his buddy doing the same. Before taking cover, Hector and I make eye contact. His second-hand man pulls his gun, putting Hector behind him as he tries to get him to safety. That shit won't be happening.

The surprise in Hectors eyes as he realizes all that bullshit he was spewing to Auggie was wrong, made manic laughter bubble to my chest in glee. I want to see him realize just how wrong he was when he told my girl that no one was coming for her. I want to see fear in his eyes as he realizes I'm going to make him bleed in every spot that he dared to touch my girl.

Cillian's returning fire on the two guards and a bullet lands one in the gut; blood spewing everywhere. He falls.

Now it's more even. Three on two.

"Come out, and show your face." Hector calls out tauntingly.

"Don't worry, you'll know exactly whose hands you will die by." I call back. Taking aim, I rid the world of that creepy motherfucker who I now know was watching Auggie getting interrogated and beaten.

"Jonas, wait." Hector puts a hand up, motioning for him to hold his fire. The man, Jonas, looks conflicted like he doesn't want to follow the order, but eventually, I see his gun lower. Just slightly, but I saw him submit nonetheless.

Not willing to take the chance, I keep my gun aimed directly for Hector's head as I step out of the shadows and into the room. My eyes never leave Hector and Jonas, trusting Cillian to survey the rest of the room, and watch my back.

"And who might you be?" Hector asks. A sinister smirk crossing his pocketed, tan face. He looks like he relishes a challenge. The promise of violence too much for him to resist.

"It doesn't matter who I am. What matters is that, that girl is leaving with me. I suggest you put your hands up, and hand your weapons over. Your death may be more painless than I want it to be if you cooperate." My voice was calm and clear, much calmer than I felt for sure.

Hector cocks his head to the side like he's studying me, and I can't help it anymore. I glance over to Auggie, taking in her injuries, and white-hot anger licks up my spine and through my body at the state of her – bound and naked, covered in bloody marks and bruised cheeks.

She stares at me like I'm her savior. Like she can't believe that I'm here for her.

The rainbow waves that I had run my fingers lovingly through not even eight hours ago, while I was holding her tightly as I fucked her passionately, were matted and tangled, sticking up all over in disarray. No one had bothered giving her clothes when they stole her from my bed and I could kick myself for not sliding her panties back over her slim legs after I'd left. But at that time, I didn't want her to wear a stitch of clothing because I had planned to be back in less than five minutes and wrap her up in my arms as she slept. I had wanted to feel every inch of warm, soft skin against my own as I fell asleep.

But this asshole in front of me took her before I could get back to her.

I didn't think it was possible for me to get any angrier. To demand more blood than I had already felt. And then I saw her. I saw what he did to her.

My jaw clenches, my grip on the gun tightens, and my nostrils flare as I struggle to control my breathing.

"Now, why would I do that?" Hector asks, that fucking smirk still on his face.

"Because if you don't, I'll make sure that your last moments will be agonizing, excruciating. And because of what you've already done to my girl, you should really want to try to do whatever it is that you can do to make your death as quick as fucking possible."

"Big words from a man who has, what, 6 bullets left in his magazine, and one other man for backup. You don't know who you're going up against. All for a girl who isn't even yours to begin with. She was Marcos's, and betrayed him. Her betrayal caused his death. Los Muertos demands justice. She was the cause of his death, so she will pay for her misdeeds with her own death."

"Yeah, that's not happening." I snap, recentering his skull in my sights.

"Should we reunite the sisters before they die? I think it's fitting, don't you?" Hector said, pulling his phone out and dialing a number. I shoot the phone out of his hand, but the damage is already done. He's called backup. Jonas raises his gun and goes to take a shot, but Cillian's faster. His body drops to the floor with a *thunk*. I can see Auggie jump with the surprise, her hands coming up to try and provide a shield. Her reaction time is off, she's slower and her eyelids are drooping slightly.

Something is wrong.

"You're all alone now." I say slowly, stalking closer to Auggie while keeping my eye trained on Hector. Cillian does the same, moving to the other side.

I have to give it to him; Hector doesn't seem phased. He kicks one foot out slightly so that he is resting his weight on his back leg, and put his hands in his pockets like he's talking at a party.

"You got this?" I ask Cillian gesturing to Hector with my head. I need to get to Auggie and unbind her hands and feet, pull her into my arms, and beg for forgiveness.

"No problem, man." Cillian steps closer to Hector, his gun never wavering. "Don't fucking think about it."

"Of course." Hector shakes his head slightly, pursing his lips, and holds his hands up in surrender. "It would seem that you've bested me."

That's shady and suspicious as shit, but I can't focus on his words right now.

I tuck my gun into the back of my pants, and dart over to Auggie, sliding on my knees to get to her faster.  I pull my pocket knife from my pants pocket and flick it open, quickly slicing through the ties.

"Auggie," I breathe her name, pulling her to my chest and holding her as tightly to my chest as I can.

17

# Chapter 17

Auggie

He's gorgeous.

Riding into danger like a knight in shining armor with red hair and a chiseled jaw set to the side with rage. The moment that he looks to me, I feel tears of relief flood my eyes. Trent runs to me – sliding on his knees to get to me faster, freeing me from the binds, and pulling me into his arms. I sob harder when his arms wrap around me, bringing me home.

"Auggie, I'm here. You're safe, baby. It's okay." He murmurs in my ear, the deep rumble of his voice making me calm. I grip his arms tighter, and push my face into his neck, breathing his comforting scent in. I can't get close enough.

"Talia?" I ask softly. I can't bring myself to leave Trent's arms, but I need to make sure she's okay.

"She's fine. She's not even here. He was just messing with you." Trent leans back, using his thumbs to brush the tears

149

off my face, and I can see him taking in every mark, every bruise, every touch, from Hector on my face and body. Trent's feather-light touch moves over my skin softly like he is trying to erase every mark made of anger with a touch of love.

"Are you okay?" The moment the question left his lips, I can see him mentally kick himself.

"I don't think I'm okay, big guy. But I will be." I answer him with attitude, reminiscent of how I used to answer any question he'd ask me when we first started living together.

He smirks, but closes his eyes, and shakes his head.

"There's my Princess. Always has to have a fucking attitude." He cups my jaw softly and I try not to wince. That last hit really did some damage.

"You love it." I tease with a smile, but I'm sure it comes out more like a grimace with how my lip feels split and I'm sure I have a cut on my cheek based on the burn I feel when I try to smile. My head is still throbbing, but I'm so relieved that he's here and I'm safe that I can push the pain aside. The way the room is slightly wobbly is a little concerning though.

"I do." He says, his words full of emotion and earnestness, and I know we are talking about something more.

"I do, too."

The door flies open, and Trent immediately steps in front of me, shifting to put himself between me and whatever is coming. His gun raises so fast I don't see him do it, and I can feel how taunt with tension his muscles are. He's completely in 'shoot now, ask questions later' mode. Cillian has tied Hectors hands behind his back with some kind of tape he must have found, and positioned him so that Hector is a human shield, showing whomever walks in that Cillian and Trent have the upper hand.

"Auggie," Kieron's voice rings through the room, and I see my brother-in-law storm in, his gun also raised with another man covering his back. "Thank fuck."

Kieron quickly surveys the room, glancing around, but seeing that Cillian and Trent have it under control, he storms up to me and tries to pull me into his arms in one of our typical big bear hugs. But Trent doesn't move. If anything, he pushes me farther behind his back so I'm completely covered.

"Get out of my way, Trent. I need to make sure she's okay." Kieron snaps. I know enough about their dynamic to know that when Kieron gives an order, all the men in the room have to listen to him immediately.

Trent still doesn't move.

"She's taken care of. I've got her." Trent answers gruffly, and he wraps his arms around me, pressing my body into his back. His leather jacket feels cool against my nipples, and that's when it dawns on me.

I'm still as naked as the day I was born.

I wrap my arms tighter around Trent, pressing my front to his back hard to try to cover myself.

"Trent, move." Kieron's voice is booming and full of authority, but Trent holds strong.

"No," he growls.

I can hear Kieron start to advance, and as much as I like my brother-in-law, I don't need him seeing me like this. I didn't want anyone but Trent to see me like this. Kieron starts to physically remove Trent from me, and Trent shoves him away. Before a fight breaks out, I have to stop it.

"Stop! I'm naked!" I scream, but peak my head around Trent's side so I could show Kieron I'm okay.

Kieron, the behemoth of a man my sister had fallen in love

with, was goofy most of the time. He'd always been up for a joke or a fun hang out with me and Talia, making moon-eyes at my sister like she was his very reason for living. And seeing me, the only other person my sister cared for, like I was... He went from protective to murderous.

"Get her out of here." Kieron's voice is low and dangerous. Every inch the powerful, mafia man he is.

It didn't instill the same reaction from me as when Trent came in and demanded they let me go.

"Wait, Talia!" I cry out, squirming around in Trent's grasp as his hands and arms held me to keep me from any eyes other than his. I know the other men in the room wouldn't try anything, wouldn't even look, as they are so loyal to Trent and Kieron. The way that Trent is shielding me, how he is looking around like he would fight each and every one of them if they dare to look too long, how he is holding me so protectively and so possessively... He's claiming me. Showing everyone, I'm his.

Coming from a possessive relationship with Marcos, and now dealing with the consequences, I can tell the difference. There's *such* a difference. I'm not a trophy with Trent, I'm something precious to him. I'm something that he wants to safe-guard and protect, something to help nurture and thrive. Trent's possessiveness is deep-rooted in protection. Not ownership.

It makes me like him so much more. Love him so much more.

I feel like if I want to be independent like I so desperately want and need, Trent will be on the sidelines cheering me on. Not holding me back in fear that I might become my own person.

"Talia's fine, I promise." Trent says over his shoulder to me.

"Talia's in the safehouse somewhere in the city. I brought her with me. She's with a five-man protection detail. Talia is safe, I give you my word." Kieron put his hand to his chest as if he is trying to prove the truth of his words through the reassuring action.

"But he said…" I look to the side, where Hector is standing with a malicious smile on his face as he takes in each and every word said around him like a snake in the grass.

"He was lying." Trent emphasizes.

"What did he say?" Kieron asks, but I notice that this time, he's looking at Trent and Cillian. The other man who walked in with Kieron, the big burly man with a thick black beard and dark hair, is walking around making sure there isn't anyone that is going to pop out. They didn't need to worry about that in this room, Trent had shot them all. All, but one.

"That he had her. That he had her trapped for months, and no one had come after her. That she had been working with the Russians." Now that my brain isn't swimming in adrenaline, I can realize that it didn't make sense… I knew Talia was with Kieron a few months ago. We'd visited them.

So, who was he holding captive? My head hurts.

Trent lets go of me for a moment, turning me around so we're face-to-face. He pulls off his leather jacket, hands it to me, then shrugs out of his long t-shirt. He hands me the soft, worn material and slips it over my head. I'm immediately enveloped in the warm, spicy scent of Trent and all my muscles relax. He's so tall, and I'm so short that his t-shirt hits my mid-thigh.

"There, I can think now." He whispers and bends down to kiss my lips softly. Sweetly.

"But now you're shirtless and I can't think."

Trent smiles widely, and his eyes spark with cautious consideration. Almost like he knows I'm teasing to keep myself from falling apart.

"Don't worry, baby. I'll take care of you." Trent says in a half-whisper, and takes the jacket from me. He slips his arms through the sleeves, and I notice that even when he turns to talk to Kieron again, he moves to the side so I can see and people can see me, but he still subtlety positions himself between me and the rest of the room.

"He has someone at another location. From what Auggie has said, and what this piece-of-shit has threatened her with, someone from the Russian Bratva. A woman. I don't know how their wires of information got crossed, but that's above my pay grade. He did call someone, demanding they bring her here." Trent explains to Kieron, in a very militant tone. It's obvious they're in work mode now, and I can't help but rub my thighs together at Trent's voice and demeanor. He's just so... take charge.

"Well, well, well." Kieron booms after a moment, his dark eyes calculating, and I can see them turn dangerous. Dangerous for one specific person in the room.

Hector.

He turns on his heel and puts his gun into the waistband of his jeans, then pulls out a switch-blade that apparently all the men in the Irish Mob carry. He flicks it open, and inspects the blade a little too intensely. I can feel my heart beat a bit faster, and anticipation lick along my spine. Kieron truly looks a bit psychotic at the mention that this man had used his wife as bait. That Hector thought he'd captured Talia, and no one cared enough to get her. I can see it messing with his mind and turning him into that protective beast for my sister.

"Hector, is it?" Kieron asks in that fake tone. Everyone in the room knows that Kieron knows exactly who he is dealing with. I may not know a lot, but the fact that Trent was able to find me so quickly means that they know their shit and have top-notch information.

"You thought you had my girl. So, you took my baby sister-in-law as well. That's a bad move, my friend." Kieron twists the knife in his hand, the light glinting off the blade.

Trent walks forward, gesturing for me to stay back, as he joins the interrogation. His shoulders are so tense that they're hunched slightly as he approaches Kieron, and stares down the man that hurt me.

"And I'll tell you, Hector, it's not even a bad move because of *me*." Kieron put his hand to his chest and raised his eyebrows. "It was a bad fucking move because you took *his* girl. And I'll let you in on a little secret, this motherfucker went downright crazy when you took her. Promising murder and blood. Can you imagine what he wants to do to you after seeing the marks you've left? After hearing the threats you've issued? I can only tell you to pray that it's quick. Because he doesn't let the bloodthirsty side of himself out often, but when he does… it's art."

Trent looks back at me, clearly gauging my reaction to Kieron's words. Like hearing that he's murdered or tortured before is going to sully the image I have of him. But little does my sweet giant know, I don't mind it at all.

I smile at him, pushing warmth and adoration into my gaze as I nod once at him, not to give him permission, of course, but telling him that nothing has changed. That I still want him – crazy bloodthirstiness and all.

He turns back to Hector, his face flushed, and the color blooming across his skin makes his hair look even more red.

"Why'd you take her?" Trent demands from Hector, taking his own switchblade out and pushes the tip on Hectors chin.

"There's no surprise there as to why we took her, *hermano.*" Hector answers, unfazed by the imminent threat to his life. "She killed my brother. I demand her head."

"She didn't kill your brother." Trent says. "Marcos was a spineless piece-of-shit who was forcing her to play house when she didn't want to. He wasn't taking care of her. He was using her. Hurting her. Auggie has told you, told me, told everyone, that she doesn't know who killed Marcos, but that she was beaten so close to her own death by his hands, and when she came to, he was gone."

"That's a fucking lie," Hector seethes, spittle flying from his mouth as he snaps at me like a rabid dog. "He was being stalked and threatened by the Russians. It was *them.* She told them when to strike. I know it." He glares at me with such hatred and vitriol, I'm surprised I don't burst into flames on the spot.

"She isn't working with the fucking Russians!" Trent pushes the blade into his neck. "Cillian, string him up."

Cillian drops his hold on Hector, trusting the tape will keep him from running, and Cillian leaves the room without ceremony.

Trent comes over to me quickly, cupping my face with both of his hands.

"I need you to go." He says in hushed tones, forcing my eyes to stay on his, and I try to ignore the grunts and punches in the background. "I need you to get out of here. I don't want you seeing me like this."

"What are you going to do?" I ask him, not promising to leave one way or the other.

"I'm going to make sure no one comes after you ever again." He kisses me soundly, his soft lips taking ownership of mine completely.

"What about the girl?" I ask. The thought that Hector had some woman trapped and bound like I had been, for *months*, weighs heavily on my mind and heart. I want to make sure I help her as much as I can.

"I'll make sure we help her. My priority is you, baby. I need to make sure *you* are safe, and as far away from that asshole and his followers as possible."

I nod in understanding. "Where do I go?"

"When Cillian gets back, I'm going to have him take you to Talia. You'll both be safe there." He takes the time to explain to me what he's thinking and what his plans are for me, and I appreciate that. It keeps me calm, when I can feel how close I am to truly freaking out. I need to know what the next step is. What to do.

"You're going to go with Cillian, see Talia, let her take care of your injuries, take shower, and go lay down. I will take care of this, and then we will be home to you guys as soon as possible."

"You'll come lay down with me?" I ask, my voice shaky, and I can feel shock and exhaustion starting to set in.

Trent takes his leather coat off, leaving him shirtless, wrapping it around my shoulders.

"I promise, the moment I can come home to you, you'll be wrapped in my arms. I'm not letting you go again." He says earnestly, running his hands up and down my arms to warm me up. But the thing is, I'm not cold.

I hear a chattering noise, and look around trying to find out where it's coming from.

"What's that sound?" I can't figure it out. It doesn't sound like knuckles bruising skin. It doesn't sound like footsteps or someone knocking on the door. The closest thing I can think of is high heels clicking on a marble floor. Whomever is wearing them must be running fast and taking small fucking steps.

"It's you, baby. You're teeth are chattering." Trent says gently, holding my chin steady and the noise stops.

"What…" I ask, fearful and nervous because I don't feel it. I don't feel my teeth clicking together or my body shaking but the more I'm aware of it, the more I freak out.

"You're just in shock, Princess. It will go away, it will lessen. Auggie, Auggie," Trent holds my face softly to look at his. "It will stop. You've been so strong, so brave. Let me help you. Let me take care of you. Will you let me?"

I nod, and when I do, it's like my body gives up. My knees give out, my muscles stop holding me up, and I have no choice but to let Trent hold me up.

"What a fucking joke you are." Hector calls out, and it feels like a shot rang through my body. I turn in Trent's arms even as he tries to hold me back.

Kieron did a number on Hector in the brief amount of time Trent and I had been talking. Hector's dark hair is sticking up like the gel had just given up trying to hold it down. His tanned, cratered skin is red and already bruised, and I can tell that his skin looks like mine from the injuries he gave me. I wonder if Kieron did it on purpose.

"Excuse me?" I snap. I don't know where the strength and energy came from, but I dig deep. "Are you talking to me?"

Hector spits on the floor; his red blood looking incredibly bright as it's stark contrast against the white floor.

"Yes. You. *Augustine.*" He rolls his bruised eyes. "A joke, I reiterate. You cower behind men who don't know you, but seek their protection and attention anyway. You are disloyal and a whore, simply hopping from one dick to the next, giving your body away to whomever grants you the most protection instead of staying loyal to the ones that you care for. Don't even pretend like my brother meant anything to you after the display I see here."

My weary body snaps to attention faster than I thought possible.

The fucking gall of this man.

He doesn't know me. He doesn't know what I've given up, what I sacrificed to be with his brother. He doesn't know the abuse and trauma I suffered at his hands. He doesn't know *shit.*

And I'm not going to let him get away with it.

I stalk over to where he's standing – no longer standing as straight and self-righteous as he was before. A warm, cautionary hand wraps around my bicep quickly, pulling me back from taking another step.

"Don't give him the time of day, baby. That's what he wants. He's trying to save his skin." Trent says, but I shake his hand off. I say nothing as I continue to walk towards Hector.

I can see the resemblance between him and Marcos. They have the same crinkles around their eyes, the same strong jawed structure to their faces, the same tan skin and dark hair. But Hector doesn't have the same unhinged look in his eye as Marcos had. The only thing I can see in Hectors eyes is agony and vengeance.

"You think I'm disloyal?" I whisper. "You think I didn't care? Do you think I would have fucking stayed for as long as I did, listened to every fucking word he spewed at me, taken every mark and betrayal of *his,* if I didn't? You're fucking delusional. I wanted out, I wanted to leave him so fucking much, but I couldn't. That does not mean I sold him out. You've got it all wrong about me because you have goddamn blinders on about your brother, thinking he's gods-fucking-gift to mankind. You're just as psychotic as him." I lose control of myself and my volume, each word coming out louder and louder, and before I know it, I'm screaming.

"I just wanted out! I just wanted to be free! And he took that from me, time and time again!" Angry tears form in my eyes, but I refuse to let them fall. I want to hit him, I want to cause him pain like he's caused me, but at the same time, I want to be the better person. Or if I even can with how I'm feeling.

"I don't know who killed your brother. I don't know who sold you guys out. But I can't say I'm sad about it. I can't say that I even really care. He got what he deserved, just like you're going to."

With the last word, I can see Hector's anger rise to an uncontrollable level. I'd gotten under his skin, just like I wanted. I wanted him to hear the truth of my words, I wanted him to hear the truth about it all. Just because I said it, doesn't mean he'd listen to it though.

"You're going to die. And you're going to die by the hand of the man that I love. The man who, I know with every fiber of my being, will take care of me in each and every way for the rest of my life. The man who could kill you with his bare hands, but uses those same hands to bring me unbelievable pleasure and softncss. A better man than you, or your fucked-up brother would have ever been. So, enjoy your death. I'll see you in hell."

I step back, my chest heaving with emotion and anger. The three men in the room stare at me in varying degrees of awe and shock. The guy Kieron came up with, is smirking like he is going to tease Trent about my outburst later. Kieron is staring at me with his jaw dropped open slightly, but pride and a promise of retribution. But Trent, oh my god, Trent.

There is so many levels to the look he's giving me. The initial reaction is shock. Shock that I stood up to my kidnapper, but I could also see understanding. He knew I'd fuck Hector up the first chance I got. I may not be a danger physically, but verbally, Trenton knew well enough that I was dangerous. Underneath that, I could see the pure, raw *need*. My words had turned him on, and he wanted to claim me just as much as I had just claimed him.

His grey eyes were deep pools I could've gotten lost in, just staring and finding new emotions of his in reaction to what I'd said.

"Well, hot damn." Kieron says under his breath. Trent starts to walk towards me, his eyes trained tightly on me when I felt it. The pain in my shoulder and temple as I fall to the floor and my head strikes the marble again.

And my world goes black.

# 18

# Chapter 18

Trent

It was like everything happened in slow motion.

One moment, Auggie's ripping into Hector, screaming all the truths about what she actually went through. Listening to her, I wanted nothing more than to go find Marcos's dead body just to fucking kill that sad sack of shit again. She was looking at me almost shyly, like she thought standing up for me, and for us, would make me embarrassed or some shit.

It was the cutest expression ever; one that showed me she actually felt the words that she said. She wasn't only trying to fuck Hector up, she really felt that way about me.

And out of the corner of my eye, I saw Hector lunge. Arms tied behind his back, he acted out in pure rage.

Kieron reacts at the same time, Bryan aims his gun, and I stand there in shock. I can't move fast enough. It feels like I'm moving through molasses. It's one of those things where it happens so slowly in your mind, that you don't know how to react. You can't make your body move any faster, and it feels like you're running through sand. Try as I might, I can't force myself to move any faster, even though my heart leaps out of my chest and my hands inch up to grab my girl.

"No!" I scream, and time speeds back up. I'm falling by Auggies side, reaching my hands out to try, and catch her before she hits the ground.

I'm not fast enough.

Auggie falls to the floor, her head hitting the ground with a sickening crack.

Her eyes don't open. She doesn't move.

Agonizing despair fills my whole being as I realize this was my fault. I was a millisecond too late to catch her. I hear a gunshot, some brutal punches being thrown, and Kieron snarling as Bryan scuffles with Hector. None of it matters though, my attention is solely on Auggie.

She's not opening her eyes.

I gently check her neck for any bones out of place, thankfully not finding any, before I move her head onto my lap. Her rainbow hair flops over her face, and I see dark red staining the strands. I do my best to investigate softly, not wanting to injure her any further. My heart is beating so goddamn fast, and I'm so fucking scared that my hands are shaking.

"Trent?" Kieron calls out from across the room where they seem to have successfully restrained Hector. His nose is now without-a-doubt broken, and his eye that was bruised before is now swollen shut. Kieron has his reddened hand wrapped around Hectors neck, holding him just enough off the ground wedged against the glass of the window that Hectors gasping. I relish the fear I can see in his one good eye.

He *should* be scared.

He *should* be praying for his life right now because regardless what happens, he's dying the cruelest death I can think of.

"She's bleeding." I whisper, hoping someone can hear me. I can't speak any louder.

"Bryan." Kieron orders, gesturing with his head to come to my side. Bryan is the one of us most equipped to handle medical emergencies. He's the tech guru and medic on our little impromptu team even though he looks like he'd be the muscle behind any situation.

Bryan kneels by me, his dark eyes taking in everything from the way she's laying to the soft breaths she's taking. I prod around her head where I see the bloody strands and breathe a little easier seeing that there isn't a pool of blood forming.

"She's alive. She's breathing." Bryan says, he picks up her wrist and takes her pulse. "Her heartbeat's strong. We won't know the extent of the head injury until she wakes up. Help me roll her to the side." Bryan straightens out Auggie's legs, and I'm too fucking scared out of my mind for her wellbeing that I don't even think twice about him seeing more of her skin than I would prefer.

I gently lower her down to the floor, holding her head as softly as I can, so it barely touches the floor before moving my hand away. I swivel her head to the side, resting it so I can see the half of her face that was resting on the marble, my stomach drops. The blood is incredibly visible through her thick blonde hair, and I clench my jaw. This is so fucking bad.

I will not freak out right now. Not while she needs me.

Taking a deep breath, I push the soft hair out of the way of the injury, and see the cut from where her skin split. Bryan moves his hand by mine, gently – surprisingly gentle for a man of his size, and he prods the bone around the wound.

"Get it together, man. She needs you. And we need to finish this." Bryan snaps at me under his breath. At first, I don't understand why he's being so harsh, but then I see my hands. They're gripping Auggie's shoulder and hand so tightly, she's probably going to have a red handprint from my hand. I force my hands to loosen their grip, not wanting to hurt her any more. It's like my body thought if I wasn't holding onto her tightly, she might slip through my grasp again.

"Where the fuck is Cillian?" I call out in frustration. We only sent him to get some rope, and he's taking his sweet fucking time. He needs to get his ass back here so I can unleash my anger onto Hector. His time on his earth is ticking away faster and faster. The bloodthirsty part of me is running through idea after idea on how best to inflict torturous pain. I think pulling his fingernails from their beds with pliers sounds like a good starting place.

"Come here, man." Kieron says, gesturing me to join him. I'm reluctant; looking down at Auggie. I can't leave her. I just can't. I know that she's going to be okay with Bryan, and I know that he will do absolutely everything in his power to keep her safe and alive, but taking my eyes from her sounds fucking awful. My hesitance is obviously clear to everyone in the room because Kieron snaps.

"Trenton." Kieron's voice changes, and I know it wasn't a request.

With a growl and a mental promise to kick Kieron's ass later, I give Auggie's hand a squeeze. "I'll be right back, beautiful."

"What?" I snap when I get close to Kieron. He's holding onto Hector with one hand, new even tighter restraints are around his wrists and feet this time. Kieron added another set of zip ties, and he has tied them so tightly that I can see Hector's hands turning white.  He's got what looks to be a ripped piece of fabric in his mouth, and it's tied equally tightly to his head. It's tied so tightly that the skin around his mouth is red, and he can't close his mouth or move his jaw.

Good, serves this fucker right.

"I want to know what you want me to do." Kieron says softly as I approach him.

"What?"

Kieron looks at me with equal parts sympathy and revenge. His brown eyes narrow when he looks to Hector, his top lip snarling.

"I know what I would do if he had actually taken Talia. I know the rage I'd feel. The blood I'd demand. I know exactly how I'd make him pay and suffer for even touching her. After seeing Auggie, after seeing what he did to her, what he was going to let other people do to her," Kieron pauses, and my rage reignites like an inferno in my body.  I try to breathe through my nose, try to calm down, but it's pointless. He put his hands on my girl. He saw her vulnerable and naked. He denied her any sort of shield or shelter. He drew her blood and cut up her skin. He was going to let others do unspeakable things to her. He took her from her home. He was going to kill her. *Kill her.*

My chest heaves with my labored breathing, and my hands twitch with the need to cause him more pain than he's ever known. Then he's ever even thought of.

"I know what I would do. But Auggie is *your* girl. So, I want to know what you want me to do." Kieron finishes. He looks at me, dead in the eye, and raises his eyebrows. "You tell me and I'll do it. No judgement. No issues. Whatever will make you, and Auggie, sleep better at night."

There's nothing I want more than to tear Hector limb from limb. Shove a knife through his eye socket, and call it a fucking day. But I need to think about Auggie's future. I don't want any other person from Los Muertos to think they can fuck with her, there needs to be an understanding that she's my girl now. That she's under the protection of the Irish Mob. The Clan's. *Mine.*

In order to do that, we need to see how deep the plan to obliterate Auggie goes. I need to ask questions and manipulate him into revealing more information. That comes from time and torture.

"Take him back to headquarters. The basement. We need to make sure that when we cut off the head of Los Muertos that no one else steps up to take his place." I say, passing judgement and planning his execution without mercy.

"I was hoping you'd say that." Kieron said with the same sick smile I'm sure I'm sporting on my face. Just because we were saps around the Jones sisters, doesn't mean we aren't accustomed to a certain degree of violence and don't relish in justice being served. However it was served. But preferably with the greatest pay-off for us.

Kieron slams his fist into Hector's face over and over again until his head hangs forward lifelessly and his eyes closed, dark with bruises already.

Both of us stand there, letting the man drop to the floor and breathing heavily with anger and vengeance.

"Cillian better have a good fucking reason as to why it's taking him so long." Kieron says, looking over his shoulder and walking over to Auggie.

"I do." Cillian's voice rings through the open room, and we

all turn to see him walking in. He's sporting a bruise on his jaw, and most shockingly, he's shirtless. Just like I am.

He has one arm wrapped around his back as he walks first into the room, and in the other hand, he is carrying a bunch of USB and extension cords we'd sent him for.

"I ran into the guards that asshole called. They sent two, but one of them had a burner that he was calling backup. I disabled him and made sure that he called off the cavalry. The other one was towing her." Cillian shifted so we could see the black-haired girl, shivering in his oversized t-shirt behind him. She had a square jaw, and bright blue eyes. Her skin is decorated in a bunch of varying degrees of healing bruises. Her fingers were gripping onto Cillian's leather jacket tightly like she wasn't sure if she should put her trust in him, but it had to be better than where she had been.

"It's okay, I promise. These are my friends." Cillian said softly, gesturing at us with the cords. "Bryan, Kieron, Trent. Oh fuck, is she okay?" Cillian looks over, and sees Auggie on the ground, I move through the room and hold her hand in mine.

"Bryan?" I ask.

"We won't know until she wakes up. She's alive though." Bryan reports.

"He won't be for long." Kieron juts his chin out, indicating to Hector. The worthless lump laying unconscious on the floor.

The girl peaks around Cillian's arm, seeing Hector bound and passed out, and even from across the room I can see her relief.

"Thank you," She whispers and burst into tears.

# 19

# Chapter 19

Auggie

Fuck, my head hurts.

What is that annoying beeping?

It's like when you hear a fly buzzing around the room, never landing on anything, but just when you think you're getting used to the noise, it changes speed or position. It's the most annoying, anxiety causing, sound in the world.

I peek one eye open to see the whole room shrouded in darkness. Due to the strong smell of ammonia and antiseptic, I know exactly where I am.

Back in the hospital.

This is definitely not where I remember being last, at that awful apartment with the guys after I'd just told off Hector.

"Ow," I groan. When I roll my head to the side, my neck screams in protest, and my eyes screw shut in pain.

"Wait, wait. Don't move." Trent's voice is soft and reassuring, and his hands come up to my face and move my neck back to center. It was painful even though he was so gentle. The ache and soreness of my bones and muscles through my neck bring tears to my eyes.

My eyes open fully to take in Trent's face. I'm so fucking happy he's here. That I'm not alone.

"Trent?" I whisper, the throbbing in my head is really overpowering everything.

"I'm here, baby." He leans over the side of the bed, holding onto my hand and the railing of the hospital bed.

"What happened?"

"Well, you fell. Actually, you were tackled and hit your head on the marble really hard. The doctors have said that you probably were hit in the spot before we got there for the second hit to affect you this much. Back in the apartment, Bryan got you stable while we waited for Cillian to come back, and Kieron and I took care of Hector. After Cillian came back, we brought you to the hospital." He explained, bringing my hand up and locking it tightly against his chest. "It's a Clan-owned hospital so you're safe. You're safe, and getting the best care possible. I'm so glad you're awake."

"How long have I been out?" I ask, my whole mouth is dry and feels gritty. Like I fell asleep with my mouth open, and didn't move for twelve hours. Which I probably did. "Can I have some water?"

"Of course, sorry." Trent flutters around. He grabs a plastic cup, the little hospital pitcher, and pours water into the cup before putting a straw into it for me. After bringing it to my lips and taking a few sips, my mouth and throat feel better, but I realize he still hasn't told me how long I've been unconscious.

"How long have I been out, Trent?"

"A day and a half." He answers softly, so softly it's almost a whisper. After hearing how long I've been here, I take a better look at him. His red hair, usually gelled and neat is unkempt and sticking up all over. Like he's been running his fingers through it constantly, and napping on it on and off without really *actually* sleeping. His pale, soft skin looks like it's thinner, more paper-thin like. The dark circles under his eyes are deeper and more sunken in, like he hasn't slept since I've been here.

"Have you slept at all since I've been here?" He shakes his head, moving to put the cup back on the small hospital table. He moves the table closer to me so the cup is within my reach. "Couldn't take your eyes off me, huh?" I smile, try to let him know I'm joking. But the smile that he gives me doesn't quite reach his eyes.

"I've grabbed a few hours. Talia wouldn't accept anything less, we've been taking turns off and on, but I've never left your side." He sits back down in the chair that must be where he's been taking up residence next to me. It's across from me so I can see his little nest without actually having to move my neck, thank god. He's got a blanket, and his phone cord plugged into the wall. A cup of coffee and an energy drink on the small table in between us. And one of the romance books he'd given me so much shit about liking.

He follows my gaze, and I freaking love the blush that covers his cheeks.

"They aren't so bad, are they?" I say, teasing him and enjoying it immensely. "Did you learn some things? I remember some scenes I'd love to recreate."

Trent laughs, a true belly laugh that brings joy to my heart. He leans onto the side of my bed with both elbows, with one eyebrow raised, and the sexiest smirk on his face. If I wasn't in so much pain, I'd be seducing him right now.

"You know, Princess, maybe I did. This book of yours is pretty worn. I think Talia said it was one of your favorites." He leans in and speaks lowly, "Next time I get you alone, I know exactly what your fantasies are, and how to fulfill them."

"Glad I could teach you something new." I say, gingerly trying to roll my head a little with a groan. "Talia's here?"

"She is. The Clan headquarters is just down the block, less than two minutes ride from here. She's been here from the moment we brought you in, but I keep sending her home to sleep."

"I thought I asked you not to get Kieron and Talia involved." I groan. He did save my life, but I'm not happy that my sister now is involved.

"Auggie," Trent rolls his eyes, and huffs like he's exasperated at my antics. I know that tone, I've heard it so many times. I used to roll my eyes at him when he sounded like that because it was almost always followed by a snide comment.

"Trenton." I snap. Instead of like before, where I could see the annoyance and frustration in his eyes at my tone, I just see humor and love. He stands up from the chair and leans over me to look me in the eye.

"Baby, I needed help. I needed information, and a way to get to you. I'd never really cared about the information I'd heard about Los Muertos before, so I had absolutely no Clan information on hand to use in order to find you. I had no information from you about Marcos, or whoever the fuck it was that tried to take you from the club. I had nothing, but the information you gave me before, and that wasn't enough. So, I called in help. I'd rather you be pissed off that your sister knows, than you be fucking dead because I couldn't get to you in time."

Well, shit. My eyes close painfully, and a whine leaves my mouth.

I guess, that makes sense. It doesn't mean I have to be happy about it though.

"I get it. Thank you." Reaching up, I hesitantly grab the neck of his shirt, and pull him into me for a kiss.

"Anytime. But, please, let's not have any more kidnapping or near-death experiences." He rests a forearm above my head to make it easier for me to rest my head and neck while still looking at him.

"You're in the Mafia. I don't think you're able to avoid near-death experiences."

Trent smiled, his mood never dimming, his eyes bright as he looks down at me. "You're such a pain in the ass, you know that?"

"But I'm *your* pain in the ass."

"That you are, baby." He leaned down to kiss me again, softly, sweetly, with just an edge of desperation.

"So, you still haven't told me what happened. You tried to distract me, but I cannot be distracted. Much." I smile, releasing the hold on his shirt so he can sit back down, but he doesn't. Like he doesn't want to be any farther away from me than he has to be.

"After you rocked my world and pretty much pissed on me to claim me in front of everyone," He teases me but I smile, softly wincing when I discover that rolling my eyes seriously fucking hurts, "he took you to the ground." Trent's energy and demeanor changed. His eyes narrow and he sighs, moving back to sit in the chair by my bed. It is like what had happened was too much for his body to be able to hold himself up as he thought about it. His hand never leaves mine.

"The fucker actually thought he could get to you with us in the room, and he did." Trent sighs again, looking at me like the sentence, and the knowledge that it happened, brings him pain.

"He tackled you, and you didn't get up." He stares down at our hands, his thumb running over my knuckles again and again. *"And you didn't get up."* He whispers and his voice breaks.

"I'm okay. I'm right here." I squeeze his hand a little tighter to pull him back.

"But we didn't know that. You hit the floor, and the sound of your head hitting the floor will forever haunt me. When I got to you, your head was bleeding and... I..." His eyes are far off, unseeing me in the present, but clearly reliving the fall. "I couldn't do anything. I was terrified to even hold you, let alone make sure you weren't bleeding out on the floor in front of me. I know enough about head injuries; I've seen enough happen in the field, have had the butts of guns snapped across my own head enough times to know that one wrong move and I could've caused you permanent damage. I was too chicken-shit to do anything, but be there. Bryan checked you over and made sure that you were still alive." Trent drops his head to the mattress, like he's too ashamed to look at me at his confession.

"Trent, look at me." I whisper, the pain in my chest intensifying with his sadness. It physically hurts me that he feels that he didn't do anything for me. It kills me to think that he feels guilty about anything that happened.

"I can't, baby. I just... I've done terrible things for this job. I've killed, I've tortured, I'm secretly a bloodthirsty fucker. But

I've always been the one the guys rely on to have fast reflexes and I'm the one that doesn't break under pressure. I'm always the one to keep a clear head and get shit done, however it needs to get done. That's why Kieron put me on your detail. Because he trusts me so much; to do whatever needs to be done for the mission to be successful and keep others safe. But when it came down to it, to protect the *one thing* that means more to me than anything ever has, I couldn't do it. I failed you." He speaks into the mattress. I let go of his hand and run my fingers through his unkempt hair.

"Trent. Look at me." I say stronger. My hand never leaves his hair, and I rub from the back of his head down to the nape of his neck, feeling the strong, tense muscles beneath my fingers. He shivers slightly, like he's trying to hide it, but it works. He looks up at me, finally. My strong man; the man who is soft and silly with me, but hard and dangerous to everyone else.

"What did you do to Hector?" I ask. There's surprise in his eyes that tells me he wasn't expecting me to ask him that.

"Not enough, I'll tell you that. I think if I had killed him right then and there I'd feel better. That I'd done more for you." He snarls at the mention of Hector.

"You didn't?" I'm surprised. With how pissed off he was, and still is, I was sure that Hector would be six-feet under by now.

"No. I'm, well *we're*, trying to get as much information out of him as we can. It's slow going, especially since I want to be the one to pry information from him. Kieron told me that he's been setting the groundwork for the interrogation. I want to make sure that no one ever comes for you again. That means I need to know each and every one of those fucks, and know the weaknesses of the organization. We're going to take it down and take all their assets." Trent was angry, he was fuming. "We're going to take them all down, and no one will ever come after you again. I can promise you that."

His eyes went from sad and filled with guilt, to angry and fierce. I love how open he is with me now. How vulnerable and emotional he is with me. I love how much I can read Trent by now. His eyes truly are windows to his soul.

The cool grey color is sharp and powerful, like what he's vowing to me is something he will do come hell-or-high-water. That he'll do exactly what he said, he'll burn it all to the ground. For me.

"I love you; you know that right?" I cup his cheek, enjoying the scruff that's formed from him letting his beard grow. "I want you to let all this guilt and sadness go because, in my mind, you saved me. You *saved* me. You were the one to find me, you were the one to cover me, you were the one to hold me and make me feel protected. You were the one to make sure it didn't become worse. So, what if you froze for a moment? I probably would've done the same thing."

"It's never going to happen again. I swear to you."

"I know." I reach up and push a stray, limp hair off his head. "I trust you."

"Good." He stands up and kisses me again, the peck emphasized his thought. "Speaking of which, don't think you're off the hook for not telling me about this whole fucking situation in the first place, baby."

"Oh yeah? What are you going to do about it?" I smirk, thankful that the lightness and teasing is back in his voice.

"The minute you're feeling better, your ass is going to be red. It'll teach you not to keep things from me again." His nostrils flare and he takes a deep breath in, holding it for a moment before letting it go softly. Regardless of my pain, I can feel my pussy throb with need and want.

"You promise?" I bite my lower lip, and the look on his face when I do that makes the need flare higher within me. There's electricity sparking between us, and it's only a matter of time before one, or both, of us snaps. Regardless of doctors' orders or what would be best for me. Right now, the thing that would be the best for me is getting Trent on top of, and inside me, as soon as fucking possible. I open my mouth to ask about any restrictions I have from the doctor, but I hear a scream instead.

"Augustine Rosalie Jones, you have some explaining to do!" My sisters voice rang through the room, and I winced again at the loudness.

"Keep it down Talia, jesus. She has a concussion." Trent snaps at Talia, turning to her and glaring. His posture screams, 'how dare you', and I can't help but giggle.

"I'm so tired." I whisper, gripping his shirt again. "I'm so tired."

Talia crosses the room quickly, her hand resting on my forehead softly, and I start to tear up. My big sister is here, and I know she'll take care of me.

"Just sleep, Auggie. We'll be here when you wake up." Talia coos, pushing my hair back. Her cool hand feels reassuring against my forehead, and the last thing I see before I let myself fall, is the faces of the two people most important to me, watching over me and keeping me safe.

# 20

# Chapter 20

Trent

"How long had she been awake?" Talia asks me, her eyes did not meet mine as she tried to fix Auggie's hair. I want to scoff because honestly, it doesn't matter one bit how she looks. I just want her awake and healthy.

"Not long. Maybe five minutes."

"You didn't think to call the nurse or doctor? Me?" She looks at me, and I can feel her disappointment and hostility coursing through the air threatening to suffocate me.

Talia had given me a fucking earful when Auggie was brought to the hospital. She screamed at me so loudly; throwing obscenities, threats, and finally, she threw a few punches.

My jaw still hurt thinking about it.

When I carried Auggie through the emergency room and placed her gently on a stretcher, I started to call around for help when I saw Talia storm in like a Valkyrie intent on burning down the entire hospital to protect her sister. Obviously, Kieron had called her and let her in on what had happened.

When the doctors had taken Augie back, prying her from my arms, Talia gave me a beatdown that only a big sister could. The minute the hits were thrown, Kieron wrapped his arms around her waist and hoisted her to him, whispering softly in her ear until she calmed down a bit, but I still can't get the words she screamed at me out of my head.

*"I trusted you! I trusted you that you would watch over her and keep her safe. I won't make that mistake again."*

Since then, it's been awkward between us. The tensions are high, and every hour that Auggie didn't woke up had made it worse. Maybe I should have called her the second Auggie had opened her eyes, but I was just so fucking relieved.

"I didn't think about it. She asked questions, needed water, and we talked."

"Hm." Talia raised one eyebrow, and I could tell she was holding in a lot of things she really wanted to say. I'm so sick of this. I'm beating myself up enough, but I know that I deserve all the vitriol she's sending my way. It's just too much right now. I haven't slept longer than 45 minutes in the last two days, I'm exhausted and delirious, and I snap.

"Look, I'm sorry. I'm sorry I didn't protect her better. I'm sorry she's hurt. I'm sorry you're upset. But I did the best I could. I didn't know anything about Los Muertos until the day she was taken, I swear. I would *never* put her in danger like that, had I known. I love her." I snapped, running a hand through my hair while the other held tightly onto Auggie's.

I'd let her scream and yell, I'd let her get some shots in, but

I'd be damned if I was going to continue to take this bullshit from Talia.

"You didn't know?" Talia's head snapped to look at me so quickly, I thought she'd broken her neck.

"No. I had no fucking clue. I was monitoring for the Italians, for any one from that camp coming after us. But because of how they'd retreated, and we had consistently not been tailed, I relaxed a bit. Any surveillance I found around us, I assumed was from the Italians." I pointedly look at Talia. "I didn't think any of this was even possible. I didn't think any of this would happen."

"Oh Trent…" Talia says, her anger and ice thawing back to friendly and warm. "I know. I don't think any of us did."

I plop back down in the chair that has become my bed and home for the last few days, letting my head fall back against the rest, my hands on my thighs, and I sigh loudly.

"You don't think I feel shitty enough? The woman I love got taken from underneath my nose because I didn't catch all the signs of someone else following us. All because I dismissed them because they didn't have Italian connections. I could've done so much more to keep her safe. But I didn't. The first thing I did when she woke up was apologize, and tell her I love her. Apologize that I fucked up so badly. And she wouldn't listen to any of it, spewing some concussed nonsense that I saved her. But we know the truth, don't we Talia?"

I stared at her with my eyes burning with emotion and hatred. Hatred for myself. Talia looks at me with softness, understanding. Her lips curl and she nods slightly, but shakes her head before exhaling.

"Look, Trent. I know I was hard on you, am still being hard on you. But what you guys don't understand is this is my baby girl right here. We had great parents who loved us, but they were gone a lot, so it was just me and Auggie. During the work week, it was just us a lot of the time. I'm only a few years older than her, but was forced to grow up and take care of her pretty quickly. Leaving her to go to college and then meeting Luca and going through all that shit, it was the worst thing and the hardest thing I've ever had to do. She's my baby sister and even though I like you and we're good friends, when I said I trusted you, I really meant it. I was putting my sister in your hands and trusting that she'd be in the best care possible. That *nothing* was going to happen to her." Talia sits down in the foldable chair next to me, dropping the duffel bag of stuff to the floor.

My chest hurts with understanding.

"From now on, I swear to you nothing will happen to her. I will prove to you, however I have to, that she is safe with me." I lean my elbows on my knees and look at her. "I love her."

Talia smiles softly, and puts her hand on my shoulder, squeezing gently.

"I know."

* * *

"Trenton Ross Connor, back off. I need to shower and I can do it myself." Auggie snaps at me, walking slightly bent over to the hospital bathroom. I was less than half a foot behind her, not letting her out of grabbing distance in case she got dizzy.

"There's no need to middle name me, Princess. I just don't

want you to fall." We had spent some time just talking and the topic of our middle names come up, now that she knows my middle name, she's been using it all the damn time.

I want to be pissed about it, but I just can't.

Auggie huffs, and through the reflection in the mirror I can see her roll her eyes. She takes a deep breath and lets it go in a very controlled manner. I can tell I'm obviously getting on her nerves, but the sharpness in her tone brings a smile to my face. I fucking love when she gets feisty.

She turns to face me, and the stiffness in her neck is still concerning to me, even though the doctor said she was okay. That the stiffness would go away with time and some therapy, but that didn't mean I was okay with it.

"I understand that you're just being careful with me, and I love you for it. But you've gone from hot protective boyfriend, to overbearing dictator who controls my every step. I can't live like that. I won't live like that. There needs to be some balance." She cups my cheek, and I lean into her touch. Her blue eyes are piercing me deeply, and I reluctantly nod.

"It's just so hard. I need to be here. For you." I can't fully explain this *need* without coming off like some creepy controlling dickhead, but it stems from fear and guilt. I know that much.

"Honey," She says softly and her small little body curls into mine. We both need to shower, it isn't a pleasant smell, but fuck, it's a pleasant moment. It feels very much like a powerful moment.

She reaches up as best she can with her pain and muscle tightness, and grabs my face with both hands.

"I know you're carrying around a lot of guilt. If Talia's been here as much as you've said, I'm sure she's not been nice. That's just my protective older sister for you. But I'm going to say this one time, and one time only; nothing, *nothing*, that happened was your fault in any way. **I** should've told you sooner. **I** should've connected the dots. **I** was the one to tell Hector off and intentionally make him angry when I was fully aware how on-edge he was. My injury is just that; mine. I still want you to dote on me because I secretly love being taken care of, but I don't want you doing all these things just out of guilt."

I take a deep breath. As I release the air in my lungs in a controlled manner, I feel the guilt lessen.

I lean down and rest my forehead on hers before taking her lips in a gentle kiss. She winces slightly, and I pull away quickly, bringing a hand up to support her neck and head.

"Thank you," She whispers with a smile.

"Anytime. Now, go take your shower, but leave the fucking door unlocked in case you need help. I swear to god, Augustine, if you feel even a little wobbly, you call out."

"Sir, yes sir." She smirks. The little brat.

When she turns around, I swat her ass and she giggles, but I can tell her mood is so much lighter. She's still my feisty spitfire, but I know how to handle the flames better now.

Walking back to my chair, I pull my phone out and see the messages that Kieron's sent.


**Kieron:**

He's ready to talk. I know you're still at Auggie's bedside, but I just wanted to let you know.


**Kieron:**

How's she doing? Talia said she'd give you one more day before she's kicking you out to see her sister. Just a forewarning.

I smirk at his 'warning', when I know how whipped he is for his girl. Probably just as bad as I am for mine.

**Trent:**

She can come over any time.

**Kieron:**

She wants to tell Auggie the whole truth.

My eyebrows shoot up. Talia had told Kieron and I that she never wanted Auggie to know the lengths she'd gone to protect her. It wasn't a pretty story, but it was one that had brought us all together.

**Trent:**

Oh shit.

**Kieron:**

Yeah, she says it's time. But I think she wants to tell her alone.

**Trent:**

Understandable.

**Kieron:**

Hector is ready for interrogation. He's spent time in the hole, sleep and food deprived, we've cut off his senses and he's definitely fucking losing it.

**Trent:**

Good, I'll be able to get my answers and then he'll be gone.

**Kieron:**

I'll tell Talia to go watch Auggie this afternoon, sound good?

We are riding the fine line on friends and leader/follower, but after Auggie's talk, I can tell she won't mind some space.

And maybe cutting off some fingers and toes might make me feel better.

**Trent:**

Tell her to be here at 4pm.

**Kieron:**

Understood.

"Trent," Auggie calls from the bathroom weakly, and my whole-body lurches forward for her. My feet find purchase with the floor, and I nearly fall as I try to get on my feet and run at the same time. Pulling the door open so quickly, I was worried I might rip the door off its hinges to get to Auggie.

Expecting to find her in danger of slipping or hurting her head more, my eyes dart over her to scan for injuries or danger. But what I saw, was not what I had thought I would walk in to see. Far, far from it, in fact.

Auggie sits beneath the water spray; her rainbow hair darkened with the water, her head propped by the corner walls, her eyes closed, and her fingers of one hand disappearing within herself quickly, with the fingers of her other hand circling her clit.

The fear immediately melts into feral need knowing that she was getting herself off *to me*.

"Didn't think to invite me, baby?" I lean against the doorframe crossing my arms as I enjoy the show, watching her lose herself in the sensations.

One of her eyes peaks open, and I see a ghost of a smile on her face.

"It was just going to be a quick one."

I step inside the bathroom, closing and locking the door, before turning back to face her. Auggie pulls her fingers from her tight pussy, and I can see her clenching around nothing. She readjusts her legs so they're spread wider, putting on a little show for me.

"Hmm. A 'quick one'." I pull my shirt off over my head, and toss it on the ground. "The question still stands. Did you not think to invite me?"

"Of course, I did. Why do you think I moaned your name?" She smirks, shifting her waist so her hips move in a slow shimmy.

"We do both need to shower." I say, like it was the logical decision as to why I was going to fuck her as gently as I could against the tile wall under the warm water.

"We do." She nods.

"And it wouldn't be nice of me to leave you wanting, would it?" I ask, pulling my jeans down as my cock bobs up in my briefs. I was hard the moment I walked in and saw her fingering herself. The moment I realized he was calling my name in pleasure and not in pain.

"Not at all." She says with a breathy tone that makes me so

fucking hard my dick is threatening to rip my boxers.

"That wouldn't be taking care of you, would it?"

"No." She says the one word in that same breathy voice, like she can barely breathe from tension, from the want, and it sends a shiver down my spine.

"Baby girl, there are going to be a few rules, do you understand?" She starts to nod, but her eyes close in pain. "I don't want you hurting your head anymore, so if you don't, or can't, talk, blink once for yes and twice for no." She blinks once.

"Good girl." I pull my boxers down. "Are you going to let me take care of you?"

Auggie looks bright, and I smile darkly.

"It's only been a few days since I last had you, and I'm going out of my mind. I need to feel you again. I need your tight, wet, heat wrapped around my cock as I show you how much I care. How we belong together. I need to feel that you're okay and alive and safe and *mine*." I do my best to cup her chin softly, being very aware of the bruises that are just starting to heal across her beautiful face.

"I'm yours, Trent. I'm yours, and I need you." Her whine goes straight to my dick, I swear to god.

"Alright, Princess. I've got you." I step into the spray, letting the hot water roll down my back as I crowd her. She's listened to my orders and stayed cradled in the corner, and I love that this feisty, spitfire of a woman, has chosen me to give her vulnerable side, her submissive side, to. It turns me on more than I can even tell her.

I lean back and let the water saturate my hair fully before running my fingers through the wet hair and push it back off my face.

Water drips down my face, my nose, my skin, as I let the water wash over me. I keep my eyes trained on Auggie. The water hitting her face, gathering in droplets and sliding down her body. I watch one drop form on her collarbone before it starts it descend down her chest, to the valley in between her breasts, down to her stomach, and lower. I can't take my eyes off her.

She's watching my every move; her eyes are wide and unblinking, and her mouth is dropped open slightly. She's turned on, and she wants me to be the one to fix that.

Oh, I will. I'll make her come over and over until she doesn't know anything but my fucking name. She'll be so fucking satisfied when we leave this bathroom that everyone will know what we did. I want her to squirt all over me and leave me drenched in her release so I can smell her on my skin for hours.

I'll take the dirty looks from the nurses and doctors, as long as she has a loved and satisfied look on her face.

"Spread your legs and show me my pussy." I growl.

Auggie does exactly what I say, spreading her creamy thighs open as wide as she can, and I barely manage not to fall to my knees when I see the glistening pink flesh of her cunt and see how wet she is. She's positively dripping.

I slowly get on my knees, resting right in front of her, and bring my hand up to her pussy, and spread her wetness all over.

"You're so ready for me, baby. Got yourself so worked up before I got here." My hands are so much larger than her toned thighs, and I push them apart even further, spreading her open obscenely.

Auggie starts to lean over, to meet me in the middle for a

kiss, but I pin her back with a look.

"Do. Not. Move."

She blinks once, showing me sweetly that she understands and rests her back against the wall.

"As much as I want everyone to know exactly what I'm doing to you and how much you love it, I need you to be a good girl and be quiet. Can you do that?"

A blink.

"Good girl."

Auggie's eyes close and she shivers despite the warmth of the shower. My mouth descends on her; licking her lower lips, just tasting her. Lapping up the cream that had seeped out from her earlier activities.

"Fuck," I groan as her flavor bursts on my tongue, and I aggressively dive back in. I lick and suck and nip and *eat* until I can feel Auggie's thighs quivering as she tries to do what I said and keep them open.

My fingers grip her legs tighter, keeping her spread and at my mercy as I push her closer to orgasm with my mouth. Her wetness is dripping off my chin and I can feel her grind against my mouth, and fuck me, it's sexy as hell.

"Trent, please," She moans, her voice echoing against the tile.

"I know, baby." I coo, and push two fingers into her gripping heat.

Holy hell, it felt like her cunt was holding my fingers in a vice.

"So tight." I whisper, pushing them in farther before scissoring them inside of her.

Auggie starts to sit up a bit, and I quickly pull my fingers from her.

"What? Why?" She whines, and I give her a pointed stare.

"You know why. Shoulders and head rest against the wall. Now."

She gives the cutest *hmph* and I swear, if she was standing up, she would've stomped her foot like a little brat.

"Against. The. Wall."

Her dark eyes give me a deadly look, but she follows my demand.

"I'm only trying to take care of you." I whisper, not giving her the chance to say anything before I resume what I was doing and feasting on her sweet cunt.

"I know," She moans to the ceiling, letting her body go limp as I bring her close to her peak. "Fuck me, Trent."

"Not yet, Princess."

"Why?" She whines again.

"Because I'll be damned if you haven't come at least once before I fuck you. You'll come once on my tongue, and then once on my cock." My fingers move faster, curling and scissoring while I watch her tiny movements, trying to see which feels better to her. Auggie breathes deeply; her full tits hanging and heaving as she breathes. Her nipple sways tauntingly in front of me, teasing me. I lean up and take the pink bud in my mouth, sucking softly.

"You… don't have to… God, that feels s-so good." Her words are stuttered and breathless, like she's trying to prolong her orgasm or, at the least, hold it off.

That won't do.

I sling one of her thighs over my shoulder and bring my mouth back to her core. I circle her clit with my tongue – first softly, then harder and harder, while I add another finger into her fluttering opening. She wants to come, I can tell, but she's holding back. Making me work for it.

I fucking love it. The harder I work for it, the more satisfying it is when I finally push her past the end and see her cry with pleasure.

"Come on, baby." I growl, curling my three fingers and finding the spongey texture against her front wall. Auggie's legs shake against my ears. She lifts her hips up and starts to impale herself on my fingers, helping me fuck her hard, and then suddenly, violently, she spasms. Her whole body is wracking with movements she can't control and her thighs lift as her release rains down all over my face.

"Oh, *fuck me.*" I nearly come at the sight, at knowing what just happened. Her body starts to sag, but I don't let her stop. "Keep going, Princess. I know you can." I straighten my spine, holding her body up, as I finger her faster, watching with rapture as I see her hole fluttering and leaking so deliciously.

"Sexiest thing I've ever seen in my fucking goddamn life. Oh my god." I murmur, talking her through everything even though I can see that she's so relaxed she's like jelly. She's trusting me completely to be this vulnerable.

As I feel her start to slow, I slow my own movements and pull my fingers out of her softly.

"Auggie?" I whisper. Her eyes barely open as she looks at me through her wet eyelashes, and she takes my breath away. There's want and lust in her gaze, but love and adoration are shining so much, it takes my breath away.

"Holy shit." She whispers back to me.

"You're amazing. Perfect. A fucking vision." I kiss down her neck and take her other nipple into my mouth. I suck and tug as I feel her arms come around my head, holding me close.

"You're pretty fantastic yourself. You know, that's the

second time you've made me do that. I've never been able to do that with anyone else."

I groan and my eyes roll back in pure feral possessiveness. My dick is so hard primed to come, her words make me shudder. She's never squirted with anyone but me before, and I never want her to do it with anyone else.

"Can you fuck me now?" Her dark eyes full of need and want. It doesn't matter that she'd just come, my girl's greedy and I love it. How fucking lucky girls are. They can come back-to-back, but guys, no matter how fast our refractory period is, we still need a refractory period.

"Is that what you want? You want me to fuck you in the shower, holding you close, and making you come on my cock?" Wrapping my hands around her thighs. I start to stand, bringing her body with me. She slides right up, the water and condensation from the shower helping move her easily against the tiles.

"Please," She moans. I shift my hips up, and we both moan when my cockhead slips through her wetness.

"Okay baby, I've got you." Reaching between us, I position my head at her entrance and let gravity help slide her down onto me, groaning in unison.

"Trent," She sighs. Everything but Auggie falls away. All that matters is her.

"I know,"

Thrusting shallowly, I try to get a tighter grip on my control but she feels so good, so tight, so warm, so *wet*.

"What do you need?" I say into her neck, biting down on her shoulder gently. No matter how out of control I feel in this moment, I will not hurt her. I *will* remember to be gentle and conscious of her injuries.

"You, just you." She says breathlessly. My fingers bite into her thighs, and her ankles lock around my hips. She wraps her arms around my shoulders, with one hand pulling at my hair.

Fucking perfect.

Perfect fucking.

I start to thrust into her deeper, the wall keeping her pinned and immobile against me. With every thrust I'm able to grind against her clit, and she must like it because I feel her walls clenching down on my cock. The humidity and steam swirling through the air make everything heightened.

"Right there, right there. Don't change anything." She moans, her fingernails digging into my shoulders so hard, I'm sure I'll have little cut from her nails, and I want it. I want her marks on me.

I keep moving exactly how she told me to, staying slow and steady, but deep and hard, and with each pass, I can feel her getting tighter and tighter.

"Oh my god, oh fuck. Faster, faster." She starts to wiggle in my grasp, but I hold her tightly, forcing her to stay against the wall and not move her head.

"You don't need faster." I grunt, grinding deeper. "You need deeper. You need my cock to rub against that spot inside that my fingers always hit and makes your eyes screw close."

The water on the shower walls works as a lube and I slide her up, only to have her fall down again as I grind. Her eyes close and her nose scrunches as her mouth opens with a sigh, and her head barely tips back.

"Again." She pleads. "Please,"

"Anything for you, baby."

I hold her tightly, and do it again and again. Moving her

body like it's an extension of my own and working us both towards our peak. Auggie's eyes open in alarm as her cunt squeezes me tightly, almost pulling me over the edge.

"I can't stay quiet." Her eyes widen in fear, and as gently as I can, I put my hand over her mouth.

"Fuck, I don't want you to have to be quiet. I want all your sounds, your dirty words, your sighs and groans. I want them all. But I don't want to share them with anyone. So, scream, moan, do whatever you need to do into my hand and if that doesn't keep you quiet, I'll swallow them myself."

Her eyes roll back as I talk to her. Her body tenses, but she lets me use her.

"Come for me, baby." I grunt softly in her ear. I feel, more than hear, her scream into my hand as her cunt grips my cock so tightly, I almost black out. I thrust faster and faster, working her through her orgasm as I chase my own.

"Good girl. Good fucking girl, coming all for me. That's it, keep going." I mutter, my movements getting sloppier as I feel the tightening in my balls, the tingling in my spine.

I tuck my head in the valley of her breasts and bite down, not hard enough to break skin, but just enough to enhance what we're both feeling, and she groans. I come inside her, hard, and groan her name.

My movements slow to a stutter as I come so fucking hard I see stars.

After what feels like minutes of coming, we both stay still. We don't move, just holding onto each other for a moment; letting our chests rise together with each breath and our wet skin touching each part of each other while the water runs over my back.

"Will there ever not be a mind-blowing time with you?" She

asks, and I can hear the bratty smile in her voice.

"Not if I can fucking help it."

21

# Chapter 21

Auggie

Trent sets my feet to the floor gently and holds me like I'm precious. He makes sure I can support my weight and that there is no way I could fall before he lets go. Which is a good thing, because my legs feel like jelly.

"I'm going to need help washing my hair now." I tease, letting my neck muscles relax and fall back against the tiles for support again.

"Anything you need, Princess." He wraps his arms around my waist and tucks his face into my neck, hugging me tightly. There's nothing sexual about it, just intimate and full of emotion. An intimacy that I wasn't aware I needed, and judging by the sigh of contentment, a moment that Trent needed as well.

"I'm so glad you're okay." He whispers in my ear, and I pull him in tighter.

"I love you."

"I love *you.*" He says softly, tightening his arms around my waist before stepping back and grabbing the mini-bottle of shampoo on the ledge.

From then on, we don't talk. We stand together in silence; a peaceful, restorative, loving silence. He squirts a bit of shampoo into his palm, and gently starts massaging it into my hair. His fingers work efficiently and quickly, softly cleansing my hair around my injuries. It's hard for me to hold back the moan I want to let out. It feels so great, so relaxing, and through my barely open eyes I can see him smile. I feel him slide his hand over the injury softly, cleaning it gently.

I barely feel it with how relaxed I am.

Trent reaches up and takes the shower handle down, rinsing the shampoo from my hair with the warm water. When he's satisfied that the shampoo is cleared from my hair, he grabs the bottle of body wash and begins to clean me all over.

Trent's methodical, gentle, soothing. I don't need to do anything, at all. He makes me feel loved and cherished. When he stands back up, I grab the shampoo and try to return the favor. I want to show him just how much I care for him, but he takes it from my hand, holding me close.

"I didn't do this because I want you to reciprocate. I *want* to take care of you. I always have."

"I want to take care of you, too."

"You can, just not right now. Okay?" He says it so strongly, his light eyes begging me to understand. He needs this. Just as much as the sex, the declaration of love, he needs to take care of me, to make sure that I'm alright.

Trent makes super quick work of washing himself and I get to sit back and enjoy the show. Suds gathering across his wide chest, catching in the patch of hair right under his belly button that leads downward. The soap sliding down his muscular thighs. It's a sight to see, this man. Breathtaking. And he's all mine.

We stay quiet until Trent's completely finished, and he turns off the water. I step into his space, putting my hands on his hips and look up as much as I can at his grey eyes before we move.

"Thank you," I look at his lips as he parts them.

"Always." He leans down and kisses me deeply. I try to deepen the kiss, licking the seam of his lips with my tongue, but he pulls back.

"Let's get out, baby." Trent pulls open the curtain and grabs a towel, wrapping me up tightly before rubbing his hands over my arms to keep me warm.

I'm warm enough inside at his care. This… This version of Trent is completely different from the one I knew before. Sure, he's always been protective, always looking out for me, but now, it's deeper. More meaningful and powerful.

No I can look back at the beginning few months we lived together, and truly see how the small actions proved he cares. Putting his arm around my shoulders when we would walk back from the stores, checking me over so panicked when I would call out for him when I was scared, making sure I drank water and ate when I couldn't bring myself to, and so many more. He's been taking care of me in his own way this whole time, no matter how much his words had said otherwise.

"I'm going to need to get going soon. Talia is on her way over." He said offhandedly and fear temporary struck my chest as I thought about him leaving.

"Where are you going?"

"To finish this, once and for all." He said darkly, kissing my forehead and wrapping a towel around his waist before opening the door.

* * *

"Talia's downstairs." I finally had my phone back, albeit with a time limit and they told me I had to put the blue-light filter on, but Talia messaged me to let me know she was on her way up. I hope she and Trent have talked, and she isn't mad at him anymore. Her anger is displaced, but I can't say that if the roles were reversed, I wouldn't have screamed at Kieron.

"That's my cue to leave then." Trent stood up, looking sexy as hell in his all-black outfit. "Easier to hide the blood stains," he had said with a sexy smirk when I asked. I don't know exactly what he's planning, but I'm also fairly sure I don't want to know the details.

With his red hair styled back and the scruff he had yet to shave off his handsome face, I was going to need to brand him in some way to keep other girls away from him.

"Come here," I whisper, fisting the front of his shirt and dragging him to me. I kissed him deeply, loving how he relented and kissed me back with as much fervor.

"I love you. Be safe." I whisper after releasing his lips from mine. "Come back to me soon."

"As soon as I can." His light grey eyes sparkle.

"Give him hell for me, alright?" I smile and peck him on the lips again. I've only seen him bloodthirsty one time, and that was the night I was hurt, so I couldn't act on how turned-on it made me. Now, I can see the transition on his face. The soft, warm-hearted Trent is leaving, bringing the dark, twisted, out-for-blood Trent that I've only met once.

His eyes sharpen, his nostrils flare, and his jaw clenches tightly.

"That's exactly where he's headed. I'll make sure of it." Trent promises, leaning in to kiss me again before standing up and grabbing his phone and duffel bag.

"My phone will be on loud. Anything happens, and I mean *anything*, you call me. Understood?" He points a finger at me, his tone dominant and commanding, leaving no room whatsoever for discussion.

"I know, I know." I wave him off with a smile.

"Seriously, Augustine. Don't fucking tempt me." He moves the duffel bag over his head so it sits across his body.

"I won't. If anything happens, I promise I'll call you immediately. Happy?" I ask, bratting back to him, teasing and pushing, but I know he loves it just as much as I do.

"Immensely." He smiles softly and a soft knock raps on the door. Trent crosses the room and opens the door for my sister before looking back at me. "I love you."

"I love you, too." I smile, watching him leave.

"Hey, hun." Talia walks over to the bedside, putting a small grocery bag at my feet. Her long purple hair is up in a high-bun today and she looks a little green, like she's the one that isn't feeling well. Against her dark wardrobe, she looks even more sickly. "How are you feeling?"

"I'm a lot better. My head still hurts, obviously, but I can hold my head up for a long time without pain. I have a bit of a headache, but it's manageable with the pain meds."

"Good," She lets out a deep breath. "That's really good."

"How are you?" I ask. She's acting weird as shit. Normally, Talia calls me out and we tease or start joking with each other. We're loud and rambunctious together, but right now, she looks like she's scared I'm going to break.

"I'm... I'm okay." She says softly. She has a light sheen of sweat over her forehead, and is clutching a water bottle in her hands.

"Bullshit, what's really happening?" I snap. It's annoying because it's like she doesn't think I know her so well.

"I have some things to tell you and I don't know how you're going to take it." She sits in Trent's chair, and hunches her shoulders.

"Fuck. You didn't tell Trent something embarrassing from high school, did you? I thought we were past the sabotaging-giving shit to the little sister stage of life, Tali." I smirk. It's a stupid joke, but it works. She laughs.

"Seriously, it's probably not as big as you think. What's up?" I fluff my pillow awkwardly while still laying on it, pushing it more behind my neck so I can sit up more and still see her comfortably without holding my head up myself. After my shower activities, I'm fatiguing fast.

"You know how Marcos died? How you woke up and everyone thought you did it?" She says.

"Yeah, but I didn't. You know that." I say, my eyebrows coming together in confusion.

"I know you didn't... I know." One of her hands shoots out to grab mine.

"Do you remember how I was at the hospital when you woke up?" She stares at our joined hands.

"Yes,"

"It's because I did it, Auggie. I killed him." She whispers.

At first, I think I heard her incorrectly. There's no way she killed him, she wasn't even there that night. I mean, I know I had invited her over, but she never let me know if she was coming over, so I always assumed she hadn't. My eyes close tightly and scrunch as I try to figure out what this means.

"What?" My voice is hoarse and it sounds like a whisper, but really, I'm at a loss for words.

I believe her. She has no reason to make it up. She looks like she's in pain as she's telling it to me.

"Why?"

"I walked in and you were unconscious on the ground, but he didn't care. He was punching you over and over, even when you laid there completely immobile and passed out. I thought you *were dead*, Auggie. Your body wasn't moving at all. No reactions when he hit you, no noises coming from you except for the sick sound of his fists on your skin. I saw you laying there, lifeless, and I lost it. I attacked and got him to leave you alone, but then he turned on me." She stares off in front of herself.

"What did you do?" I whisper, starting to feel sick to my stomach that she's been holding onto this for so long. A dirty little secret that she thought she couldn't share with me.

"I grabbed the closest thing which just happened to be a fire poker, and I hit him. I hit him as hard as I possibly could and he fell. He just never got up again." She sat up straighter, no sympathy in her words, but I could see she was struggling.

"I made a call and got you to the hospital. You stayed there for at least three days before you woke up and I didn't leave your side, until I was forced to."

"Who did you call? The Irish? Is that why you and Kieron got married so fast?" I swallow the lump that's forming in my throat. A sick feeling intensifying because I inadvertently ruined my sister's entire life.

"No, no. Nothing like that. Kieron saved me, Auggie. Saved me." She grips my hand tighter.

"Luca?" I guess next. I never really liked him. Talia never seemed happy with him, never seemed *in love* like I thought she deserved after the newness of their relationship had woren off.

She nodded. "He was a bad guy... I didn't know how bad until I had to ask him for help."

"How bad are we talking about here? You're married to the son of the Skipper for the Irish Mob." I chuckle weakly.

"He was the son of the Italian Don. The rival mafia in Boston." My jaw drops. My sweet, loving sister, is a magnet for mafia trouble apparently.

I guess I can't say anything.

"And what," my heart beats faster in fear for what she is going to say next, "what happened?"

Talia took a deep breath and takes a big drink from the liter of water in her hand, before taking another one out of the grocery sack before handing it to me.

"And he promised he'd take care of Marcos's body and cover-up, as long as I stayed with him and I understood I owed him."

What does that mean?

What *the fuck* does that mean?

"Talia... Did he... Are you..." I don't... I can't... I don't know what that means and what she had to do. My mind races with each and every thought that is flying through my mind, each scenario worse than the last. She shakes her head and I can tell that she doesn't want to get into details. I let it go now because honestly, it's a bit too much for me. My headache has started to increase with the stress. I don't want to start this conversation and then not finish it in one sitting because she can tell I'm in pain and forces me to take heavier medicine. The fucking pain pills they have me on will knock me out. I don't want to do that right now. Her dark brown eyes plead with me to let it drop. Her eyebrows scrunch together like she's in pain at having to think about everything she went through. And that makes me ache.

One day, I'll find out exactly what my sister went through. I'll find out exactly what she endured for me. And one day I'll make sure to repay her, for everything.

"I'm okay. Everything is okay now. But I wanted to tell you because this is all my fault. You've been in Los Muertos crosshairs for something that I did, you're here right now because of me." She says softly. "I'm sorry."

"What the fuck, *you're* sorry?" I ask incredulously. "Why the hell are you sorry? You saved my life. If anything, I should be sorry. I fucked up your whole life."

"No, Auggie, no. You didn't do anything wrong. We've just had some bad luck when it comes to guys." She wipes the tears that have fallen under her eyes, and gives me a watery chuckle.

"We have. But maybe our bad luck has run out." I squeeze her hand and touch the biggest engagement ring I've ever seen in real life that adorns her finger. "I'm surprised Kieron let you out of his sight long enough to come check on me." I tease her, knowing just how protective Kieron is. And for good reason, apparently. Secretly, I love it. I love it for her, and I want it for myself. She's always been the one taking care of people, and I'm so unbelievably happy that she's found someone who wants to take care of her.

She deserves it.

"Seems like we both have that." She smirks, looking down at my phone that lights up – yet again – with a message. Probably from Trent. Isn't he supposed to be torturing someone right now? "I heard him in the hallway getting you to promise to call him if anything happens." She teases me, and I can feel my cheeks blush.

At least that's all she heard.

"Kieron's overprotectiveness is going to get worse here for a little bit." She looks at me expectantly before pulling a small bag out of the grocery bag and handing it to me. "Open it."

It's a sweet little pink and blue bag with dots all over. Curiously, I open it and pull out the gift. It's a shirt of some kind.

I look over at Talia, confusion written all over my face, but she's so excited I can practically feel her vibrating.

"Look at it." She nudges.

**Best Aunt Ever**

"No, really?"  I look to Talia with such happiness and excitement, I yank the covers off and practically tackle her myself in a big hug. "Oh my god, Tali! Congratulations! How far along are you? How are you feeling? Does Kieron know? Is he excited? When are you due? Are you stuck on 'Aunt' or can I pick my own nickname? I think "BAE" has a good ring to it. You know, for 'Best Aunt Ever.'" I ramble and clap with happiness.

"Get your ass back in that bed or your boyfriend will kill me." Talia laughs, helping me back into the hospital bed. "I'm so happy you're happy about this."

"Are you fucking kidding me? *Of course* I'm happy about this! Wait, are you guys?" Damn, maybe I screwed up and read the situation wrong. Maybe she wasn't thrilled with the surprise baby.

"We are over-the-moon happy. Kieron is…well, Kieron is *very* happy, and I'm so ready. I'm safe, I'm loved, I'm protected, and I know our baby will be too. Kieron will be such a great dad." She says wistfully, her hand resting on her still flat stomach.

"You're going to be a fantastic mom." I tell her, leaning forward to hold her hand. With the movement, my head and neck protest as shooting pains go from the top and side of my head down to my back. The pain is so sharp, so severe, it takes my breath away.

"Auggie?" Talia's voice has gone from happy and jovial to scared in a flash.

"It hurts." I whine, holding my head with one hand and trying to shift my position to take the weight off the parts of my back that hurt.

"Fuck," She swears, running out the door and calling for a nurse.

"Call Trent. I promised." I gasp, the pain not dulling in anyway. If anything, it's getting worse, making me feel nauseous as a black haze starts to fill my vision.

"I will. Don't worry, Auggie. I'll take care of it." I hear Talia promise from the far side of the room, and more footsteps come walking in quickly. Talia's comforting voice tells them what happened, how I moved, and what I've said and then I feel cold hands on my neck, poking and feeling.

"I'm going to give you more pain medicine, okay? Don't fight it, just let it take you under and let your body heal." The nurse says kindly. The darkness filling my vision is creeping up faster and faster and the cool sting of the medicine entering my IV tells me I'm going to be asleep really soon.

"Tali?" I call out weakly, too afraid to move my head or eyes at all.

"I'm right here," She holds onto my fingers and enters my line of sight.

"I'm so fucking happy you found Kieron. You deserve... the... world." My words become slower and slower as the medicine starts to take over. "Please call...Trent..."

"You deserve the world *and* the stars, Auggie." Is the last thing I hear before the pain goes away and I fall into a dreamless sleep.

## 22

# Chapter 22

Trent

The fucker broke so much faster than I was expecting.

I know that Kieron said he's been laying the ground work, but damn, I thought I had a good few hours of fun time before we got the information we needed.

"Who is next in line?" I snarl, the knife in my hand dripping with blood from the letters and shapes I've dug into his skin. Like a fucked-up learning activity. A circle here, a hexagon there. The letters of Auggie's full name stretched deeply across his abdomen so he won't forget in the few hours he has left *exactly why* he's here.

"There's no one next. You killed my right hand. No one else would try to take up as leader." Hector spits out the blood that's pooling in his mouth from the hits I've given him, and a tooth goes flying. It's a sick sight; blood, piss, and sweat seep into the concrete under my feet. It's only going to get worse, ad that makes me smile.

"Who is in charge of your finances, your payroll?" I snap. Hector shakes his head, biting down on his lip like he doesn't want to squeal and give up secrets like the little rat he is.

"Tell me!" I roar, punching him as hard as I can in the kidneys, making his whole body sway on the chains he's hooked up to over his head. The fucker wheezes, coughing again and spitting more blood.

"I'd tell him, Hector. His girl is in the hospital because of *you*. That's a lot of anger he has and it's all directed at you." Kieron says behind me. He's resting his shoulders against the plastic-lined brick wall. "Not to mention, that's *my sister-in-law* and I made a promise to my wife that nothing would happen to her. I'm not okay with breaking a promise." He kicks off the wall, coming to stand right by me.

Where he's cleaned and polished - as polished as Kieron can be in his black jeans, leather jacket and biker boots - my hair is wet and out of place, the small amount of skin that's showing is littered with speckles of blood, and my knuckles are going to be purple tomorrow. A small price I'm very willing to pay.

I carve the S into the Rosalie I've started on his stomach.

Kieron keeps his promise and lets me handle Hector how I choose. Hector cries out, screaming like a little baby as blood flows down his front. He's gasping and even paler by the time I'm done.

"Alec, Alec Michailkov. He's a Russian accountant that we turned.  He's in charge of all the money for Los Muertos." Hector cries out.

Well, I didn't see that coming.

"Let me get this fucking straight." I snap, turning his chin to face me.  "Your asshole brother is so fucking paranoid that the Russians are after him that he converts one of their accountants to work for his gang, only to then go on a rampage because he thinks someone in his camp is working for them. He's so paranoid that he takes it out on my girl, almost *kills* her. And you, you stupid piece of shit, you think that she is still the one feeding them information?"

"He's not talking. I know for a fact." Hector groans. I drop his chin and his head falls forward, hanging between his strung-up arms.

"And how do you know that?" Kieron asks putting his hand on Hector's shoulder where I'd thrust a blade in between the joints earlier. It had to hurt like a son-of-a-bitch, but Hector doesn't scream. He's near the end of his pain tolerance.

"Because, we have his brother under surveillance. He knows one wrong move, and he's gone. Alec got into the wrong stuff, and owes Los Muertos his life. When he tried to get out, we gave him a deal. Help us or die, he chose to help us. Having his younger brother under our thumb is just a little extra motivation." Hector pants, the exertion of talking becoming too much.

"Who is the girl you brought to the penthouse?" Kieron asks. I'd almost forgotten about her in my haste to get to Auggie.

Hector thought some black-haired, blue-eyed girl was Auggie's sister and honestly, there isn't any resemblance. Maybe they had similar stature, but so did a lot of people.

He's a stupid man that let revenge and paranoia bring him to where he is now... at the end of my knife.

"She's some Russian girl, one that was sniffing around our gang. She got a little too close for comfort. Information started to slip, and they figured out plans, figured had her." He was starting to mince words and pass out again. Fuck. His words don't really make sense, but that's to be expected at this point.

Kieron pulled his hand off from Hector's shoulder and smacked Hector across the face.

"Who is she?" He yelled in his face.

"Mila... Smirnova..." Hector said as he passed out again.

"Smirnova. Of the Smirnov's." Kieron said, his eyes widening with recognition.

"He really liked to fight above his weight class." I said, shaking my head at the dying fool. "Trying to take on the whole fucking Bratva with his little gang. What an idiot."

Kieron stayed silent. He shook his head and ran his non-bloodied hand through his long hair. Hector had dropped a bomb on us. We had a member of the Smirnov family in our safehouse, being watched after by two of our own... This could get ugly real fast.

"What do we do, Kieron?"

"Fuck. I don't know yet. I need to think this through. But what I do know is, if they find out we have her, and they think we've taken her hostage instead of Los Muertos, it's a war. A needless war."

I nodded.

"Kill him, get rid of the body, and let's figure this out." Kieron said, going back to the spot against the wall he'd claimed when I'd started. I turn back to the table, going to grab my nine-inch serrated blade thinking that one shot to the kidney, one to each lung and a good slice across the throat will do just fine, when my cell-phone blares. The trilling *ring ring ring* cuts through the air like the knife I was going to use.

My stomach drops. My heart beats too fast. My palms start to sweat. Something's wrong. Something's happened.

I drop the knife in my hands and scramble to grab the phone out of my back pocket.

Talia's name blinks across my screen, and I'm nearing a full panic attack.

"Talia, what happened?" I snap in the phone, already making my way towards my jacket, ignoring Kieron's attempts at asking what's going on.

"She... she's okay." Talia's broken, watery voice comes through the speakers. "But she moved too fast, she was excited and moved too fast. Her neck, she said her neck popped or something and she was in so much pain that I had to get the doctor."

"What did the doctor say?" I get into the elevator, Kieron hot on my heels as he listens intently to everything I say. He's pulled his phone out now, probably getting someone to take care of Hector and his body. I don't even care that I'm not the one to ultimately end his life anymore, I just want to be there for my girl.

"That she needs to be aware of how severe her injuries are. He doesn't want to put her in a neck brace, but he will if she continues to aggravate the injury. She's okay, I'm sorry I'm crying it's probably making it sound a lot worse than it is. She just needs to sleep and to not strain her neck or head for a while." I would trust her words a lot more if they weren't punctuated with sobs.

"Talia, we are on our way."

"Kieron's with you?" She asks, her cries getting louder. They're so loud I have to hold the phone back from my ear for a moment before I respond. Her words aren't making me feel better. She says Auggie's fine, but the reaction she's having proves that something serious happened. Shit, is it worse than she's letting on?

"Talia, is Auggie alright? You're scaring me here." I say, trying for a calm tone, but my heart is beating so hard it feels like it's going to beat out of my chest if she doesn't reassure me that she's okay.

A wail is my answer.

"What the fuck is happening," I whisper and drag my hand through my hair so hard my roots start to protest. "Is Auggie okay?" I snap, but the hysterical sobs are my only answer.

"Give me the phone." Kieron says strongly, his tone sharp towards me, almost like he's pissed at how I talked to his girl.

"Tali, baby. It's okay, just breathe. Is Auggie alright? Trent looks like he's going to punch a hole in the elevator doors and rip through space and time himself to get to Auggie if you don't tell him she's okay." I flip him off.

"Okay. Okay. I know. You knew this was going to happen. I told you I read it in one of the books. I know. It'll level out, don't worry. Yes, I love it. I do. Because I love you." I listen to his side of the conversation and am about to deck my best friend if he doesn't tell me what's going on.

"Okay, baby. Take a deep breath. There you go, good girl. We are stepping out of the elevator at headquarters now, we'll take our bikes and be to you in no time. Less than five minutes." He says soothingly. "I love you, baby. We'll see you soon." They hang up and he hands me my phone.

"What was that? I haven't seen or heard her cry that much, ever. Not even when she killed her ex."

"So, we have some good news." Kieron tells me with a smile; a bright, blinding, proud smile. "Talia's pregnant. That's why she's a little... out of control with her emotions lately."

"Holy-fucking-shit! Congratulations, man!" I pull Kieron

into a tight hug, clapping him on the back a few times before we separated. "That's such great news."

He pulled his keys out and swung his leg over his bike. I mirrored his movements, my own bike roaring to life between my thighs.

His smile told me just how perfect it was, and how great he felt at becoming a Dad with the love of his life. He looked calm, excited, at peace. He looked like he finally found his meaning for living.

Is it fucking crazy that I want that, too? That I can see that with Auggie? Starting a family of our own?

That thinking of her belly rounded with my baby drives me fucking crazy?

I shake my head to clear the image from my head, the vision of Auggie carrying my baby, happy and safe, and us together forever, making my heart swell in my chest.

It would be our future; I won't accept anything less.

23

# Chapter 23

Trent

I walked into Auggie's room, ignoring the looks from the nurses and doctor at my

bloodstained hands. There were soft gasps and murmurs as Kieron and I stormed through the floor of the hospital like we owned the place. I don't really know why they were so fucking surprised. They knew who we were. What did they think we were, benevolent mafia members?

I call out her name as I push open her door and rush to her side. Talia was sitting in the chair I'd used and she jumps up like I scared her.

"She's not woken up yet, they said it could be a little bit. They had to give her some heavier pain meds." Talia's face was all red, her eyes puffy from crying. She looked like a racoon and had obviously tried to wipe all her makeup off. "I'm so sorry, Trent. This is my fault."

"It's not your fault." I said as I breathed in deeply, my heartrate already calming down as I get closer to Auggie and am able to see with my own two eyes that she's safe. "She's going to have to learn to let us take care of her, and acknowledge her own limits."

Kieron takes Talia in his arms and hugs her close, letting her sniffle into his chest as he ran a hand over her purple hair to calm her down.

"Congratulations, Talia. Kieron just told me the news." I say with a smile as I thread my fingers through Auggie's unconscious ones. I'm not leaving her again, no matter what. Hector is taken care of; Kieron can figure out anything else that needs to be done.

"Thanks," She says with a smile. "We're pretty excited."

"I take it Auggie's excited, too?" I smirk. Knowing her and how much she loves her sister, as long as Talia was excited, Auggie was probably jumping up and down.

"She is." Talia smiles brighter. "So now that you know, you can probably tell that I've been a little…emotional lately. I'm sorry I snapped when she was first admitted. That wasn't fair of me. I was scared and pissed off and I unfairly put all the blame on you."

I look to Auggie, knowing what we had talked about and I can't help but think that if I had put Kieron in her hands like she'd put Auggie in mine, I'd have reacted the same way.

"We're good, Talia. No worries. I only want her to be okay."

"Me too."

"Fuck, can you guys stop talking? My head hurts enough and your jabbering over me isn't helping." Auggie groans and the hand that isn't holding mine covers her eyes.

"I thought you were going to stop scaring me like this." I

sigh dramatically. "You know I'm barely thirty, I don't need to be getting grey hairs already."

Auggie chuckled. "You'd look sexy all salt-and-peppered mixed in with your red hair."

"Let's not find out for a while, huh?" I smirk and lean over to kiss her. She tries to sit up to reach my lips, and I gently nudge her shoulders back.

"No more moving for a while. You might feel good right now, but your body doesn't. Let take care of you a little longer."

"It's not like I'm intentionally pushing through the pain, I just forget." She nestles down into the flat looking hospital pillows. "Can you turn off the overhead light please?"

Talia scurries over to the wall where the switch is, and dims the lights so it's comfortable for Auggie. She's still sniffling. Is this what she's going to be like for the next nine months? Shit, Kieron has his work cut out for him. Not that he seems to mind at all.

"I'm sorry," Talia says, leaning over and giving her sister a kiss on the cheek.

"Don't be. It's not your fault at all." Auggie smiles weakly. Her eyes make contact with mine and I can see the burning question in them. "Did you.."

"I didn't, but I'm sure he's gone by now." I answer, threading my fingers through hers. "I got Talia's frantic call just as Kieron and I were deciding how to handle it."

"You might not have delivered a final blow, but Bryan said that he bled out within minutes. He's well and truly gone." Kieron says, pulling his phone out for me to read the message from Bryan.

**Bryan:**

Went down to the playroom not never three minutes after you messaged. No heartbeat. Shot him once between the eyes, just to make sure that fucker really was dead. Hope Auggie's okay.

Relief floods my entire body.

Relief that my girl will never have to deal with that asshole again.

I just need to make sure the rest of Los Muertos is gone right along with Hector.

I hand the phone back to Kieron. And as if he can tell what I'm thinking, he smirks.

"Already on it." He mumbles low enough for just me to hear.

"Are Cillian and Bryan," Auggie looks at me with a questioning look. I make a mental note to introduce her properly to my friends, and nod. "are they okay?"

Kieron smirks and pulls Talia to his side. But I look to my girl. This sweetheart of a badass with attitude that will make the most patient man snap, and I know I'm such a fucking goner.

"Yeah, baby. They're okay. Like I said before, Bryan checked you over after Hector tackled you, and Cillian had left to get something to bind Hector better. Do you remember the 'sister' Hector was going on about?" I ask her. I could see her start to nod and I squeeze her hand to stop her.

"Blink once for yes, twice for no." I smirk at Auggie, and am insanely satisfied with the blush that covers her cheeks. There isn't a doubt in my mind that she's not remembering how I took her in shower. Her light eyes stare up at me in equal parts embarrassed and lust, and she bites her bottom lip. Fuck, if Kieron and Talia weren't here...

"I don't want to know." Talia shudders. Kieron kisses her temple, putting his hand on her waist.

"I don't think you have any room to be teasing them." He stage-whispers in her ear, kissing her temple.

"You don't!" Auggie points a finger at her sister. She's still red and flustered, but putting on a good show of trying to turn the attention off of them. I chuckle, but cover it with a cough. Or at least, I try to. My girl turns back to me and points the same accusatory finger in my direction. "Don't start."

I hold up both of my hands in a gesture that portrays my faux innocence with a surprised look on my face. I'm not trying to hide or withhold anything about my relationship. I want to scream to the world that she's mine. I have no shame at making her remember what I do to her and making her tremble with the memories.

I want her to always remember who she belongs to.

And who belongs to her.

"Anyway," Auggie side-eyes me like she knows I'm not sorry in the least about making her blush and be embarrassed – I'm not – and returns to the conversation at hand. "I remember Hector making me think he had Talia. Who is the girl he had?"

"She's the sister of one of the Russian spies. She's latched onto Cillian, not letting him out of her sight for longer than it takes for him to go to the bathroom. We don't have a whole lot of information, we haven't been able to talk to Cillian yet, and the information we got from Hector proves his paranoia was affecting his ability to think logically. Just like his prick of a brother." I want to explain it all to her, but I also don't want to overwhelm her. Her brain is injured and she's been through so much.

Kieron stays quiet the whole time, but it is fairly obvious to me that he knows more than he's shared with me. I wonder what intel Bryan has been able to uncover since we got some actual information from Hector.

That man is truly our jack of all trades.

Auggie didn't seem to buy that it was all we knew right now, like the observant, smartass she is. She narrows her eyes at me accusingly, but thankfully, lets it go. Sighing, she closes her eyes again, bringing a hand up shield her eyes from the remaining soft glow of the dimmed light.

"All you need to do right now is rest, baby. We can focus on everything else when you get better." I put my hand on her forehead to smooth the stray hairs there, but my blood-stained hands are such a stark contrast against her soft, clean skin that I ball my hand and drop it to my side. The last thing I want to do is stain her with my deeds, even if they're bloody for a damn good reason.

Instead, I kiss her forehead.

"There's so much more to talk about though," Auggie says sleepily.

"There's nothing that needs to be fixed right now. Nothing that can't wait for a bit." I say softly. Talia's hand is on my lower back as she moves me to the side to talk to her sister.

"We're going to go, hun. Do you need anything?" She asks softly.

"Nope, Trent's going to be overbearing and take care of everything for me." She rolls her head gingerly to look at me and smile. I swear my heart beats just for her.

"Don't pretend you don't like it, Princess."

She rolls her eyes, but doesn't argue. She might put up a fight about how she's independent, but she wants to be taken care of in each and every way. And I want to do that for her.

Kieron comes up to me and gestures for me to follow him away from the girls.

"I'm not even going to ask you to come in for a while. Get Auggie set up and then we can talk. But I do want to know what you want to do about Los Muertos. Do you want to be the one to break it down or do you want me to pass it to someone else?" Kieron asks. He's passing the responsibility to me, and I'm once again floored at how seamlessly he's able to switch from leader to friend and back again. He's probably – most definitely – not supposed to let me make a decision of this magnitude, but he knows it's important to me.

The last thing I want is him in trouble with Skipper because I take too long or aren't able to give it as much attention as I usually do.

"Give it to Cillian or Bryan. I'm going to focus on getting Auggie set up in her new apartment, and then I'll be back and help them wherever they're at with dismantling it."

Kieron nods, hitting my shoulder once before he says, "Good man. No problem, it's what I was expecting. I'll have someone on Los Muertos and then we need to look into the Bratva. If Cillian isn't going to let the Smirnov girl go, or she won't go, then we have another fucking problem brewing."

Another fucking war. And one that will not be solved as easily as the one with the Italians.

"Understood." I nod. "Is he not wanting to send her back?"

"From the check-in's, what Cillian has told me is that she's hesitant to go. She won't talk about her family, and that he's certain there's some kind of bad-blood happening there. Cillian refuses to send her back to a bad situation. I need to do more research into it, put some feelers out."

"That's not for me, Kieron. Not this time." I shake my head

and cup the back of my neck. It's not that I wouldn't go for Cillian, I would, but I have Auggie to worry about now. Going undercover like that… It's not something to be taken lightly. I volunteered to help Kieron and Talia when they needed an undercover man into the Italian mob. I can't do that again. Not with Auggie. Not that I'm just now healing from before.

"I know. I'd not ask that of you." Kieron didn't ask me to do it the first time, either. He knows how fucked in the head it can make you, especially if the group you're watching goes against your own morals so much. Especially if you have to do things like I did to prove you were on their side.

"She needs me and I need her." I look over to my girl and see her chatting softly to her sister, her eyes still closed and Talia brushing her hair back like I wanted to.

"I have to wash my hands. Get this blood off of me." I mutter. The fear of tainting Auggie, of potentially doing something that's unforgivable in her eyes, of being left alone after falling so hard, is terrifying.

"She loves you. All of you." Kieron says, drawing my attention back to him. "You don't think that I felt so shitty about myself when I had to show Talia the bad side of me? But once I did, I was very surprised how much she loved that side of me too."

I don't say anything. I don't really think there is anything for me to say, but I understand what he's trying to tell me.

"Go wash up, we'll stay with them until you get back." Kieron tips his chin up to gesture to the bathroom. I walk to the bathroom quickly and immediately turn the water to scalding.

As much as I'm scared Auggie might see me differently with the actual blood on my hands, I can't find it within me to feel sorry or regret ending Hectors life at all. It's what needed to happen and I'm fucking glad that even though it wasn't by my hand, I tortured that fucker for what he'd done. I scrub with the hospital soap roughly, trying to erase any drop of dried blood from my fingers or arms. My clothes are fucked, but at least I can clean the remnants of his gruesome death from my skin long enough to kiss and hug Auggie.

I wash my face, scrubbing my new beard to get any blood that was trapped there, and dry myself off as best I can. It's as good as it's going to get without a proper shower, but I'm itching to get back to Auggie.

I open the door and Talia's waiting right by the bathroom, her hand jutting out to hand me something. A plain black t-shirt.

"Thought you might need one." She smirks, and ducks in for a quick side-hug. "We're going. Kieron had to take a call, he's right outside. If you need anything, call me. We're staying at headquarters until she is discharged and decides what she wants to do. She was asking about apartments and stuff, so you might have a long few days of apartment hunting for her ahead of you." Talia steps back towards the door. "Let me know what the doctor says, he wanted to talk to her about discharging her when they left last time."

"Will do." I say and hold up the shirt. "Thanks."

"Anytime."

* * *

"I swear to god, Trent." Auggie said under her breath and I knew a blow-up was coming. "Give me my book back. The doctor said I was fine and didn't need that much monitoring anymore. Everything is healed and I'm good! I can read a damn book now, Trent." Auggie damn near growls at me. She had been discharged from the hospital the evening after Talia and Kieron announced they were pregnant.

I had argued with the doctor for a bit about if that was really what was best for her, but he assured me, upon threat of his life, that she was perfectly fine and her brain needed time to heal. That she could do that in the comfort of her own home, as long as she followed his recommendations.

Auggie had then threaded her fingers through mine and pulled me down so I leaned over her and asked me softly to take her home.

I was a goner.

All our stuff from the safehouse had been moved to head-quarters and Kellan had put her up in Talia's old apartment for the time-being. It was kind of him to do. I was more than willing to have her stay in mine with me, but Talia had suggested her old apartment before I'd even opened my fucking mouth. It didn't really matter since I wasn't going to let her sleep alone ever again.

"What's it about, baby?" I smirk, and flip through the pages of one of her newer romance novels.

She mumbled under her breath and held out her hand for me to give it back to her.

"Oh no, doll. That's not how this works. What's your book about?" I lean over her little nest on the light grey designer couch where she was resting. I bracket each side of her with my arms and wait for her to answer me. The blush that crosses her cheeks makes me weak to the knees, and I push forward. I want to hear her talk dirty.

"It's about a guy and a girl. There. Give it back to me."

"Details, details."

"You're impossible. Terrible. Annoying." Auggie sits up, pushing herself into my space. No complaints here.

"Yes, yes, tell me more." I love seeing her last nerve and stepping right over it.

"It's about a girl who was best friends with four guys and she has to leave. Then she gets mixed up with some bad people and they try to kill her and they end up dumping her back in her hometown. They all blame each other for everything, but slowly fall back in love. The main man in her harem reminds me of you. Bossy. Possessive." She leans over and grabs the book from my hand, tugging it close to her chest.

"Four guys to one girl?" I'm shocked.

"They share." She holds it close to her.

"I couldn't do that." I shake my head and run a hand over her shoulder, down her arm, pushing her softly back into the pillows. "I'm a selfish son-of-a-bitch and you're mine. All mine. I won't be sharing you with anyone, so don't even think about it, doll."

"Not even with your best friends?" Her eyes sparkle with laughter and I start to sweat. Does she actually want to be with other people? I look deeply into her eyes and search. I search for any kind of indicator that she wants more than just me. I don't want to share, but I don't really think I can be without Auggie. So, I guess I'd have to do what I'd have to do.

"Relax, big guy. I don't want anyone but you. You're more than enough for me. Not yucking someone's yum, but I'm a one-man kind of girl." I drop my head in relief.

"Thank fuck. I don't know if I could watch you be with others. But, then again, I'm completely screwed." I say seriously.

"What? Why are you screwed?" Her rainbow hair is piled on top of her head in a loose bun that wobbles as she talks. So fucking cute.

"Because I'd do anything for you." I lean down and kiss her deeply. "If you told me that was what you needed, I'd figure out my own shit to give it to you."

"You'd do something like that for me?"

"Baby, I'd give you the world if you asked."

She lets the book drop to the floor with a *thunk,* and both of her arms wrap around my neck. She pulls me down against her body, wrapping her arms and legs around me like a koala, as she kisses me. I wrap my arm around her back and shift her so she's straddling me, and pull her by her thighs to be as close to me as possible.

"I just need you." She whispers against my lips. Her words make my heart soar and my smile makes it difficult to deepen the kisses she's giving me. "I just *want* you."

"You've got me, baby. All of me." I say against her lips. "Are you wet for me?"

Auggie nods, sitting back so there's a small space between us and I can look up at her. She must be feeling better because the movement to her head didn't make her wince. Instead, she bit her lip and rolled her hips against me.

"I think I should check, don't you?" I slip two fingers along the waistband of her sleep shorts. They taunt me, showing off her long legs and always just a hint of her ass. I'm going to buy her one in each color, I fucking love seeing her wear them.

The soft waistband rests against her skin, and I slide two fingers along the band before dipping them lower until I reach her heat.

"Oh fuck, baby, you're dripping. That book really got you going?" I ask.

"Does that bother you?" She whispers.

"Not in the slightest. As long as you come to me every time you've worked yourself up." I wanted to groan at the thought of her reading her little book, sitting there looking like an innocent angel, but making her panties drenched. "Fuck, that's so hot to think of. You with your ruined panties, turned on, but can't do anything to get relief… No, baby. It doesn't bother me at all. If anything," I take her hand and bring it to my hardened cock. "If anything, it turns me on too."

Auggie whimpers and rolls her hips again.

"In fact, you ever find something you want to try, you let me know. Except for the sharing, I want you all to myself." I bite her shoulder. I slide my fingers all the way into her core, and I curl my fingers. Auggies head falls forward against my chest and I start to thrust in faster.

"Is this what you want, baby girl?" I whisper in her ear and am rewarded with a shiver.

"Yes," She moans. "Please."

My fingers move quicker; scissoring and curling, until I can feel her tense. When her thighs start to quiver and shake, I know she's on the edge. Instead of letting her tumble over it, I pull my fingers from her and slip them between my lips.

Auggie's eyes are wide as she watches what I'm doing. I moan at the taste of her on my tongue and lay her back on the couch.

"Please," She whines, begs. And I fucking love it.

"Shhh, baby." I shush her softly and unbutton my jeans with one hand. "I've got you." Auggie's pulling at the drawstring of her shorts and has them, along with her underwear, off in seconds.  I bend down and spread her knees open, pushing one up to her chest and I bend down to take a long lick of her pussy, gathering her wetness in my mouth.

"Fuck me," I mutter.

"What do you think I'm doing?" I mumble, speaking directly into her cunt. The vibration from my words makes her moan louder. Auggie pushes against me; forcing me in deeper, and I groan.

I can't wait. I can't.

I pull back from the warm, delicious space between her thighs, and free my cock from my pants, just pulling my pants down far enough to slide into her.

"Fucking hell.  Every time.  Every time, Auggie, you feel so fucking good." I groan. It's never going to be enough, I'll always want more of her. "You're mine, Princess, do you hear me? Mine." I growl in her ear, reveling in the shiver that runs through her body. I move my mouth to her neck, sucking on the pulse point until I know that she'll wear my mark for days to come. Proving to everyone that dares to look at her that she's mine.

I pull back and slam home, pushing in and grinding into her as hard as I can. When I slide back in, I shift her hips so that her clit grinds on my pubic bone with each movement. She clenches around me tighter and I know it's worked how I wanted it to.

"Oh god," She groans, her eyes closing.

"No, no, no, baby. Eyes on me." I put my hand on the arm of the couch above her head so that the angle changes just slightly, and she squeaks.

"Eyes on me." I repeat when she doesn't immediately open

them. "Now, Auggie."

Only then does she open those gorgeous eyes of hers and stares at me with hooded eyes.

"Hey, beautiful." I smile and thrust into her shallowly. Just enough and in just the way I know will push her over the edge fastest.

"Trent," She gasps. I shift my hips so my cock moves a bit more at an angle to where the head of my dick will rub against her g-spot with ever thrust. I slowly rock into her.

"That's it, isn't it. That's the spot, right there." I don't even need her to answer me, the way she moves and how she won't stop shifting her hips tells me I'm right.

"Please," she whimpers and it's music to my fucking ears.

"Imagine that, Auggie Jones saying please."

"Maybe you're doing something right for a change. I was going to - *oh fuck again* - be good instead of smarting off... I told you those books would – *Trent, oh god,*" Her eyes roll back and I smirk at the sight. She can talk shit all she wants, but we both know that I'm rocking her world. "I told you those books would help you. You just needed a little bit of help." She cries out as I thrust into her harder.

"I don't think I needed the help, and you know I didn't, but I sure like how they gave me an insight into your head, baby." I pull her thigh up and around my waist, making the angle even deeper. Fuck me, she feels so good.

In the beginning I was too emotionally drained; hiding behind snark and facades to get me through each interaction. Watching Garzino do what he did and not being able to do anything about it, basically playing God and deciding who lived and who died for even that short amount of time made me question everything.

But then, she was there. Kieron and Kellan giving me this assignment changed everything for me. It gave me my light back; my life, my sense of self. But most of all, it gave me her.

She is like a beacon of hope and independence in a small little package that did nothing but piss me off and sass me at every turn.

And I loved it even then.

I loved her fire and her desire, her passion and her drive, even if I didn't show it. It was what made us such good friends. It's what makes us such good lovers. It's what will make us such good… forevers.

"Like I said, help." She says with a smile and runs a hand down my back, making me shiver. When her fingers get to my ass, she squeezes and pulls me in closer. "But right know, I want you to fuck me like you hate me."

I almost come right there. Jesus christ, she wants to kill me.

But what a way to go.

"Is that what you want?" I feel the feral part of myself start to come to the surface, the part of me that wants to hurt, that wants to drive her mad like she does to me.

"I always wanted to know how you'd fuck me when we were fighting." She confesses and I swear my dick gets even harder. I stop moving and sit back to look at her in surprise.

"Really?"

"Really." I remind myself of her injuries, of the doctor's recommendations, but I can't help it. My hands shake and my heart beats faster. I squeeze her thighs a little tighter as I try to control myself.

"I can't." I thrust deeper, slower. I have to control myself. I'll never forgive myself if I hurt her.

"You can." She nudges closer to me, shifting her hips up

to take me in again. My head drops to her chest as I take a deep breath. My mind, my heart, and my dick are all saying separate things.

"Please, Trent, be gentle with my head and neck, but other than that, I want to know. You know you want to." Her soft, sultry begging is what does me in.

Let's be honest, I would give her anything she'd ask of me.

"You'll tell me red if it's too much, do you understand? If you can't talk, and it's too much, you'll tap my forearm twice, *hard.* Do you understand?" I pull out of her and grasp my shiny dick at the base. I have to hold back, I don't want this to be over just yet.

"Yes," She breathes the word like a sigh of relief.

I adjust her body the way I want it; one leg propped high on the couch, the other spread wide so I have a great view of her pretty, wet pussy.

"So fucking pretty. So wet." I say mesmerized, and I slide two of my fingers through her wetness, dragging some down to her ass, making it slick all over.

Auggie's eyes close, and she lets me take over completely. Her surrender showing me how much she trusts me in every way.

I drag my finger up to her clit, and I circle the small, hard nub that I find there. Without warning, I pull my fingers back and slap her.

"What the fuck, Trent!" Her eyes fly open and a sinister sense of achievement flows openly through me.

"If you're going to be mouthy, you're going to get it."

Her eyes darken to match mine. And she nods.

I don't waste any more time as I plunge into her heat. I don't even try to be sweet about it. I know she's wet enough; I know she wants it; I know I want it.

Auggie cries out, a guttural groan that I can tell is from both shock and relief. Her whole body jumps with the force of my hips, and I do it again. Just to watch her tits bounce and her head move up the couch. A wince crosses her face, from the force or from her head I'm not sure, and I quickly shove a pillow above her head.

That's the last kindness I'm going to extend to her for a bit, though.

"Hang on, Princess." I tell her and grab both of her thighs to wrap them around my waist, and lean one knee on the couch to shift us up and her waist is pulled up off the couch.

"Hold your legs here." I order and move my hand so my fingers rub over her clit, fast and furious.

"Trent, fuck, oh my god." She whines, and it's perfect. Her thigh starts to slip, and I smack it.

"Keep it there. Do what I say. *Now.*" Her eyes blaze, but she holds her thigh back where I placed it.

She's fluttering around me already; her hands shaking with the effort to stay where I placed her. But then something inside her snaps and I know she's going to fight me. She's going to push back, and I hope she does.

I feel a smirk cross my face, but I'm sure it's more of a snarl. I can't wait.

"No," She starts to fight against me, pulling both of her legs out of my grip, but that shit isn't going to fly. The defiant streak in her is rising to meet the fighter streak in me. She wants to fight; she wants to bring us back to the beginning of our relationship where we argued just for the sake of arguing.

I grind into her harder, snacking her ass for defying me, but I can see she likes it. She likes my mark on her.

Good, I fucking like it there too.

"Yes," I snarl and go faster, and faster. I don't want her to be able to think about fighting me. All I want is for her to take it, take my cock, take my come, and *thank me* for it.

I laid down over her, holding onto her ass as we move as one. Auggie's moaning and crying out in my ear, pushing me that much closer to my orgasm. She's there, she's *right fucking there*, but still won't come. I can tell she's holding back.

I lean back and grab her cheeks in my hand roughly, forcing her to stare at me.

"You're going to do what I say, and you're not going to fucking argue with me." I say through clenched teeth. Feeling her fight me as well as her giving this to me, is perfection.

"I'm so fucking sick of you arguing with me and if you're going to continue to, the moment your neck is healed, I'm going to find a better use for that mouth."

"Oh, fuck off." She says breathlessly playing along, and rolls her eyes.

I move my hand down to her neck, not putting any weight through my palm, but I tighten my grip on the sides of her slender neck, as I grind into her harshly, making sure that may each movement grazes her clit.

"Say that again, baby. See what happens."

"Fuck. Off." She stares at me defiantly with an edge to her voice, and in her eyes. Auggie may seem like she's unaffected, but I know her body by now. I know she's close.

Her pussy's fucking pulling me in, and holding me tightly like it doesn't want me to leave with each fast pace thrust.

My orgasm is quickly approaching, but I refuse to go before she does. That shit isn't going to happen. My fingers tighten on either side of her neck, restricting her airway just slightly but never putting any weight on her neck.

"Good?" I ask, giving her the chance to tell me that it's too much.

My strong, brave, horny girl blinks once.

"Good." I hold tight to the sides of her neck, and grind harder against her. I pull out and thrust in again and again. Her whimpers and gasps push me closer and I grit my teeth.

"Trent," She cries out, grabbing my forearm and holding on tightly. I'm sure I'll have angry, red half-moon fingernail marks on my arm, but I don't change anything; not my speed, not my angle, not my position. She's gripping me tighter, and her breasts jump with each thrust, her chest rising and falling with the breaths she's trying to take.

She comes with a cry, her voice breaking into a groan as her cunt clamps around my cock like a vice. She pulls me over when her hand snakes between us and drags my mouth to hers.

Together we're hurtled into our pleasure, not able to hold back anymore and our kisses go from angry and desperate, to soft and sweet as we come down. I want her to know how much I love her. How much I'll care for and protect her with each breath I take.

Because even though we started off rocky, I wouldn't change our foundation a bit.

# 24

# Chapter 24

Auggie

It was a good two weeks later that I finally talked Trent into letting me look for my own apartment. He wasn't a huge fan of me living in Newburyport when he had to be in Boston for work. I'd fallen in love with that little coastal town. I'd fallen in love with Trent there, too.

"Tell me again why you demand being so far from Boston?" Trent took my hand, a grumpy look on his face as we walk through the little apartment complex. The apartment we had just toured was cute. More importantly, it was affordable. Even though this town was where I wanted to be, it was crazy expensive.

"Honey, we've had this conversation." I groan, and roll my eyes.

"Just tell me again. Humor me."

"Because I love it here. I feel comfortable, and I love seeing the sun rise over the water when I wake up." I look over my shoulder wistfully. This apartment is right on the beach so I can see the water from where we are standing. The weather is cooler than the last time we were here. Winter is quickly approaching, and soon the water will be icy and the waves will crash into the beach leaving ice behind. I can't wait to see it.

"But it's so far." He whines, and I laugh loudly.

"It's not that far, Trent. 45 minutes max. And I know how you drive. You'll be here in 20." I thread our fingers together, and pull him towards a little café around the corner from the apartment building.

Trent stays silent through the short walk, and I can see the gears turning in his head. He's broody and pouty and *thinking,* which means something big is bothering him.

He opens up the glass door as the bell rings, signaling our presence. It smells fantastic; like fresh baked goods and coffee. Trent didn't smile to the teenager working behind the counter, but I did. The minute the pimple-faced teenager smiles back at me, Trent glares. I smack his stomach with the back of my hand and whisper, "be nice".

"I will when he doesn't make eyes at my girl." Trent growls and pulls me close.

"Trust me, caveman, they all know I'm yours." As much I tease him, I love the possessive side of him. He looks at everyone as if he will singlehandedly fuck up their world if they harm me in any way. On the same hand, I love that Trent lets me be free. He is always standing right behind me with his arms crossed, like he is still my personal guardian and not my boyfriend.

After being 'protected' from the world and hidden away for

so long, being stripped of every choice and care, I love that Trent somehow perfectly combines what I love and what I need, naturally.

We walk to a table in the back; the old, worn wood of the well-loved table was soft under my hands as I slid into the booth. Trent slides into the other side and he takes my hands in his.

"You could stay in my apartment in Boston." He said softly. His voice is so soft and vulnerable that my decision to live on my own waivers just a bit.

"Are we ready to live together?" I counter.

"We did for months, here in this very town." He holds his hand up towards the air.

"That was different and you know it."

"How?" Trent's voice is calm, but I can tell he's desperate to argue with me. His fingers curl into a fist, and he rests it right next to the hand of mine that he's holding.

"Because, we didn't want to be together then. We barely tolerated each other. This is… This thing between us is so much bigger. I don't want to rush into anything, and then have you regret it." I couldn't have that. My heart clenches tightly in the imagined sorrow that he could potentially regret anything about us.

His fingers squeeze mine tighter, and his clenched fist relaxes enough to cover our joined hands. His mouth opens, probably to try and tell me he wouldn't ever regret us, but I can't listen to his reasoning. The fact of the matter still stands that I want to, I *need* to, do this on my own for just a bit.

"I need to do this." I whisper.

Trent doesn't say anything, even though I can practically *feel* how much he wants to make me see his point of view. I do see what he's saying, I understand why he doesn't think it's a big deal. But, to me, it is.

"I just need to be a bit independent for a while. Especially now that Hector is gone, now that you've ensured I'm free," I cup his beard-covered chin, and gently nudge him to look at me. "I need to find myself a little more. And I think you do too."

I knew all about what Trent had endured while undercover with the Italian Mob. And I can honestly say that after hearing what he went through, I understand why he was so… hollow when we met. He was still beating himself up and feeling like he didn't know who he really was.

"That sounds a lot like a goodbye there, Princess." His brown eyes drop as a weak smile that doesn't quite reach his eyes crosses his lips.

"It isn't. At least, not for me." I promise. "I want to be with you. And I don't need to be single to find myself. Do you?"

He shakes his head quickly.

"I love you. If you need some space, I'll give you what I can. I'm not a patient man though, Auggie."

"I love you, too. What do you have to be patient about? You have me. I have you." My head tilts in confusion.

"As true as that is, until you fall asleep in *our* bed every night, until you call *our* house home, and until my last name is *ours*, I'll be working on getting you to accept it. To accept that our future is going to be here sooner rather than later." He says, so strongly and surely, like it's a done deal. Like living together and marriage between us is inevitable.

He holds his hand up to stop a barista passing by and orders us two coffees, a chocolate croissant, and a cinnamon roll, all while my jaw is dropped.

Trent smirks at me, and shrugs his shoulders.

"You honestly think that I'm not going to lock you down as soon as I possible? You're perfect. You're amazing. And by some odd stroke of luck, you love me like I love you. You must be crazy if you think I would let you get away from me at any point in our lifetime or the next. I won't accept anything less than forever. And that won't be enough."

I guess he's right. Any, and all, of the next steps of our lives will be together and it's inevitable.

————-

"Why can't I just hire you some movers?" Talia says, watching the men move around the small space of the apartment Trent and I had shared, packing my stuff, and taking apart the few pieces of furniture the Clan bought for us. Kellan, Kieron's Dad and the Clan leader, had graciously let me keep it all. It wasn't the best quality, but it did the job. And it meant I didn't have to buy anything with my very limited budget.

"We're moving two blocks." I open my bedside drawer and start to pack the stuff there.

"I feel terrible." Talia moans, putting her hand over her stomach; her still completely flat stomach, and goes to pick up a box.

"Don't you even fucking think about it!" Kieron roars from the other room. That man has a 6th sense about when Talia was going to do something she shouldn't.

"Oh, shut up! I can lift a little box, Kieron!" My sister yells back to him completely unaffected by his tone.

"Tal, his face is turning red. I wouldn't do it." Trent calls to her, his voice shook dramatically like he's scared.

"Talia, I swear to god, you pick up a box and-" Kieron's footsteps are like thunder as he walks towards the room.

"Oh, please don't. I don't need to deal with any more male egos and possessiveness than I already have to." I take the box from her hands, ironically labeled blankets and was super light, but I wasn't going to argue with her baby daddy.

"Fine, but you will let Kieron and Trent do the heavy stuff." Talia laughs, and I stop packing to watch my older sister laugh. She'd always been free with her emotions, free with her determination, and her laughter. But there was that pocket of time where both of us were so stuck, and her light died. She's let it die. For me.

I'm so fucking thankful that Kieron found her and saved her. Even though he didn't know it at the time, he was saving me too.

Trent walks through the door, his eyes wide like he's trying to see how much trouble Tali is going to get in and wants to watch the drama unfold. I chuckle at how much of a Papa bear Kieron's becoming and I love him more for it. He's going to be a great father, and I can breathe easier knowing my sister is completely taken care of. Trent comes over to me, and pulls the dark romance novel I'm holding out of my hands, gently placing it in the box for me.

"What's wrong, baby?" He says softly, his dark eyes meeting mine. I'm astounded at how well he continuous to show me how much he pays attention to me, to my needs, to my emotions, and to my wants. How he takes care of me is totally different than what I'm used to, but I'm sure as hell loving it. It's the kind of care I'd always wished for. The kind I've always read about, but never experienced.

"How do you know me so well? It seems like you can tell

my emotions from just my expressions. Stalker." I say the last word with a sing-song tone, and I look at him out of the corner of my eye warily.

"I had to get good at telling when you were uncomfortable or nervous just by watching you, baby. You weren't exactly forthcoming before." He smirks, pulling me in close to kiss my forehead.

*Swoon.*

"What are you talking about? I'm very vocal about how much you pissed me off." I smack his chest lightly, and am rewarded with a big, warm smile. He's so much lighter these days. So quick to smile and joke and love.

He's no longer hiding or bogged down.

He's free.

"And as much as I enjoy our banter, I did have to become somewhat of an Auggie Jones expert to be able to guard you effectively. I can tell you're thinking some big thoughts there. Need any help carrying them?" He's looking at me so intently, that there's not any doubt that he would carry every worry, burden, hope, and dream I have on his shoulders, if it meant I didn't have to be weighed down. He'd take all the bad stuff so that all that I was left with was the good. Selflessly, honorably, lovingly.

This. This right here, what we have between us, is what I've always needed, always wanted, always craved. My heart threatens to beat out of my chest and present itself to him, but I manage to keep my heart in my chest. At least for the moment.

"I'm just really thankful. For everything. You saved me, in more ways than one." I say, my eyes watering with the tears that I'm trying to hold back. Trent wraps his hand around my waist, his hands are so big they span most of my back, and he pulls me to him in a hug. My nose tucks into the exposed skin right above his t-shirt and I close my eyes at the comforting scent of him.

Talia must have left the room because she's always one to jump in and help comfort me when I'm crying. I'm relieved she's gone for the moment, to be honest.

I'm glad it's just me and Trent. This is just our moment.

He leans back just enough to look at me, all while keeping our bodies pressed together as his hands run up and down my back. His eyes soften, the corners of his lips tip up just slightly, and he rests his forehead against mine. We both close our eyes as we hold each other. I don't know why, but I know this is a life-changing moment. One I'll look back on for the rest of my life as the moment that changed my life.

"You saved me, too." He says, and I stop trying to hold the tears back, as a tear drops down my cheek, one drops down his.

———-

"It's so cute!" Talia cries excitedly when she climbs out of the pickup holding my few boxes and furniture. Trent had informed me when we started the moving process that Kieron had wanted to use the SUV he just got for the baby to help me move, but Talia had won the argument that a pickup truck would be easier to move more things. Apparently, they hadn't completely hung up the phone with Trent when they started to resolve their agreement either.

"I thought so." I smile, excited about this new adventure I'm starting on.

"I thought my apartment looked pretty good." Trent mutters under his breath like a toddler who hurt his knee. Even though he's acting like I sore loser, I know he understands why I'm doing this. He's supportive and understanding, but I think he hopes if he teases me enough, reminds me enough that he's asked me to live with him, that I'll magically change my mind.

Would it be easier? Of course. Trent makes more money than I ever will. He's already promised that he would take care of my every want and need, and moreover, he's showing me that he *wants* to do that. But this is something I need to experience. Something I *want* to experience.

I know Trent and I are endgame; I know that he and I are solid, and he's my forever.

I'm not in any hurry.

"Poor baby. Need me to kiss it better?" I purse my lips and wink at him, sending just enough of a smirk and sway of my hips that he darts to grab me. His arms wrap around my middle, and he pulls me into his chest with a growl.

"If you're going to tease me like that, I'm going to be forced to show you why that's not a nice thing to do. Especially not to me." He growls in my ear. His words send a shiver down my spine. I fight to keep my eyes open when I really want to lean my head back, and let him ravish my mouth and neck, leaving his marks all over.

"Oh yeah, what are you going to do about it?" My words are meant to be bratty and sharp, intended to drive him wild. But they come out like a sultry whisper, a siren song begging for him to keep whispering to me.

He looks around quickly, taking in where Kieron and Talia are standing against the truck, whispering to themselves, and he slides his fingers up my neck, threading them into my hair to expose my neck to him.

Trent meets no resistance. I let him use my body however he wants to, and he knows it.

"Bad girls get punished. Is that what you want? To be a bad girl?"

I shake my head as much as I can, the bratty side in me wanting to see just how far he'll take this. Trent bites down on my neck, probably leaving a red mark for the world to see, but I don't care. I want to wear his mark.

"If you're going to be a bad girl for me, I'll send Talia and Kieron home right now. I'll send them home, and throw you over my shoulder and we will go christen your new apartment." He says, and honestly, with how damp my panties are, that sounds like a fucking fantastic idea.

"But you won't be coming for a good, long, while." The last three words are punctuated with a nip to the soft skin at my throat, and his warm hand tapping my ass.

"Yeah, right. You'd feel me tighten around your cock or your fingers and you'd be happy to give me an orgasm." I whisper, wrapping my fingers in his dark t-shirt and bringing him closer. To anyone on the outside it looked like we are just embracing, but to the two of us, it's a little power struggle that serves as foreplay. I'm demanding my dominance be heard, and Trent's trying to assert his own.

Do I make it easy for him?

Of course not.

"Oh, Princess." He chuckles darkly. His grey eyes narrow, and his tongue darts out to wet his bottom lip. All my attention is zoned into that movement. The wet shine that's left behind on his lip is calling to me. I can't look anywhere, but at the lips I so badly want to taste.

He nuzzles his face into my neck, and the fucker licks – actually *licks* – from the juncture of my neck all the way up to my ear. I squeak, and go to pull back in shock, but he holds me in place, his grip in my hair tightening.

"Don't think for a second that watching you be pushed close to the edge, and then brought back down over and over again until you're crying with need and *begging* me to let you come isn't something that I won't do. Some days I crave it, baby. You giving me complete control over your pleasure and begging me so sweetly to let you come, knowing that it is going to be a mind-shattering, squirting, screaming, orgasm…" He groans softly, his fingers loosen in my hair, but he wraps the fingers around the nape of my neck, digging in just enough to make me moan.

"That will be a sight that I will see soon. How soon I see it," Trent takes a deep breath, and let it go slowly, breathing me in "is completely up to you."

I swear my knees start to wobble, but he's holding me so closely that I know if I'd fall, he'd catch me.

"That doesn't sound so bad to me." I whisper back to him, and just as I see his eye widen in excitement, we hear Kieron yell at us.

"Can you stop with the PDA, my god." You can hear the eye-roll in his voice. I snort, very unladylike, and pull away from Trent, but I keep our fingers laced together.

"Like you haven't been taking this moment to feel up my sister!"

"She's got you there." Talia smirks and crosses her arms over her chest while Kieron mumbles something about smart-asses.

Trent smiles widely and it takes my breath away. His smile lights up his whole face, and you can practically see the happiness radiating from him. The fact that he's so relaxed, so joyful, it makes my heart swell with love for these people around me even more.

"Let's go move you into your apartment." Trent says, and he pulls me towards the direction of the stairs. Towards my independence, towards myself, towards my…now.

We get to the bottom of the stairs, with my love, my sister and my friend behind me and it feels monumental. Like it's the first step to the rest of my life.

I flick my hair over my shoulder to look at everyone, and I see them all already looking at me. No one is rushing me, no one is trying to get me to go up those stairs. They know how big this is for me, and are just supporting me. Waiting for *me* to take my first steps.

I look at Trent, and have a moment of fear. Maybe I should just move in with him. I love him, I know we are going to be heading in that direction anyway, his apartment is closer to my sister, I wouldn't have to worry about bills or such, and most importantly, I'd be safe and loved all the time. I always have, and always will, have shelter in his arms as he has shelter in mine.

In the dark amber of his eyes, I can see his support. I know I could change my mind right here on the spot and he would do whatever it took to make sure I'm okay. He'd move all my shit wherever I asked, make sure I didn't have to pay for breaking the lease, and take me home. I know it.

But I can't. I need this. And he knows it just as much as I do.

He nods, and swats my ass before gesturing up with his chin. "You've got this."

And with those three words, I feel like I can do anything with him by my side.

# 25

# Chapter 25

Trent

*Two months later...*

"What are you wearing, Princess?" I whisper into the phone, my hand on my cock as I jerk off slowly to the sound of Auggie getting herself off.

Since she's moved to Newburyport, we've seen each other often but not as often as I would like. She's stubborn and independent and feisty, and I love her so much. She insists on working full-time in order to pay for everything herself, regardless of how much I offer to cover things. The most I've been able to get her to accept is me covering dinner, but that shit will change soon. I can't stand that she's working herself into the ground.

It's our first Saturday night apart. Usually I'm there or she's here, but she has to work early in the morning and wanted to "actually sleep". Like she can't sleep when I'm there. Which is bullshit, because I know that she sleeps so well wrapped in my arms, but I also know that I had to go four days without her, and that means that I have four orgasms to give her. So, she's probably right and she wouldn't be getting any sleep until the early hours.

"The little black bra and thong set you got me." She says breathlessly in my ear, and I groan. I remember that set. Lace, see-through, barely covers her nipples and it might as well be a G-string for as little as it covers. Fuck, the mental image I have of her in that pushes me closer.

"Run your finger over the lace on your nipples, just graze them enough that they push up against the lace." I tell her, "Pretend it's my fingers touching you."

"Oh," She groans. I close my eyes and can see her laying on her bed, the white comforter contrasting with the black lingerie she's wearing and the colors of her hair fanned out around her.

"With your other hand, slide your palm down your stomach and rub your pretty little clit on the outside of the lace."

"But, Trent…" She whines, and I cut her off with a growl.

"No, baby. Do what I say." I keep the pace on my cock slow, but intense. I don't want to come before she does, but just hearing her voice like this does something fierce to me.

She whimpers softly, but when she sighs, I know she followed directions.

"Good girl."

"Trent," She gasps.

"Yeah, baby? What do you need?" I ask, stroking myself faster.

"You, I need you." She moans, and my head drops back against my pillow.

"You have me. Move the little bit of ruined lace aside, Princess, and put two of those fingers into your pussy. Pretend they're me, and do what I'd do. Slide them up and down your slit, moving the wetness all around. I bet you're fucking dripping, aren't you? Tell me," I'm getting lost in the image of her in my mind.

"Yes, yes, ah." She cries out. It's music to my ears; the hottest fucking thing I've ever heard and I want to hear it daily for the rest of my life. "God, Trent!"

I can hear her squelching wetness on the other side of the phone, and never before have I wanted the ability to climb through a phone more.

The sound of her coming sets me off, and I explode into my own hand, the ropes of come fly all over me as I groan my release.

"Fuck me, that was so hot." She says breathlessly. "We should do that more often."

"I will concede to having phone sex with you every single time you decide you have to stay home." I really didn't think this through. I put the phone in between my shoulder and my ear and hold it there while I try to find something, anything, to wipe up with. My eyes land on my discarded t-shirt on the floor. I lean over to pick it up, and wipe off.

"You know, most guys wouldn't be complaining after having phone sex with their girlfriends."

"I'm not most guys." I throw the shirt to the side, and make my way to my bathroom that's connected to my room. While I can grumble and complain that I wish Auggie had moved in with me, I wouldn't have wanted her to move in here. My apartment was sterile, bland, cold. It truly was like a hotel, just a place to crash when I had to. Hell, even I preferred Auggie's apartment to my own.  If I knew that she would have been okay with it, I would've asked to move in with her and done it in a heartbeat.

"I know you're not." She says with a very audible smirk, and I felt my chest puff up a bit with pride.

Damn right I'm not.

"I just miss you." I say, a small moment of vulnerability. "I miss waking up and seeing you first thing. I miss pretending to complain about the socks in the bathroom or the hair on the shower wall.  I miss invading your space and making a place *ours*."

She's silent through the phone, but I can hear the rustle of fabric like she's getting under the covers.

"I miss you too, honey. I was going to talk to you about this tomorrow when you came over, but what about if you left some stuff here?" My heart beats faster, I swear. It's a small step, but one that is monumental. I don't want her to feel like she has to. The tension between in the silence isn't terribly uncomfortable, but it's enough to make me squirm.

"Are you sure?" I whisper.

"I'm sure. I have a drawer all cleaned out for you. A special, new blue toothbrush to put next to mine in the bathroom." She chuckles, and it warms my heart. "I'm actually surprised you haven't done it by now."

I'd thought about it. A lot. Just leaving a shirt here, a book there.  Slowly move myself in until she realized it.  But I couldn't do that to her.  I couldn't let my own selfish need to be with her overshadow what she *needed* to do for herself. Every day it was a little harder to say goodbye, listen to her lock the door, step into my car, and drive back to Boston.

But I do it.

For her.

"I wouldn't invade your space like that." I murmur softly.

"I know." The words ring true in my ear. She really does trust me, and knows how crazy I am for her. She feels safe with me, and knows that I am content to go at her pace. This small, little spitfire of a girl chose me, *me,* and I'm hit with an overwhelming sense of love and clarity.

I'm going to marry this girl.

* * *

The next morning, after a short, fitful night of attempting to sleep, I start my bike, letting it roar to life. It's way to fucking early to be up and moving, the city barely awake around me, but after the phone call with Auggie last night, I can't stop thinking about making her mine.

Permanently.

Not saying I'm going to propose tomorrow and marry her next week, it's way too soon in her eyes for that, but I would in a heartbeat if I knew she wanted that.

The crisp air is almost too cold, even through my leathers, as I sit on my bike and feel the rumble of the engine as it warms. The weather is changing quickly, and I find that I'm actually excited for the holidays. For once. I used to despise the holiday season. Everyone was all coupled up and in love, going on and on about holiday magic, but when you don't have anyone special or family to celebrate with, it's depressing.

I would tag along with the other guys out on the town, and Kieron's dad always had a party where I'd drink until I was blackout drunk, and find a willing body to spend the night with. I would always wake up feeling worse. Emptier.

This year, Kieron has Talia. I have Auggie. I won't be alone.

The drive to Kieron's beach house is calming. The rumble of the engine between my thighs, the brisk morning air whipping my cheeks, the sun peeking out over the horizon. It's the second-best thing ever. The first being in Auggie's arms.

I'm man enough to know I'm completely obsessed with my girl, and know that I don't give two shits about what anyone else says.

I signal to get onto the highway, merging quickly and the engine roars louder. After my revelation last night, I *need* to put plan into action. I have a long drive to think about what I want to say to Talia. An hour and forty minutes go by in the blink of an eye; the repetitiveness of the pavement under my tires, and the constant wind in my face… it's about as serene as I can get.

The small beach house comes into view. The sun has brightened with the morning hour, fully shining over the water as waves crashes onto the shore. A black pickup truck, the one we borrowed to move Auggie, is parked outside the house, and when I get closer I can tell it's Cillian's by the hockey stick license plate adorning the front.

I wonder why he's here so early.

I park my bike next to the truck and kill the engine. It's even colder here, right on the water, but Talia makes sure to keep the house warm. I bound inside quickly, not bothering to knock.

"Honey, I'm home!" I call out, sweeping my arm upward in a grand gesture. And the greeting I receive is much less friendly. If looks could kill, I there is no doubt that I would be dead.

"I swear to fucking christ, if you wake up Talia, I will castrate you." Kieron jumps up so quick I barely see the transition from sitting to standing, and he's angrily pointing a finger at me.

"Sorry," I shrug my shoulders, and crinkle my nose in apology. A rudely woken-up Talia is a very angry Talia, and I do not need her in a bad mood for our talk.

"What the hell are you doing here so early?" Cillian asks from the couch. He looks like shit. Cillian is the life of the party usually. The one that's always got a plan, and a smirk that tells you he's up to no good. The biggest of us in height and weight, one punch from him could knock any of us out, and he's sitting on his older cousin's couch looking like someone took him through the ringer emotionally. The dark circles and rumpled hair speak for him.

"What the hell happened to you?" I raise an eyebrow.

"I don't want to talk about it." Cillian snaps and looks down. "The situation with the Russian girl is…difficult."

"Understood." I could push him, prod and poke until he tells me what was wrong but when I look to Kieron to see the severity of whatever it is Cillian's going through, he shakes his head. "I, uh, I wanted to talk to Talia actually."

"She's sleeping. And pregnant. And both of you fuckers decided to drive over 90 minutes here, from Boston, at the ass-crack of dawn without even calling to tell me. You both just show up. What the hell is going on?" Kieron rants, his dark hair is unbound for once and it makes him look like a lion ready to pounce on the incomers for invading his space.

"Shh, man." I put my hands up to try and calm him down, but the damage has been done and I hear the squeak of the door hinges.

"You're a dead man." Kieron snaps at me.

"I didn't do it, you're the one who yelled." I step back, trying to put some distance between us in case he actually did take a swing.

"Kieron?" Talia calls out, but the moment she opens the door I avert my eyes. Cillian does the same. "Fuck, I didn't know we had company."

She is wearing the shortest t-shirt known to man, barely covered her... area. I do not need to think about Talia's pussy right now. It feels wrong on so many levels.

"Go cover up, baby. Please." Kieron says, and I have to applaud the man for withholding the growl I know he wants to let out. He's clenching his fists tightly and has shifted so that he's blocking her. Kieron didn't need to worry, both of us are making a point not to look.

The door closes again just long enough for Kieron to take a deep breath and mutter, "I need a drink," before Talia emerges again. This time fully covered.

"Hey guys," She yawns and walks over to Kieron. She rests her head against his chest and places a hand on his heart. "Calm down."

"You should be sleeping." He mumbles.

"I'm okay. It's 7 in the morning, a good time to get up." She taps his chest and sits back to look at Cillian and I.

"Sorry, guys. My morning sickness is really, really bad, and I'm getting it throughout the night. I think I got maybe three hours of sleep last night. That's why this one is being extra caveman today." She jerks her thumb at Kieron's chest.

"Do you need anything?" I flail about trying to figure out a response that doesn't make me sound like a creep, but shows that I care.

"Just Sprite, crackers and sleep. Doctor said it's normal."

She rests her head against Kieron's chest again, closing her eyes in exhaustion.

I feel like a jackass. When I look to Cillian, I see him cringe and can tell he feels the same.

"So, not that we don't love seeing you guys, but what's is the purpose of this extremely early visit?" Talia says, moving swiftly to the couch and taking a stuttering breath. Kieron is watching her like a hawk, his eyes never leaving her person in case she should need him. If I saw him like this a year ago, I would've laughed at him, called him a pussy, and told myself I'd never be like that over a girl. But now, all I can think of his how I understand every single thing he's doing because I know I would do the same if it was Auggie.

Cillian moves to sit in one of the oversized chairs next to the couch and I plop into the leather loveseat, propping my leg up on one of the armrests. Kieron's jaw clenches and I smirk, knowing I'm pushing my luck with him this morning.

"I just came to talk to Kieron about some of the new developments with the Bratva." Cillian swoops in, and I move into a more seated position, not wanting to piss boss man off anymore.

"I came to talk to you, actually." I run a hand through my windblown hair. Nerves start to prickle through me, and my eyes stay downcast.

"That's not ominous… especially at 7 in the damn morning." Kieron mutters. I look at him, rolling my eyes, but when I look to Talia, she has the biggest grin on her face.

"Alright, let's go talk." Her smile lights up her whole face, and I know right then that she knows what I'm going to say. What I want to ask.

She stands up and gestures for me to follow her to the

kitchen.

The last time I was here, Kieron had basically told me that he knew I had a crush on Auggie, even if I wasn't able to see past how infuriating she was at the time. Kieron and Talia really are a match made in nosey heaven.

"Do you want some coffee?" Talia asks, moving through the space with ease and grace. I fumbled in, and sat at the small circular table in the corner. My palms start to sweat, what the hell is that about?

"No, I'm good thanks." I wave her off.

Talia smirks knowingly and puts the tea kettle on the stove to start tea for herself. Man, being pregnant must be hard. You have to give up caffeine and alcohol.

It would be worth it a million times over in the end, though.

"So," Talia turns and rests her hip against the stove with her arms crossed "what was so important you needed to drive the hour and a half out here, at seven in the morning, without calling or texting? What's got you looking so tortured and excited at the same time? Something to do with my sister, perhaps?" She quirks an eyebrow. Teasing him mercilessly.

"Yes, I wanted to talk to you… I mean, I'll talk to your parents too, if you think I should. I mean, I probably should. But you and your sister are super close, and you've been through so much for each other, and I want to make sure that you think what I'm thinking is the same thing because I, well, I…" I know I'm rambling; the words are falling out of my mouth uncontrollably and without stopping to take a breath. And she's just… listening.

I'm breathing heavily, but don't keep embarrassing myself because she's very obviously trying to hold back a giggle.

"Don't laugh at me," I drop my head to the table with a *thunk*.

"Oh Trent," She comes over and pats my shoulder softly. "You know Auggie. Do you think that she would ever let anyone else *give their permission* to marry her?"

And she's right. Auggie would probably smack me if she knew I was asking anyone for their permission to ask her to marry me.

"But do you think she'd want to?" I sit up and look at her, completely dropping any sense of fake confidence I had.

Talia smiles kindly at me and cups my cheeks with her hands.

"Without a doubt."

# 26

# Chapter 26

Auggie


*Seven months later...*

This Boston winter is relentless.

I tuck my chin into the thick scarf I wrapped around my neck. The thick wool tickles my chin, but it's worth it to have the warmth.  I'm walking downtown to meet Trent on his lunch break. Trent's working with Cillian and Kieron on this whole Bratva thing, I don't really know what's going on, but I've met Mila one time in the nine months she's been around.

She's a cool girl, and just crazy enough to keep Cillian in check. Not that either of them said they were into each other. But anyone with eyes can tell Cillian has it bad.

I see the little café we like to frequent that's right by HQ, and run inside away from the cold that's threatening to take some of my toes.  It's just a small hole-in-the-wall that gets overlooked a lot, but it's one of the best waffle places around.

I smile to one of the waitresses and pick a booth towards the middle of the room. Not even bothering with a menu, I smile in thanks when the waitress sets down a cup of water and asks for my drink order as I take off the top two layers of winter protection.

"Two coffees. I'm also ready to order for the table." I tell her, setting my scarf on top of my coat and bag, then run a hand through my freshly bleached hair to try and get rid of the static. "I want a stack of three waffles, home fries, two eggs over easy and a side of sausage." Pausing to let her right down my order, I open my mouth to rattle off Trent's usual order when his familiar leather and citrus scent fills my nose, and I feel his protective, loving energy surround me.

"I want a breakfast burger with double fries." He says, pulling off his jacket and sliding into the other side of the booth. "And a cinnamon roll for the table." He smirks a me.

"Got it." The waitress says, not making eye contact with either of us, but her face turns red.

*That's right. He's mine.* I smirk.

"Hey, beautiful. Sorry I'm late." Trent takes both of my hands in his, holding them in his from across the table.

"I was waiting for hours and hours," I roll my eyes and fake scoff, but look to him with a smile.

"I know, I'll just have to figure out some way to make it up to you." He says softly with a smirk of his own.

I squeeze his fingers gently. It seems like we've been together forever, that this – us – is decades old. I feel comfortable, confident in him and us. I feel safe and loved, more than I ever have felt before. We make the distance work for us, not that there really is much distance at all.

"How's... work?" I settle on, well aware that we're in public, and not wanting to mention the real work he does.

"It's been hectic. Cillian is starting to lose it, I think. Mila left."

My eyebrows shoot up in shock. "No shit."

"No shit." Trent grabs my water and takes a drink.

That's surprising. From what Trent has told me, Mila was staying in HQ under the protection of the Irish, but with her ties to the Bratva, they were still ironing out everything.

So, if she left... Poor Cillian.

"How's the store?" He asks me, changing the subject.

"It's great, I really love working there." I'd gotten a full-time job that a bookstore, one of the few bookstores in Newburyport. My favorite one, actually. It was the same one where that frat boy sent me into a tail-spin of emotions and Trent saved me. It was quaint, and right on the water. It was comfortable, and it paid decently.

"It suits you." He says, bringing one of my hands up and kissing my knuckles.

"What does?"

"Happiness. Freedom. Love."

My heart damn near bursts.

"All because of you." I say softly, a small, shy smile on my lips.

"All because of *you*." He squeezes my hands in emphasis.

The moment is so charged with love and acceptance, comfort and longing, that the rest of the restaurant fades away a bit. Trent leans forward over the table, his long arms reaching me easily, and he cups my cheek.

"I love you," He whispers. I open my mouth to tell him how much I love him too, but the waitress chooses that moment to interrupt and set down the mountain of food we ordered.

My scowl at the interruption is quickly replaced with interest as the delicious smells fill my nose. Waffles, mmm.

"Here you are," she sets down the plate in front of me, then sets Trent's in front of him. Then finally, the biggest cinnamon roll there is in the middle of us.

Trent smirks at me as I pretty much drool at the sight of it.

"Do I know my girl, or do I know my girl?" He teases, and stuffs a grouping of fries into his mouth. I rip off a huge chunk of the cinnamon goodness and moan at the buttery, sugary sweetness.

"You're so good to me." I sigh between bites.

"So, tonight." Trent starts, picking up his burger, "Kieron is throwing a party. He says it's a 'congratulations' party for them, as well as a late Christmas party, but really, I think it's just an excuse for Kieron to invite all his friends and get drunk one last time before the baby is here."

"And Tali is okay with that?" I ask, somewhat incredulously. She had been very… intense with her pregnancy. My precious niece or nephew is making life absolutely awful for my sister from the first few weeks, even now, a few days after their due date. Intense, painful morning sickness, swollen ankles and face, and she's been a little…irritable. Talia is three days past her due date with no end in sight. Kieron doesn't seem to mind though, at least he doesn't let it show if he did. He is still as obsessed and in love with her as ever. It's so cute to watch.

"I'm guessing so. Kieron invited me and said she'd be there and to invite you. Who knows, maybe walking around and getting out of the apartment will help kickstart her labor." He takes a big bite of his burger.

"Isn't sex what is supposed to be the secret to starting labor?" I pour an unhealthy amount of syrup over my waffles, and cut in to the fluffy squares.

"I'm assuming that isn't a problem for them." He chuckles.

I shrug my shoulders. I don't really want to think about my older sister having sex as much as they seem to. We eat in comfortable silence for a bit before Trent asks me if I'll come with him to the party.

"Oh yeah, babe. I'm all yours tonight." I smile.

"Dangerous words, Princess." He runs the toe of his boot up my leg tauntingly. "You're mine every night."

My core heats at his possessive words and I squeeze my thighs together.

The things this man does to me.

"I'm yours. If you're mine."

"That's never even been a question." He says simply; his dark eyes taking me in and a smile crosses his face. He says the words so confidently, with so much convention that there is no room for any doubt. My heart beats for him.

And I know it always will.

* * *

I look fucking sexy, if I do say so myself.

I'm glad I'd packed this little black dress last minute. I just thought it was sexy, and on the off chance we decided to go out, I wanted something to wear other than comfy clothes. When we're at the apartment, I'm usually naked anyway so I learned not to pack a whole lot. But I'm glad I impulsively packed it.

It's a long-sleeved, velvet dress that cuts off right at my mid-thigh, and has a high neck but a dangerously low back. It shows all my curves in the best way. When I saw it online, I'd immediately put it in my cart and checked out. It was sexy in an understated, intriguing way.

I don't know what the dress code was for tonight, but it was either this dress or my sweats… or the lingerie I'd also packed.

And I really don't think that Trent would be cool with me showing up to a party with all his friends and coworkers in a black bustier and thigh-highs. Although, the show of dominance and possession he would for sure give might be worth it.

"So, I'm definitely getting into a fight tonight." Trent says, his words are gruff as he leans his shoulder against the door frame and looks at me while I'm dabbing lip gloss on my lower lip. Our eyes meet in the mirror as I take him in. He looks mouth-watering.

In the past few months, he decided to keep the beard and let his hair grow out. Not as long as Kieron's, thank god, but shaggy and rugged. It's a *very* good look for him. He's styled it tonight so it's pushed up and out of his face, looking messy on purpose. He's wearing a black henley with the sleeves pushed up to show his forearms, his dark, fitted jeans that sculpt his ass just right, and his black boots. The all-black look really works for him. Trent's standing there, arms crossed over his chest, and a feral look on his face as he stares at me, just staring at him.

"Already planning on debauchery tonight?"

"I have to. Have you seen how unbelievable you look? Someone's going to look a little too long at you for my liking and I'm going to kill them." He says simply, like planning a murder wasn't a big deal.

"No fights, please. Just let them look, as long as there's touching it doesn't matter." I tuck a fly-away hair behind my ear and turn to face him. "I'm coming home with you. I don't want anyone else."

He pushes off the door and wraps me in his arms.

"You better not. You're it for me, Augustine. I hope I'm it for you."

* * *

"This is just friends?" I yell at Trent, trying to push my voice loud enough that he can hear me over the music and other conversations in the club. That's right, *the club.* Because Kieron had rented out a nightclub and filled it completely with people like it was a regular night out.

"We have a lot of friends!" Trent yells back with a smirk on his handsome face. The room is dark and flashing with the strobe lights that illuminate different spots around the room just enough to see where we're walking. Trent's hand is in mine and thank god I'm wearing my boots because there's no way I wouldn't have fallen if I was wearing heels.

This is ridiculous. We're pushing through people in a crowd just to try to get to Kieron and Talia, who I can see on a small stage, nestled in the back. Kieron has his arm around Tali, holding her close to him while he's taking a sip of amber liquid, and resting the glass back on his thigh.

It's nine at night, and they both look as if they're ready to leave.

It takes us twice as long to get to them because everyone

and their brother seem to stop and talk to Trent, shaking his hand, and catching up. His hand never leaves mine, and it doesn't pass my notice that the looks I'm getting are extremely reserved and guarded. Like people are afraid to look at me too long, to take too much of an interest in me.

After we leave the last three second conversation, I tug on Trent's hand.

"What did you say to everyone?" I say pointedly. And that fucker knows exactly what I'm talking about too because even in the dim light I can see his sheepish expression.

"I didn't say anything."

"Liar."

"Okay, okay. I may have expressed that you were mine and not to test me tonight to a few of the prospects. They got the word around nicely." He shrugs like it was a perfectly normal thing to do.

I'm torn between being livid and being aroused because he knows what this caveman bullshit does to me. I settle for smacking his arm halfheartedly, and try my best not to smile too brightly.

I don't want to show him that I condone this behavior, but I secretly love it.

He tugs me closer and barrels through the rest of the people. We finally make it to Kieron and Talia, the latter smiles brightly at me, but is very obviously trying to hide a yawn. Cillian is there, talking to Bryan seriously in what looks to be a very tense conversation. Both of them are strained, and their shoulders are raised like their hackles are up. Or a fight is going to break out in any moment. I haven't got to hang out a lot with either man, but they definitely look angry. Bryan is a few inches shorter than Cillian, but the anger emitting from him makes me think that Bryan would dominant if a fight does break out. I wonder what it's about, but I'm not going to pry.

"Auggie! I'm so glad you're here!" Tali tries to stand up, but it's difficult with the beach ball she's sporting.

"I'll come to you! Just stay resting." I race over to her, and give my sister a big hug. It's been such an amazing thing, how much our relationship has improved thanks to these mafia men we've found. They brought us back together when others tried to tear us apart.

"What the hell are you doing here?" I ask her as I lean back, "You could give birth at any time."

"I know, I know. But I'm so sick of just waiting. I wanted to be out with everyone." She leans back against the couch, cradling her bump lovingly. How my sister manages to look so good at nine months pregnant, I have no idea. She's glowing and goddess-like, regardless of the bloating.

I wonder what I'll look like pregnant. If I'll have half her grace and beauty.

"I tried to get her to let me cancel this. I'm antsy just being here." Kieron tells me, and that makes me feel better.

"You should've let him cancel it, Tali. Or at least you guys stayed home." I argue. Trent hands me a cocktail, I hadn't noticed that he'd run to the bar.

"Look, when it's too much I'll tell you guys, okay? Satisfied?" She snaps. Her eyes narrow and her nostrils flare in anger, so I hold my hands up in surrender. Kieron pulls her closer to him and he turns to nuzzle into her neck.

I take a big drink of my cocktail, pleased to find Trent got me a vodka with Sprite. He pulls me to him, sitting back on the couch next to Kieron and Talia, then shifts us so I'm sitting on his lap, content to just let the world continue around us.

"Do you want something like that?" Trent whispers, his beard tickling my neck.

"Something like what?" I look at him, and see where he's staring. Kieron is holding Talia, one hand splayed protectively over their child. He's whispering in her ear, and my sister is so happy. The biggest, brightest smile is on her face. You look at them and can plainly see how happy they are. How in love. How excited they are to hold their child and be a family. When I look back at Trent, I see the want in his eyes. The yearning. He wants that, too. He wants to be happy. He wants a family.

"I do." I answer quietly, but I know he can hear me.

"With me?" There's a bit of hesitation, a bit of disbelief, and a hint of hope in his words.

"With no one else." I kiss his lips softly, cupping his cheek and smiling down at him. "Is that something you want?"

"Princess, if you'd let me, I would put a baby in you right now. I want everything you want, I want everything together. Living together, the same last name, a little baby with blond hair and grey eyes that smiles like the sun. I want you. Forever." His fingers grip my waist and thigh.

"I want all of that, too."

27


# Chapter 27


Trent


Auggie is still sipping on that first drink I got her. Ever since she told me she wants to have my babies, I've been hard as a rock.

I run my fingers along the hem of her dress, wanting the contact, all while cursing that we have to hang out here. She won't leave until Talia leaves, just in case. As the evening has progressed, Talia has started to grimace more and more. She thinks no one sees it, but really, the three of us are hyper-tuned to her.

"I think it's time to go." Kieron says suddenly, jumping up out of nowhere and holding Talia's hand.

Auggie stands up and nods. "I think that's a good idea, let's go."

Talia looks up at both of them, then looks to me like I'd be the one to say she should stay. I don't know why she'd think

I'd do that. I told her earlier she should've stayed home and we would have all come to her if she wanted company, but no, she felt she had to come out. "I agree with them."

She takes a deep breath and nods. The three of us release a held breath. Thank fuck she was listening finally.

Auggie and Kieron help her up, and as soon as Talia is vertical her expression changes. Her eyes widen and she looks horrified. I quickly do a glance around where she's looking, looking for any threat or anything that could be harmful.

"Oh my god, Tali!" Auggie says excitedly, her voice loud to be heard over the thumping of the bass. "It's time!"

"Time for what?" I ask, dumbly.

"We have to go, right now." Kieron's face has gone from relieved to more stressed than I've ever seen him. His eyes are surveying around them, searching for any threat and I join him, trying to defend our little family from an unknown threat.

"Do you guys need help, or should we just wait to hear?" Auggie asks, helping Talia move around the table when I see what they're talking about. Talia's legs are soaked, a small puddle at her feet.

The baby is coming.

"Oh my god." I say shocked, my mouth drops and I'm so surprised that I don't know what to do.

"I've got it." Kieron says, taking Talia under his arm and starts pushing them through the club. "Can you call Kellan and let him know? We've got a bag in the car, the car seat already installed." He's going through a list in his head out loud, and I do my best to listen to everything he's saying. They might not want us to be there – and we'll respect their privacy and wishes – but I'll do everything I can to help my friends.

We make it to the front of the club, and Kieron hands Talia to Auggie and I while he fishes his keys from his pocket. "I'll be right back, baby. Hold on." He kisses her forehead and runs off. The tension mixed with excitement is rolling off of him in waves. Talia accepts my arm, letting me hold her weight for her and leans forward with a low whine.

"Talia?" Auggie asks while I tighten my grip on her to help keep her standing.

"Oh my god, this is fucking painful." She groans.

Contractions. Shit.

"Where is Kieron?" I mutter, looking for the flash of his headlights.

"Fuck, that was awful." Talia stands straight up, a slight sheen of sweat covering her face.

"You've got this. You're the strongest person I know, and your baby will be here in your arms in no time." Auggie says to her sister, giving her the pep-talk and strength she needs. Talia's a strong chick, one of the strongest I've ever met, but the pain she's in must be awful because she looks scared. Terrified.

"My baby." She whispers breathlessly, and Auggie nods enthusiastically.

"Your little baby who is going to be so fucking loved by everyone. They're going to be a little smush ball and love you so much. It's worth a little pain, right?"

I feel so helpless because I have no idea what to do or say to help this situation, to help calm my friend's fears, but listening to Auggie comfort her sister just makes me love her all the more.

"Right." Talia whispers, the strength and resolve returning to her expression. A set of tires squeal to a stop in front of us as Kieron slams the car in park and runs around to help Talia into the passenger seat.

"Thank you, guys. We'll call you when we get set up there." Kieron says, while Talia grits her teeth and lays her head against the headrest.

"Love you," she says on an exhale, talking to Auggie with a tired smile.

"I love you," My girl leans over her big sister and cups her face. "I'm so proud of you."

The smile on Talia's face is thankful, grateful even, and she closes her eyes before Auggie steps back and closes the door.

"See you later, Daddy." I call to Kieron, who scowls at me.

"Don't you call me that. That's a reserved nickname now, fucker." He says with a wide smile. A smile that tells me how proud he is, how excited, how ready he is to start this new chapter.

"Get out of here!" Auggie laughs and smacks the top of his car.

Kieron smirks and stomps on the gas, the tires peel out and Auggie and I are left in the wake of their hasty, exciting exit.

"Well, shit." Auggie sighs after a few moments and I can't help but laugh. "What should we do with the rest of our night?"

"Oh, baby. I have a few ideas." I give her my best panty-dropping smirk, and lean down to pick her up. Auggie squeals, wrapping her arms around my shoulders to hold on as I hold her to my chest. Her ankles wrap around my hips, and my hands grip her ass to keep her against me.

"Let's go home." I say before I take her mouth in a passionate kiss that promises more.

* * *

"Baby, you have to stop doing that, or I'm going to fuck you right here outside my front door." I have to grit my teeth as Auggie nips at my neck and grinds her hips harder against me. She'd jumped into my arms after the elevator opened and kissed me, hard, deeply. Open-mouthed and desperate. My favorite kind of kisses.

The key keeps missing the fucking key hole, but I can't, won't move her away from me.

"Do it," she groans.

"I'm not going to fuck you out here where everyone could see your perfect body. No, I'll fuck you inside where only I can see you. Dirty girl, wanting to give everyone a show that's reserved for me."

I finally, *thank fucking god*, feel the key move into the thread of the hole and unlock my door. Kicking it closed, I make quick work of walking through the small apartment to my bedroom. I want her in my bed, spread open and dripping, for me. The moment the door opens, Auggie is tugging at the sleeves of her dress, pulling it off so the top of her dress hangs around her waist, giving me access to her tits.

In the time we've been together, I can definitely see a difference in my place. Auggie's touch and presence. No longer is it a place to simply catch a few hours rest and store my clothes. It feels more and more like a home. The only thing missing is her here, permanently. But I'm not going to open up that argument right now, I figure she will tell me when she's ready.

Or it'll be five years down the road, and I won't take no for an answer. In my mind that's the amount of time I think I can last before breaking down and picking her up like a caveman to take her back to my shelter for protection and love.

Auggie has taken my bare, cold, lonely apartment and made it warm and inviting. Even though she doesn't live here full time, I've made it as clear as can be that she can do whatever she wants to my place. In my eyes, it's hers too. And all of a sudden, pictures started to be stuck to my fridge. A throw blanket on the leather couch. A welcome mat. Small little things that I didn't even think could add much, but the fact that *she* put them there means something.

I try my best to not toss her on the bed, but I'm so keyed up that I'm sure she hits the mattress extra hard. My vision narrows as she immediately starts crawling back towards the head of the bed and her knees close to cover my line of sight to her pussy.

"Oh no, no, no, baby." I growl, and yank her thighs apart and hold them apart while I look unabashedly at my girl. My pussy. She's wearing a barely-there piece of black lace that's completely ruined and I lick my lips. "Keep them spread for me."

The fire in Auggies eyes is mouthwatering. She wants to fight me, the little brat, she wants to deny me what's mine. But with a swift swat to her outer thigh, I grip her chin between my thumb and finger.

"You know you want me to take you, Princess. Don't fight me." I growl and I can feel her melt into my touch. "Stay just like that." I order and sit back on my knees, grabbing the hemline of my shirt and pulling it over my head in one motion.

A small gasp brings my attention to Auggie's face in alarm. Her eyes aren't on mine anymore, they're on my body. She always makes sure to check me out, always drinks in her fill of my naked body, and fuck if it doesn't go to my head. But this time, I know exactly *what* she was staring at.

My first tattoo.

"When…" She breathes out the word like she isn't able to full form a sentence. It's a big piece, taking up most of my side, and it hurt like a motherfucker, but it's beautiful and mine. It's a phoenix spreading its' wings proudly, about to take flight. I chose to do it in black and grey, the details coming from the linework and stippling rather than the colors. I take a deep breath and feel Auggie's warm fingers trace over the still-healing flesh.

"I got it on Monday. It took basically all night, but I only had to sit once." I tell her, the awe striking her.

"Why didn't you tell me? I know how big this is for you." She traces the lines up to the beak of the bird softly.

"Because I wanted this. To see your reaction. It's the first of what I'm sure will be many more tattoos on my body, but this one, this one is ours. I'm the phoenix born from the ashes of myself before you. You, Augustine Jones, you pushed me from the ashes, and brought that fire back to my life. You ignited me, brought me to life. And I can never thank you enough for it." I take her lips in a deep kiss, sliding my tongue over her lips, begging for entrance.

She opens her lips and I take no time at all in plunging my tongue into her mouth to taste her as we fight for dominance. A growl leaves my throat, and I pull her thighs down so her whole body slides on the bed until she's directly under me, her legs hanging off the bed. Her dress is bunched up above her hips, and I'm about to lose my fucking mind if I don't get to touch her soon.

"I love you," She says as she pulls back from the kiss, but I don't let my lips leave her body. I kiss down her neck, over her collarbones, down her sternum. I cover her in heavy, wet kisses that make her shiver with every swipe of my tongue against her skin.

"I love you, too." I promise, and take one of her nipples into my mouth giving it a hard suck. Auggie groans and I smile, with a mouth full of her, when I see her eyes roll back at the pleasure.

"Take your pants off." She orders me, and I raise an eyebrow, surprised – but not really *that* surprised – that she's taken to ordering me around. And I'll follow her to whatever end.

I snake a hand down to my belt and the metallic clinking of my buckle being undone is what fills the silence. I slide the belt off in one quick, snapping motion and drop it to the floor. Auggie bites down on her lower lip before shimmying out of her dress.

"You looked so ravishing tonight, baby. Stunning. But the fact that I get to see you like this, bare and open and mine… it's breathtaking." With one hand, I pop open the button of my jeans and drag the zipper down. My other hand starts to slide up her thighs, inching closer to the warm wetness that's waiting for me.

Auggie doesn't say anything, and she doesn't need to. The look in her eyes, the way her bare chest is moving up and down quickly with her breath, the squirming she's doing to try and relieve some tension, it all tells me what she wants, what she's feeling.

And right now, my girl needs to be fucked.

Successfully getting completely naked, I crawl onto the bed over her. One of my knees goes in between Auggies legs and I take care to apply just a little bit of pressure. Just enough to take the edge off. She shivers, and her eyes scrunch close as her mouth drops open just a bit.

"Yes," She moans.

"I've got you." I whisper. Then, I grind my knee against her clit.

"Oh my god,"

That's fucking right, 'oh my god'. I slide a hand under her to cup her neck, and kiss her again. The deep, possessive kind that leaves me breathless. When I know that she's out of her mind and can feel her grinding back on me, trying to get closer to the edge, I take away my knee and rest between her thighs.

"What, why?" She whines and I love it. I love it when she lets her guard down and just let's herself be true. She's a little whiney in bed, and a whole lot of bratty.

"Hush now, baby." I push two fingers into her, sliding her wetness all around so her clit it wet under my thumb. The moment I start to move my fingers she sighs in contentment and she meets my movements with a roll of her hips.

I curl my fingers with each press inside her, and use my thumb to circle her hardened clit in time with the movements.

"Yes, yes, please. There, right there!" She cries out, grabbing my arm between her legs as I speed up my hand. She curls her body up just as she lets out a warrior cry and her release floods my hand.

So. Fucking. Sexy.

"That's it. Fuck me, Princess. You're soaking the bed, look at you. Doing such a good job." I make sure to keep the same pressure, same rhythm, same angle and keep going until she pushes me away.

She looks so strung out, so spent. But we're not done.

I line myself up at her entrance and kiss her softly before I push in all the way to the hilt.

Auggie groans under me, her eyes closing again and her walls clench around me. Shit, she's so wet, so warm from her orgasm that if I don't control myself, I'll be coming in no time.

"You feel so good, Auggie. Fuck," I groan and start to rock into her softly, slowly. I know she's overstimulated; she always is after she squirts, but that also means she's more likely to come again for me. I love pushing her to her limits and bringing her to new heights of pleasure.

"Trent," She whines softly and I can feel the familiar tingle at the base of my spine, the tightening of my balls with her breathy moan. She's dragging her fingernails down my back and thrusting up in time with me.

"Come on, baby. One more for me." I bite her neck, and she throws her head back with a groan. I slide a hand down and play with her overly sensitive clit, rubbing it in soft circles. The way that we're connected, my hand puts more pressure against her with each thrust into her. It's driving her crazy, I can feel it. Her cunt is holding like a vise and she's getting wetter than before.

"Come for me, Auggie. I need to feel you come on my cock, and then I'll fill you up. Come on, I'll fill you up and give you that baby we both want." I groan in her ear, my own body tightening as I try to fight off coming so soon but my words and the image it's bringing to my mind is pushing me closer and closer.

"You're not wearing a condom." She whispers. I'm holding on by a fucking thread.

"If you have a problem with it, tell me now. I'll pull out, but there's already a chance…"

Her eyes burn with a taboo fire and I know that I'm coming inside her tonight. That it's going to happen and she wants it.

"Come inside me, Trent." She whispers in my ear. Goose-bumps erupt down my back and I struggle to hold back. "Do it. Fuck a baby into me."

And my control snaps. A man can only hold out for so long when his dream woman is telling him to come inside her, possibly, hopefully, getting her pregnant with his baby. Everything I've ever wanted right within my grasp.

The mental picture of Auggie's belly rounded with my child, her tits full with milk for our baby… Fuck.

I grab the meat of her hips and help her body move as I pound into her as hard as I can.

"Going to cum inside you, going to get you pregnant and keep you. You're mine, do you hear me? Mine. Tell me you want that, that you want my baby. Tell me, Auggie." I rasp out. I need to hear her say the words. That she wants this as much as I do. I know there's probably no way she'll actually fall pregnant tonight, but I guess I have a breeding kink I didn't know I had.

Or maybe it's just an Auggie kink.

"I want it. I *need* it." She says quickly, her hands on both sides of my face so I can see her eyes. "I want it all with *you*. Fuck a baby into me. Fuck your baby into me."

Her words are like lighter fluid to the fire that is smoldering inside me. The moment she speaks, I light up and come harder than ever. I'm completely at her mercy as I lose all control and hold her body to me tighter, groaning her name. My face nestles into her hair and I suck a mark into her hairline while I feel the edges of my orgasm as it ends.

Auggie slides her fingers through my hair and pulls, hard, as she cries my name in my ear. Her body goes taunt and she comes again for me, pulling my cock, my cum, even deeper inside her. It feels so good, even though I'm sensitive as hell now, her walls clenching around me still feel make me groan. A fresh wave of lust and want coursing over me.

We lay there, breathing heavily together, holding each other tightly. I don't make any effort to move, and neither does she. It's nice to just be together. Connected. Loving each other the oldest way known.

"I meant it, you know." She whispers into the darkness.

"What, baby?"

"That I want everything with you. Be it now, tomorrow, next year or in the next five. You're it for me too, Trent. I love you; I love everything about you and I love our relationship. Our strong foundation. As long as we're together, I know that we'll be okay. Whatever happens." Her words were so sincere, so genuine that I know without a doubt that she means each word.

"Whatever happens." I rest my forehead against hers and am grateful for whatever act I'd done in a previous life, that meant I got her in this one. "Together."

# Author's Note

I'm so excited you guys get to meet Trent and Auggie. When I started *From My Past*, I wasn't expecting Kieron's guys to demand their stories to be told as well. But, I'm so glad they did.

Thank you to the readers, it's because of you that this story has come to be. I had so many requests and DM's going; "What about Trent?", "What happened with Trent?", and my favorite; "I need to know what happens with Trent and Auggie." I hope their story lives up to the hype. I love them and am so glad I got to spend some time with them.

Thank you to my PA, Chelsi Weddle, for all you do for me and this crazy author journey I'm on. I could not survive Facebook stuff without you. I appreciate you more than you know!

Thank you to my ARC team for all your fantastic insights and help! You guys rock!

Thank you to my street team, you guys are amazing and thank you for everything!

Thank you to my family for your never-ending support and

love. Having you guys hype me up and push me to keep going is amazing.

And last but not least, thank you to my husband and my kiddos. My hubby has always pushed me to keep writing, taking the kids for me and encouraging me to follow my dreams. He's let me vent and talk the plot/spice out when I get stuck. Thank you, love, from the bottom of my heart for all that you do. My three babies are my reason for living, I hope to show them that no matter what, to keep reaching for their dreams.

# Check Out Other Works By Alina Martyn

**The Heliander Chronicles**

Secretly Born

Living In Secret

Secrets End


**The Men Of The Clan**

From My Past

Towards My Now

Embracing My Future (coming 2024)


Follow me on social media;

Instagram: @alina.martyn1

Facebook group: Alina's Spicy Angels

Tiktok: @alina.martyn1

@authoralinamartyn


Sign up for my newsletter to stay up to date on everything!

www.ingramcontent.com/pod-product-compliance
Lightning Source LLC
Chambersburg PA
CBHW070448300726
48975CB00007B/2079